Date Cute Marry Rich

Date Cute Marry Rich

Alexis Nicole

www.urbanbooks.net

Urban Books, LLC
78 East Industry Court
Deer Park, NY 11729

ISBN 13: 978-1-60162-314-0
ISBN 10: 1-60162-314-3

First Trade Paperback Printing September 2011
Printed in the United States of America

10 9 8 7 6 5 4 3 2 1

Distributed by Kensington Publishing Corp.
Submit Wholesale Orders to:
Kensington Publishing Corp.
C/O Penguin Group (USA) Inc.
Attention: Order Processing
405 Murray Hill Parkway
East Rutherford, NJ 07073-2316
Phone: 1-800-526-0275
Fax: 1-800-227-9604

Date Cute Marry Rich

By

Alexis Nicole

Acknowledgments

I can understand how actors and singers who win awards feel about their acceptance speech, because it is definitely hard to remember all those who have impacted you over time and helped you through this process. To give love to all those people in a few sentences is no easy feat, but they tell me this is a necessary part of the book, so I guess it must be done.

I always like to acknowledge God first and foremost, because without Him I would be nowhere near where I am today. He has brought me through a lot in my short twenty-two years of life, and I am thankful that He has given me a gift that can be shared with others. To love the Lord with all my soul probably doesn't even come close to how much He loves me in return but giving Him all I have to offer is my heart's joy.

To Carl Weber, thank you for taking a chance on a young, inexperienced girl and making her a published author. This process has been nothing like I thought it would be, and it has taught me so much. I have gained a great deal of happiness with writing, and I pray I can continue to grow as an author and accomplish half the things talented authors like yourself have.

To my mother, you are my everything. I don't think God could have given me a better person to mold me into a woman. Words can't express the love I have for you. You are an amazing, intelligent, hardworking, gorgeous, woman who has sacrificed so much for me, and my life's mission is to make you proud every day. I promised you your own island, and I'm going to make sure I make it happen, so start thinking of names you want to call it.

To my sister, Rachel, and my best friends, Dion and Ashley, you guys are my inspiration. Thank you for sitting up long nights with me, going over ideas and giving me good gossip to use. Thank you for the shared laughs and tears, the advice, and constant encouragement. You guys are the most amazing sisters a girl could have. I know God has great things planned for our lives, and I know we'll be able to see each other through it every step of the way. I love you.

To my church family, Pastor and Sister Goode, thank you for your continuous love and prayers. The Lord always leads me to a good church home, and I don't think there is a better one than Fellowship of Prayer International. You guys are the true meaning of people of God, and I am so blessed to be a part of this family.

To my grandparents, David and Lillian Cannon, thank you for just being you. The love you share between each other and give to your children and grandchildren is nothing but a blessing. You love me unconditionally, even when I mess up or disappoint you at times. I might hear about it for months and months, but you love me no less. Know that you are in my thoughts and consciousness in all that I do. I am so glad that I am still able to say that I have you around to teach and guide me. I love you both with all my heart.

To Victoria Christopher Murray, you have no idea how much you mean to me. To me, you are the example of excellence in this business, and I am so grateful that I have you here for me during this process. You have taught me so much, and it is definitely not knowledge that I will take for granted. Thank you for being my mentor, my inspiration, my example, my everything.

Acknowledgments

To my fans and supporters, I know there may not be many of you since I am just getting started, but I appreciate all the love and support. You guys give me so much positivity and encouragement, and this gives me the strength to keep writing for you. Thank you from the bottom of my heart.

Lastly, to those who I have loved and lost, thank you for the life experiences and the great book material.

Chapter 1

Skye

Four bad dates. No, not bad dates. Four horrible dates.

That was why I was so sure that this was going to be the one, because it was the fifth date that I'd had in the past five weeks and five had always been my lucky number. I was born in the fifth month, on the fifth day, in 1982. Okay, so eighty-two doesn't end in five, but you get my point.

So, I had endured all those bad dates over the past few weeks because of what I knew for sure, and that was that the fifth date would be on point.

"You don't have to say it, Skye. I can tell you're extremely impressed."

I looked up only because my parents, the Reverend and Mrs. Davenport, had raised me right, but really, I just wanted to keep staring at my appetizer, which was so much more interesting than the man in front of me.

"So, tell me," said Carter Wellington, leaning forward. His light brown eyes really were beautiful; they sparkled over the flickering candlelight. "Have you been out with anyone like me?"

Was he kidding me? No! I wanted to stand up and shout that for everyone in this five-star Fifth Avenue restaurant to hear. But, instead, I just gave Carter my raised-right smile and stabbed my appetizer, the Oysters and Pearls, which Carter had insisted that I have.

I pushed the white sturgeon caviar as far away from the oysters as I possibly could. Oysters I could handle, but I'd told Carter that I didn't want any part of caviar, no matter how highbrow, how sophisticated it was to chow down on fish eggs. But he'd insisted, as if he had any right to tell me what to put in my mouth. Since he was paying and I didn't want to show my butt in front of all these stuffy people, I finally agreed. If he wanted to throw away his money, who was I to tell him not to?

"So, tell me all the great things that Chyanne told you about me."

It was a ridiculous request, but a rhetorical one as well, because he never even took enough of a breath for me to get in a word. He just kept on about all the things he was sure Chyanne had told me.

Chyanne Monroe. My best friend. I was going to kill her!

"Oh, Skye, I have the perfect guy for you," she'd told me last week. "Carter Wellington. He's so cute!"

Cute he was. It was everything else about the arrogant, self-centered man that was driving me crazy. I couldn't figure it out; what had I done to Chyanne—my best friend, who was really more like my sister—to deserve this?

"I'm sure Chyanne told you that I was just promoted to partner, and that is no small feat at a company such as Bailey, Booker, and Smith."

I didn't have to say a word; Carter just went on. It was amazing, really, that he still had so much to say, since he'd been talking like this from the moment I stepped out of the cab.

When the cab had first stopped in front of Ocean Blue, I'd been impressed that Carter was standing right there. He'd opened the door for me, given the driver a twenty, even though the ride hadn't even hit ten dollars on the meter, and then he'd given me one of those Sunday church hugs, where our pelvises were miles apart.

Impressive was the word that came to my mind. But I wasn't surprised. It was my fifth date . . . on point, remember?

But right there, in those thirty seconds, that was when the good part of the date ended.

"You really are a lovely girl," Carter had complimented me as we stood at the bar, waiting for our table. He nodded as if he approved of the tight navy blue dress that I'd carefully chosen to wear tonight.

But then, when his eyes did a slow crawl up my body, then down again, it began to feel old man creepy. I'd crossed my arms in front of my body, trying to hide myself, until Carter finally looked me in my eyes.

"Yes," he said. "Lovely. And that's important for a man like me because of how handsome I am."

What?

He went on. "You know, if I weren't a top attorney, I would be a top model—the male kind, of course." And then he chuckled, as if he'd said something funny.

I just stared at him.

From that point on, he talked. Even as they escorted us to our table, in the exclusive restaurant that sat only twenty-six, he talked. As we settled, he talked. As they brought our drinks, he talked. As the waiter tried to take our orders, he talked.

We were only eating our appetizers and I already knew that the native New Yorker came from a long line of talkers—he was a sixth-generation attorney who had attended the best private schools from kindergarten; had graduated at the top of every class, in every school; just missed being president of the *Harvard Law Review* by a few votes; and was now well on his way to having Wellington added to the masthead of the law firm where he'd worked since graduating from Harvard seven years ago.

When Carter began his soliloquy on his early days at the law firm, I let my mind wander. If he was just at his first day at his job, he had many more years to go and I needed to fill my mind with happy thoughts.

But it was hard to—because across from me sat that man who'd become so typical of my New York dating experience.

New York—the concrete jungle where dreams were made of.

I'd come to the city with my fair share of dreams. My career was first, of course. One day I was going to be a world-renowned designer. But that didn't mean that I wanted to conquer the fashion world alone. I wanted a man by my side, someone who I could relate to, someone who I could spend this marvelous life with.

But meeting that special someone was much more difficult than getting into New York Fashion Week without any connections. Maybe I shouldn't say "meeting," because, truly, meeting, getting together, hooking up was quite easy in New York. There were plenty of guys to meet, to date, if you wanted to do that forever.

My challenge was that I didn't want to just date around; I wanted to meet someone who wasn't a tool. But there were a bunch of tools running around New York. Take my first date, Darren: He was tall, dark, and built, which I expected since I met him at the gym. He was hard not to notice, especially when his skin glistened with perspiration after bench-pressing two hundred and twenty pounds. That, by itself, was a turn-on.

The first week, I watched him, and then, in week two, we watched each other. After all that wordless flirting, he stepped to me and asked me out. I happily accepted.

We went to a little pizza place down in the Village, which was cool with me because I wanted to get to know all parts of the city. The restaurant was quaint and romantic . . . and it was also the place where Darren had the best of times with his ex.

"This is where we met," he told me.

I didn't know what to say. I tried to change the subject, asked him how long he'd been working out.

He replied, "Six years. It was Shaunte, my ex, who got me started."

By the time we left that restaurant, I knew everything about Shaunte, except for her Social Security number.

After that, I changed my workout times.

Then there was Kevin.

Ah, Kevin, the model—underwear model, to be exact. So, you know he had it going on. We bonded one day in the Starbucks line, when he asked me where I worked and was so impressed that I was a designer. By the time we both had our drinks, he had asked me out and I was thrilled.

"Let's do this, like, tomorrow," he said, as if he couldn't wait to see me again. "I'll call you in the morning."

The next day we had our date—at Starbucks! I sucked it up because, you know, he was a starving artist, sort of, and I certainly understood that. But right when I started sipping my Chai Tea Latte, Kevin whipped out his portfolio. He flipped through the pages of him in various poses—with underwear, without underwear, clothed, half clothed.

I watched, in shock and awe. I mean, we were right across the street from my job. I didn't want anyone to walk in and think that I was looking at porno.

Right when I was ready to ask him why he was showing me all of this, Kevin popped out, "So, can you hook a bruh up? I mean, I'm so much better than just show-ing off what I've got, you know what I'm sayin'?"

I was as stiff as a board, not wanting to look to my left or my right. I just kept praying that no one would recognize me and see that I was looking at this big-ass black case filled with naked pictures. Okay, yeah, not all of them were naked, but there were enough full frontals for a full spread—pun intended—in *Playgirl*.

"So," Kevin said, pressing me, even though I still sat stunned. "Can you help me out? I mean, you do all those runway shows, right?"

The only thing he could do for me was not come after me when I stood up and ran out that door.

I was gun-shy after that. But then I met Evan Mor-ris.

Okay, so who wouldn't be affected by the star run-ning back for the New York Jets?

I met Evan at an NFL fund-raiser for autism. Leigh Carrera, a well-connected party promoter whom Devin met a few months ago, had gotten our whole crew into this event. Evan was speaking when we walked into the room, and I was drawn in by the way he talked from his heart about his autistic niece. He quoted statistics, tell-ing the crowd that one in every óne thousand children is autistic. When he finished, I was one of the people on my feet, applauding his sincerity and commitment to such a worthy cause.

As the crowd mingled, he'd walked right up to me. I was shocked by the fact that, first of all, my girls and I stood out in this crowd of fabulous people, and then that Evan was most interested in me. For the next two hours he gave me all his attention, and we just talked, about everything from school to our careers, to both being new to the city. Before the night was over, he had my number, and two days after that we had a date.

All thoughts of every other guy I'd ever known in my whole life went totally out of my mind the moment Evan sent a driver, complete with the hat, to my front door. The driver, Marcus, helped me into a shiny Escalade and then took me for the twenty-five-minute ride outside of the city.

Yes, I'd agreed to go to Evan's home, but he'd convinced me that it was difficult for him to go out and enjoy a private dinner because of who he was. That made sense to me.

"And, I really want to get to know you, Skye," he'd explained.

That made even more sense.

On the ride to his home, it was hard not to snuggle into the soft leather and think about what was ahead. Last night Evan had called, put me on the phone with his chef, who asked me what my favorite foods were; then Evan got back on the telephone and promised me a night to remember.

I couldn't wait.

It had started out like the dream I'd expected it to be. Drinks in the massive living room, followed by dinner served at the twelve-seat dining room table, where Evan and I sat next to each other.

The whole time the ambiance was perfect; old-school Luther played in the background, the company was amazing, the conversation was stimulating, and this man was nothing but a gentleman. I was really feelin' Evan, and that was why when he leaned over and kissed me, it was all good, until he took my hand and lifted me from the sofa.

I asked him, "Where are we going?"

"To the bedroom," he whispered, "for dessert." Then he winked at me.

"Uh, excuse me," I said, pulling away from him, "but I'm not dessert."

Why did I say that? That perfect gentleman turned straight into the boogeyman. I swear, that man's head started spinning, and he started talking about how I had to be crazy. Didn't I know why he'd invited me to his home?

Now, it wasn't just because I was a pastor's kid that I wasn't going to jump into bed with this fool. My father and I didn't agree on too many things, but what happened on the first date was one place where the reverend and I were in accord.

That date ended up costing me a fortune, because there was no driver to take me home. And since it was too far to walk, I had to ask Evan to call me a cab. I was steaming through every mile of that seventy-five-dollar ride back into the city.

Oh, yeah, I was hot! But unfortunately, I wasn't hot enough to give up. Because next came Melvin. . . .

There really wasn't much to say about the guy I bumped into at the dry cleaners, because when we got into the movie theater for our first date and the lights went down, his hand went straight for my blouse. I tossed my box of popcorn over his head and ran out of there as if someone had just yelled, "Fire!"

But even after all that, all those hell dates, I was here with Carter because I had faith in my lucky number.

Carter broke through my thoughts. "So, Skye," he began, "I guess you're kind of quiet."

Uh, no! It was just that I didn't believe in two people talking at the same time. And since he'd talked through our appetizers and entrées, there hadn't been room for me.

"No," I said, finally answering him. "I'm generally not this quiet." I hoped he'd get the hint.

He reached across the table and covered my hand with his. "I understand," he said gently and knowingly. "You were just so fascinated with what I had to say. That happens to me all the time."

Fail! Major fail!

This fool had to be kidding me.

"Would you like to order dessert?" the bow-tied waiter asked.

"Yes," Carter said.

"No," I said at the same time.

We looked at each other.

He'd won the appetizer battle, but there was no way I was giving in this time. I needed to get away fast, and I had the perfect escape plan.

"I'm sorry. I should have told you before. I have an early call in the morning. A photo shoot. I have to be on the set before six a.m."

"Oh."

"And you understand. . . ." I waved my hands toward my face. "I need my beauty sleep."

"No," he said, as if I'd really expected him to answer that question. "I don't understand. I don't need any kind of sleep to look this way. But if you do . . ."

Somebody needed to slap this man. But since I wasn't into violence, it wasn't going to be me. Instead, I was just going to get out of there.

The check hadn't even come, and I was already standing up.

"Well, at least wait and let me walk you out," he said.

"No, that's no problem at all," I said. "I can catch a cab right out there."

He looked as if he was unsure; at least he was that much of a gentleman. But then something caught his attention at the bar. I followed his gaze to the woman he'd made eye contact with. At any other time, with any other man, I would've been pissed. But this time I wanted to walk over to the woman and tell her to take my seat.

I just gave him a short hug when he stood. I resisted the urge to thank him for nothing and thanked him for dinner instead. I almost jogged out of the place.

It was almost ten o'clock, but this was New York and Fifth Avenue was lit up like the middle of the day. Dozens of cabs zoomed past, and I only had to take a few steps to the curb before a yellow cab stopped.

I was already dialing Chyanne's number before I'd even given the driver my address. When he pulled away from the curb, I pressed the phone to my ear.

I didn't curse, but I was about to cuss my best friend out for real!

Chapter 2

Chyanne

I was halfway between apologizing and laughing my butt off.

"I don't even think he knows my name." Skye was still huffing through the phone.

"He never stopped talking!"

"I'm so sorry." I giggled.

"Oh, you think this is funny?"

Okay, it wasn't often that Skye got upset, especially with me. So, I backed up, swallowed my laughter, and apologized again. "I really thought he would be good, Skye. I mean, he seemed to be a decent guy, and he's a rising star in the corporate law department."

"I know . . . he told me."

I had to work hard to keep my laughter inside. Taking a breath, I said, "I guess I should have vetted him some more." And then, because I wanted to change the energy, I added, "Forgive me?"

I knew I had her then. Those two words—*forgive me*—were the pass that got all of us out of all kinds of trouble.

"Well, I will accept your apology on one condition." She paused, as if she was waiting for me to ask her what was the condition. But I wasn't going to say a word; I needed a moment so that the next time I opened my mouth, I wouldn't still be laughing. Skye said, "You are never, ever, as long as you are black, allowed to set me up on a date."

"As long as I'm black? That's a long time," I said, wanting so badly to bust out.

But when Skye added, "I'm serious, Chy," I agreed.

I didn't mean to be laughing at my best friend this way—it was just that the way she described the date was hilarious, though I'm not sure it was any funnier than those other dates she'd had lately. Skye really needed to consider doing a dating reality show, and after she calmed down a little, I was going to talk to her about that, because what she was going through could make *The Real Housewives of Atlanta* look like a serious documentary. Really, though, reality shows and all other kidding aside, all I wanted was for my bestie to find the happiness that I'd found.

"Chyanne!" The voice called me from my bedroom.

Speaking of my happiness, I said to Skye, "I promise I won't set you up on another date." Turning the conversation serious, I added, "But I won't have to, because I know that God has someone for you. He's just making him get right, and when he does, that man is going to walk right into your life."

"You're sure, huh?" Skye asked me.

"Positive."

"Is he going to be cute or rich?"

"Which would you prefer?"

"That he lets me get a word in edgewise," she said, referring to her date with Carter.

This time Skye laughed with me.

"Chyanne!"

"Coming, Malcolm," I yelled out. To Skye, I said, "I've got to go."

"Yeah, yeah, I heard. Go take care of your man."

"I will, girl. Love you."

"Mean it," she said, completing our own little special good-bye.

The moment I hung up the phone, my bedroom door opened and Malcolm, my happiness, strolled into the living room, wearing nothing more than a towel and a smile.

I sighed as he slipped his hands beneath my silk robe, which was barely closed, and embraced me. His torso and shoulders still gleamed from the shower he'd just taken. Or maybe it wasn't the water—maybe it was our lovemaking that had his skin, his torso, and shoulders glistening. Either way, he looked good to me. I held my breath as his embrace tightened. Was my baby ready for round number three?

"How's Skye?" he asked me, finally backing away.

"She's cool." It wasn't that I was lying to Malcolm; it was just that I didn't want to waste time talking about a date that was a bust. I stood on my toes to kiss him. It was the only way my lips were going to reach his, since he was six foot two. I wanted him to change the subject. I wanted, badly, to get this man to take me back to bed.

The kiss was much too short for me. And then came the dreaded words. "Okay, I'm going to get out of here."

He twisted to turn away, but I held him back. "No, baby. Stay." I wrapped my arms around his waist. "I want you to stay the whole night."

Gently, he pried my fingers away from him, one by one; then, without saying a word, he tracked into my bedroom. I was ready to make my argument, but he spoke before I had the chance to even get my words together.

"I've got a lot of work to do."

It was a simple argument and an effective one. I guess that was why he was a top litigator.

But Malcolm Parks was not only my boyfriend—he was my boss at Bailey, Booker, and Smith. And he had taught me a thing or two. "It's already after ten," I said, keeping it short, the way he'd taught me, though I knew my argument couldn't stand next to his. There was a reason why he was one of the firm's stars; he'd fought his way to the top, and his battle included nineteen- and twenty-hour workdays on the regular.

Like I thought, my argument was ineffective, because Malcolm didn't even bother to answer me. By the time he got into my bedroom, he was on a mission; he grabbed his pants from where they'd dropped when he'd stepped out of them. Next was his shirt, which had been tossed onto the floor right next to his pants.

I leaned back onto my sleigh bed, watched my man prepare to leave me, and sighed. It was always hard to let Malcolm go because these were the only times we could be affectionate. At the office, it was strictly professional. Not that I had a problem with that. Of course, Malcolm and I had to keep our relationship on the low, since we both wanted to keep our jobs. And at times it was kinda exciting and sexy to pretend that my boss wasn't my boyfriend.

But even though I understood, and even though sometimes I even enjoyed playing, it was getting tougher to keep up with the game. My career was lurching forward, which was a very good thing; I was assisting with the litigation of more cases, and the bosses upstairs were taking more and more notice of me. But as I grew professionally, the time that Malcolm and I could spend together was shrinking, taking our relationship in the wrong direction.

We were going to have to figure out a way to deal with this at work. I mean, the company wouldn't really fire two of its best and brightest, would it?

But even though I wanted to, I wasn't about to tackle this subject with Malcolm tonight. Up-and-coming litigator or not, I was smart enough to know the battles I could win and those that I needed to attack at a different time.

So, I just watched Malcolm tighten his tie and turn to me, looking as professional as he did when we'd first walked into my apartment. Holding his hand, I escorted Malcolm to the door, kissed him good-bye as passionately as I could—trying to change his mind, of course—and then waved good-bye when I didn't change a thing.

I closed the door and leaned against it for a moment. Ten o'clock was still early, especially since I never went to bed before midnight. How was I supposed to spend these winding-down hours when my plan had been that tonight would be the first time in weeks that Malcolm would spend the night?

Malcolm wasn't the only one with work. I had a heavy caseload and plenty that I could be doing. But it was hard to think about legal issues when Malcolm's Burberry fragrance was still all over me.

Slowly, I smiled. There would be no work tonight. I clicked out every light in my two-bedroom apartment and headed toward my bedroom. Early or not, at least I could be with my boyfriend in my dreams.

Chapter 3

Devin

Flyy Girlz was my domain.

That was what I was thinking as I strutted down the center aisle to the front of the ten-seat shop. Not that this place was mine; but it might as well have been. Arthur Moore was the owner—he owned several salons throughout the city, but this one he left in my very, very capable hands.

"Okay, now come on, Ms. Sue," I said to the sixty-year-old woman whom I'd just hooked up. She was still standing in the back of the shop, behind my chair, turning her head from side to side, checking her style out in my mirror.

"Devin, I don't know how you do it," Ms. Sue said, the way she did every two weeks, after I'd hooked her up.

"Oh, stop it," I said, feigning modesty. But then, because I really didn't have a modest bone in my body, I added, "You know how I do it. I'm just the best hot-curler handler this side of the Mississippi."

"This side and the other side." Ms. Sue laughed.

I raised my hand in the air like I was about to testify. "Tell the truth," I said as I swiped her credit card, then gave her the slip to sign.

"Devin"—she pressed her glasses up her nose—"can I put the tip . . ."

"Now, Ms. Sue . . ." That was all I had to say. My customers knew that I accepted credit cards for payment
but not for tips. I didn't want that paper trail—not that
I was gonna cheat the IRS or anything. I'm just sayin'.

Ms. Sue sighed, but still she pulled a twenty from her
purse. That was what I was talking about.

Just as I confirmed Ms. Sue's standing appointment
for two weeks, Leigh came storming into the shop. I
said good-bye to Ms. Sue before I greeted my friend.

"What's up, girl?" I asked, not bothering to keep the
what's-up-with-your-hair look off my face or out of my
tone. "What brings you by?"

As if I didn't know. All my girls lived in the city, and
they came to Brooklyn for only three things: a good
meal, a "jamming" party, and moi, the best hairstylist this side of . . . well, you know. And since we didn't
serve any food here, and there was no party going on, it
was clear that Leigh had come here for me.

My girl took the rubber band out of her hair and
shook her ponytail out. "I know I don't have an appointment, but can you hook me up?"

I stepped back and folded my arms, as if she was
asking me the impossible. But, of course, I was going
to take care of her. Everyone in our little circle, and
even beyond, knew that I was responsible for the fierce
styles that Skye, Chyanne, and Leigh wore. If anybody
saw Leigh looking like this, it would mess with my cred.

I waved my arm in a big circle and pointed to my
chair. "Sit," I said. "You need my mercy."

She laughed but didn't waste any time scurrying toward the back. She said hello to the other stylists and
their customers as she moved, and over the whirring
of the dryers and the clicking of the curlers, and all the
laughing and chatting, they all returned her greeting.

I whipped out a smock and covered Leigh. "You know, God was looking out for you, 'cause my next appointment canceled just an hour ago. I was about to take one of those walk-ins." I glanced at the four women who sat up front. Two were flipping through magazines, one was gabbing on her cell, and the other had leaned back, closed her eyes, and settled in for what she knew was gonna be a long wait. But none of them seemed to mind.

In fact, no one coming into the shop cared how long it took, because of the atmosphere I had created. I kept people talking, laughing, moving. It was pure entertainment, and no one seemed to notice that it could take up to five hours just to get a wash, blow-dry, and style, because as the number one shop in Brooklyn, we were always so busy.

"So, what's up, Mz. Devin?"

I smiled at what I called my New York name. Leigh had given it to me shortly after we met, about six months ago. Mz. Devin, just like Mz. Jay on *America's Next Top Model.* He was my hero, though I could teach him a thing or two about strutting down a runway. My stroll had become my signature; I could stop traffic with the way I sashayed up and down the street in my three-inch platforms. Men *and* women loved to watch me. Oh yeah, Mz. Tyra needed to know about me. But since I was unlikely to be discovered by Miss Oprah, Jr., I just made the most out of my shop.

"Ain't nothing up but you," I said, directing Leigh to one of the cubicles for her washing. These private rooms were one of the best features of the shop, to me.

Now, we hired girls who took care of the washing and conditioning for most of the stylists, but not for me. I was a full-service stylist. I took care of my customers from start to finish; that's why everyone kept coming back to Mz. Devin.

"So, have you started to see anyone special?"

Dang! Leigh didn't waste any time; she was starting in on me right away today. With her head in the bowl and her eyes closed, I was tempted to turn the water on cold. Full blast. Shock her a little. Maybe then she'd stop with all the questions about my love life.

But since I knew that her questions and concerns came from a cool place, I turned the water to warm and began to rinse her hair. "How many times do I have to tell you, Mz. Thing? I am totally happy with the single life right now. It's fun, and there's too much I have to do with my business before I can get serious with any-one, anyway."

"I'm not talking about serious, serious," Leigh said as I lathered her thick, shoulder-length hair with shampoo. "I think you should just be looking for some-one special, something meaningful."

"Why won't you believe that I'm not the Disney princess looking for her happily ever after with Prince Charming?"

"I do believe you. That's why I have to look out for you. Because you don't even know what's best for you."

Now I really wanted to cover her head with cold wa-ter.

She said, "Look, I have two tickets to an art show tomorrow night. The gallery owner is a friend of mine, and I really want you to go so that you two can meet."

"Okay," I said hesitantly. I conditioned her hair, then stepped back so that it could sit for a little while.

"You don't sound excited." Leigh pouted.

"Should I be?"

"Look, I'm just telling you to go, have a good time. Meet my friend, and see if the two of you hit it off. If you don't, you didn't miss anything. But if you do . . ." She smiled and then turned her cheek so that her left dimple was front and center. As if I was going to fall for that and melt the way all men did around her.

Still, there was only one way I was gonna get Leigh to get out of my business. "Okay, I'll go," I said, thinking that it might not be that bad. An urban art show—that could be interesting, and since Leigh had two tickets, maybe one of the girls could go with me. This way, if I didn't like Leigh's friend, either Skye or Chyanne could help me make a quick getaway. I'd ask them about it tonight.

"Great," Leigh said, wiggling her hips as she snuggled her head far back into the bowl for her rinse. "You're gonna have a great time."

"Well, if it's so great," I began, "why aren't you and Michael going?"

That shut everything down. The smile that Leigh had on her face faded fast, letting me know that there were still no flowers growing in her marital paradise.

She said, "We already have plans."

But I ignored what she'd just said, knowing there was much more behind those words. "Wanna talk about it, honey?" I asked softly as I wrapped her head in a towel.

Leigh paused for a moment, as if she was going to tell me something, but then she just shook her head. "No, I'm good."

"Doesn't seem that way."

"But I am." Leigh pushed herself up and then sauntered out of my room and back into the safety of my chair, where she knew that I would talk about anything except for our personal lives.

I sighed. I didn't like it when my friends had issues, but, really, I didn't see why Leigh and Michael couldn't work out their problems. In the short time I'd known Leigh, I hadn't yet met her husband, but I'd heard her talk about him when things were good between them,

and I knew they could get past whatever they were going through. That was what I had—hope for my friends.
I wanted peace in her marriage, especially since she
was the only one who had given her hand to a man in
front of God and two hundred friends and relatives. I
wanted the two of them to get back to the happy place
where they'd been the day they took those vows. And
judging from the look on Leigh's face, that was exactly
what she was hoping, too.

Chapter 4

Skye

It was time to go.

Don't get me wrong; I absolutely loved my job at Zora Davis, which had quickly become one of the hottest fashion labels in the industry. In fact, this was what I dreamed that I'd be doing since I was a little girl. From the time I was five, I had been all about fashion. So, over twenty years later to be living my dream was beyond incredible to me.

But even though I loved my job, this had been the longest day of the longest week, and I couldn't wait to hook up with the crew. I was sure the laughs were going to be on me tonight. If Chyanne hadn't already told Devin what'd happened on my date, she would tonight for sure. That was okay. If the laughs were going to be on me, the *mojitos* and martinis were going to be on them!

Not that I cared that Chyanne and Devin were sure to give me a hard time. Now that Carter Wellington was forty-eight hours behind me, I could laugh, too.

On my computer, I clicked through the last of the pictures—the layouts for the photo shoot for *StylePro* magazine on Monday. This was going to be my biggest shoot yet, and I wanted everything about it to be perfect so that my boss would see that I could handle this line and a whole lot more.

Approving all the concepts, I e-mailed the JPEGs to my boss, then grabbed my sweater. But the moment I picked up my purse, the telephone rang. Since it was my work phone, I almost ignored it—especially once I saw the caller ID. But ignoring this call would be like ignoring a toothache—you couldn't do it. My mother would just hang up and call my cell, and then she'd stalk me until I answered.

"Hey, Mom," I said, grabbing the phone and putting on my sweater at the same time.

"So, how was your date?"

Really? Before "Hello. How ya doing?" This was the first thing my mother wanted to say to me?

I sighed, but I knew I couldn't hesitate too long, or else my mom would go straight into her "you're not getting any younger" speech. And not only did I not want to hear how much she wanted grandbabies, but I was already twenty minutes behind schedule to meet Chyanne and Devin down in the Village.

So, I did the only thing I could do. I lied—to my mother, the preacher's wife.

"It was great, Mama."

"Really?" she said with hope all in her voice.

"Yup, but I can't talk to you about it now, because . . . I'm under a deadline, and I have to get this done for my boss by"—I glanced at my watch so that I could come up with a good time—"seven."

I know, I know. Two lies in two seconds. But if I'd told her that I needed to get off so that I could meet up with Chyanne and Devin, she would've wanted to know every detail of my wonderful date. But work . . . my mother never stood in the way of that. She didn't want to mess with my job—especially since I could pay my own bills now.

"Well, call me tomorrow. No, call me tonight. I want to hear all about it."

"Okay," I said, already dreading the extra lies I'd have to tell.

But, I couldn't think about that now—not when I had death on my mind. Chyanne and Devin were going to kill me. We were going to the Cellar for Spoken Word Night, and because they didn't take reservations and it filled up fast on Friday night, they never sat a party until everyone was there.

I grabbed my purse, and since I was the last one in the office, I locked the glass double doors. Trotting down the hall as fast as my five-inch Louboutin pumps allowed me, I calculated how long it would take me to get to the club. If I caught a cab in five minutes, and the traffic wasn't too bad. I would be only about thirty minutes late. Argh!

Outside, the day's light was dimming, and I could imagine Chyanne already at the club, pacing and cursing me out for not being there. Even though I couldn't see her, I needed to settle down my always-on-time friend. At least I could tell her that I was on my way. That was the last thought I had as I looked down into my purse for my phone.

And then . . . *bam!*

I walked into a brick wall. Or at least that was what it felt like.

I stumbled backward but didn't fall; the muscular arms of the man, who'd almost knocked me senseless, saved me. But, though I was still standing, all I could see were stars.

I heard the *click-clack* of heels on the pavement as New Yorkers rushed past, and then there was the blare of honking car horns that still found its way to my ears. But my eyes . . . Everything was still fuzzy.

"Are you all right?" asked the man who'd bumped into me. Or had I bumped into him?

He held my arm as if he was afraid that I might still fall. I blinked a couple of times to erase the stars and then looked up and into his eyes.

"Are you all right?" he asked again.

I wanted to answer him, but it was hard to speak. Not because I'd been knocked silly. No, really, I was fine. Or maybe I wasn't. Maybe I'd been knocked straight into heaven, because the man in front of me sure 'nuff had to be one of the Lord's angels.

"Miss?"

I didn't know what to focus on: his light brown eyes, which were filled with concern; or his moist, heart-shaped, plump lips; or his shoulder-length locks, which swayed a little as he shook his head.

Now, I wish I had fallen . . . straight into this beautiful man's arms. Because of my business, it didn't take me more than an instant to assess the six-three frame, the 220 pounds of pure, solid muscle; this man was the Adonis that I'd seen pictures of in books. You know he had to be fine—I was around models all day long, and there wasn't one I'd seen who could stand next to him.

I thought about making my legs go weak, forcing myself to drop down right then and there. Oh, yeah, I was about to fall for real.

And then my stupid phone rang, messing up my moment.

He said, "Do you need a doctor or anything?"

"No, no." I waved my hands. "I'm fine."

My phone was still ringing, and it was only habit that made me glance at the screen. Dang! It was Chyanne. But I didn't care. Best friend or not, late or not, I was going to find a way to have a conversation with this guy.

"Okay, great," Mr. Locks and Lips said with a smile that melted me. "Have a good night." And then he spun around and walked away. Left me there, gawking, trying to figure out a way to call him back.

"Dang it," I said when he turned the corner and my phone stopped ringing. Now I didn't have the stranger or my best friend. But a second later my phone rang again.

"I'm on my way," I said before Chyanne could even begin. "I'll be there in a few."

"Skye!"

"I know. I'm sorry. I had . . . an accident."

"What? Are you okay? Do you need me to come to you? Devin and I can be there in five."

"Hold on," I said, glancing over my shoulder one last time to see if somehow the stranger had come back. Since he hadn't, I stepped to the curb and hailed a cab. "I'm fine," I told Chyanne. "Just got a little shaken up, but nothing a pomegranate martini won't fix."

"Okay . . . just take your time. . . . Get here safely," she said before I clicked off the phone and slipped into a cab at the same time.

I gave the driver the address to the Cellar, then sat back. I was terribly late, but there was no way Chyanne would be on my case now. We were like sisters—if I hurt, then she did, too. If I was late because of an accident, then all was forgiven.

And I wasn't lying. When I first bumped into that handsome stranger, I felt like I'd been hit by a Mack truck. But I didn't feel a bit of pain; I guess his fineness was like medicine.

"Umph, umph, umph."

I laid my head back, closed my eyes, and tried my best to remember him. I never wanted to forget his image. If I couldn't have the man, at least I'd have the memories. And as fine as he was, that was enough for me.

***

"No bloody nose, no limp, no nothing," Devin said as he stood and greeted me with his hands on his hips. "What kind of accident were you in?" he asked, as if the fact that I was still walking disappointed him.

"A minor one." I waved my hand, then shrugged off my sweater. "How did you guys get a table?"

"We told them that the third party was in an accident," Chyanne said, handing me the glass, my drink already waiting for me.

There was nothing like having a bestest.

As I took a sip of the martini, Devin said, "Well, since you still got all your limbs, let's dish. Chyanne told me all about that mess you called a date." He laughed.

I growled at Chyanne, who was snickering, too, and then I had a flash of the stranger. My hand started to shake as I remembered his lips. Dang! Why couldn't *he* have been my lucky date number five? Because I wouldn't have cared if he talked all night—as long as I could have stared at him, I would not have had to say a word.

I didn't have to do much talking now, either, as Chyanne filled Devin in on my date with Carter as if she'd been there. Like I expected, the two laughed at my expense, but as I listened to Chyanne tell the story, even I had to chuckle a few times; it was so ridiculous.

Through dinner and dessert, we caught up on what had been going on in our lives. Chyanne was still deeply in love, and Devin wasn't thinking about anything but his shop. As we talked and drank and laughed and drank and ate and drank, I allowed my mind to drift back on memories and float to the present. What wonderful lives we led! We were in our twenties, had been best friends for our entire lives, and were living in the most fabulous city in the world. Could life get any better than this?

Well . . . maybe just a little for me, if I could be as lucky as Chyanne and find Mr. Right.

"Hey, so which one of you heifers wants to come with me to an art show tomorrow? I got tickets from Leigh, so you know it's gonna be fierce."

Chyanne raised her glass toward me. "I guess you're going with him, 'cause I'm nobody's heifer."

I laughed.

"Plus," Chyanne added, "I have to get ready for this case that I'm hoping to get first chair on."

"Really?" Devin and I asked together.

"Yup! And when I get it and when I win that case, we're gonna celebrate for five days straight. And you . . . heifers are gonna pay the bill!"

We all laughed.

I said to Devin, "I'll go with you," thinking about business, too. I get inspiration for my styles from everywhere—from TV shows, from people on the street, and especially from art. After all, that was all fashion was—if done right, it was art that we wore.

With that decided, two more hours passed as we just sat and shared, and inside, I thanked God the way I always did for my friends, my life, my blessings.

Chapter 5

Devin

What I loved about Leigh was that when there was an event with her name on it, it was always top of the line, first class. And this art show was no different.

"Dang," Skye whispered. Her arm was hooked into mine as we slowly sauntered down the spiral staircase that led into the grand ballroom of the Melrose, the new luxury hotel that sat at the base of the Brooklyn Bridge.

Okay, so Skye was impressed. Good, because it was always her or Chyanne who took me with them to their swanky affairs.

"What? You thought I'd bring you to something that wasn't up to our standards?" I said, as if I could get her into these kinds of events all the time. But, though I was acting nonchalant, trust and believe I was even more impressed than my best friend. It wasn't just the glamorous surroundings, or the two hundred or so folks who lingered about, or the paintings on the wall, or the sculptures on the stands. It wasn't even the tuxedoed waiters who balanced trays with exotic hors d'oeuvres and champagne.

The thing that had me most impressed was the men!

I grabbed one of the champagne glasses from the tray of a passing waiter, and while I sipped on the bubbliest bubbly I'd ever had, I peeked at all the "art" around me. I'd been pretty serious about keeping a low social profile and focusing on my business, but with all this sweetness around me, that was going to be a hard thing to do now.

I let my eyes wander as I took in the view. Someone should have told me that all the fine men in New York hung out at art shows. There were all kinds on display here—black, white, brown . . . tall, short, medium . . . lean, robust, and in-between. The men were by themselves and with their women, though that didn't mean a thing, with the way some of those men looked at me.

Mmm-hmm. I could tell the ones who were on the down low. It was in their eyes, the way their eyes lingered on me . . . just a couple of seconds too long.

Now, I wasn't one to mess with no married man. If a dude wasn't ready to embrace his sexuality, then he couldn't embrace me!

But that was okay, because there were plenty of other fine specimens to choose from.

Skye and I wandered through the space, both of us checking out the art that we were most interested in. Her muse was on the walls; mine was in all kinds of tailored suits.

Umph, umph, umph!

"Oh, look at this one," Skye said, stopping in front of a painting.

It took me a moment to take my eyes away from a guy right in front of us who was wearing those pants.

Skye said, "This is beautiful."

I had to work to turn my attention to the picture that Skye was looking at. What! She was staring at some painting of an old, wrinkled lady.

"Amazing," Skye whispered.

Not! I said to myself. But I stood next to my friend as if I cared about the picture. Not that I was fooling Skye; she knew how I was.

"Devin?"

I spun around in the Ralph Lauren suit I had on and looked into the green eyes of a man so fine, he made me sway a bit. "You must be Clarke," I said.

He smiled, showing me all thirty-two of his orthodontic-enhanced teeth. "It's so nice to meet you," he said as if he really meant it.

Well, Leigh had come through in more ways than one. Clarke and I were about the same height, which was always important to me—though people always said everyone was the same height in bed. Anyway . . . his cinnamon-colored skin was so smooth, I wanted to reach out and touch it just to see if he was real. The only thing that was wrong was he was dressed like one of those English butlers on one of those shows on the BBC. I'm talking the whole nine yards—from his paisley ascot to his wing-toed shoes. He was fine, but already he seemed just a little too stuffy for me.

"This is some show that you've got going on," I said.

"Oh, yes," he said in a tone that sounded like he was speaking out of his nose. When he glanced at Skye, I introduced the two. "Would you like me to show you guys around?"

I gave Skye one of those long looks, with my right eyebrow raised just a bit. It was our signal, one that we all used . . . me, Skye, and Chyanne. Skye had come up with the look back in high school, the sign that everything was cool and we wanted to be left alone to . . . explore, shall we say.

Now, it wasn't that I was all excited about Clarke—already, he didn't seem to be my type. But what could you tell in five minutes, right?

Skye got my message—of course. "No, you guys go on. I want to wander around on my own, if you don't mind, Clarke. I like to take my time."

Clarke smiled, though it looked like his whole face hurt when he did that, but when he turned around, I followed him. And really, I would have followed him all night, because I just couldn't take my eyes off his behind.

What was it I said before? Hmph . . . hmph . . . hmph!

Chapter 6

Skye

I was glad to let Devin go off and do . . . whatever. I really did want to browse through the exhibit, just take my time and see if I could get any good ideas for my line. One thing I'd learned a long time ago was that fashion and art were really one and the same—all creations began in the heart of every artist.

But though I really did want to wander through the rest of the show, I couldn't get away from this wonderful painting. Actually, it wasn't a painting—it looked like it had been sketched with charcoal. But every line was so defined, so refined, that it almost looked like a black-and-white photograph.

A photograph of a woman—a much older woman, maybe in her seventies, or even eighties. She was lying across a settee, it seemed, and was clearly nude, though nothing showed beneath the sheet that covered her completely. But my eyes didn't stay on her body. I was drawn to her face. That was where the story was told—in every line, every wrinkle that revealed the thousands of days of her life. She'd earned every crevice through not only her tragedies but through her triumphs as well.

But it was her eyes that affected me the most—in her eyes, I saw the wisdom of time. And peace, true peace.

It was just a sketch, but I felt as if I was connecting with this woman on some level, for some reason. I wanted to know all about her and learn everything I could from her. And in her eyes, I could almost see that she was willing to pass everything she'd learned on to me.

"You like this sketch?"

The voice came from behind me . . . deep and rich in its resonance. But the woman in the picture held me captive; I couldn't turn away . . . not yet. So with my eyes still on hers, I said, "Yes, I like it a lot. There's something about her. It's like I've known her. Or really wish I'd known her."

"Well, I knew her well," the voice said. "She's my grandmother, and this is my portrait."

Now, I couldn't wait to turn around and meet the artist, but when I did, I almost stumbled over my feet.

OMG! It was him—Mr. Locks and Lips. The guy from yesterday. The one who had knocked me off my feet—literally and figuratively.

"Have we met?" he asked. His eyes were squinted, as if he thought he knew me from somewhere.

I didn't want to remind him of who I was and how clumsy I'd been. It was much better if we met under these circumstances, right now, both appreciators of great art. I opened my mouth to tell him, no, we hadn't met. But a yes came out of me instead.

"We met just yesterday," I told him. "I was coming out of my building, and we kinda bumped into each other."

"Ah, yes." He smiled as if the memory of that was much more pleasant for him than it was for me. "I guess I should apologize again."

I waved my hand. "Oh, no," I said, anxious to change the subject. I wanted to get that image of me stumbling

on the sidewalk out of his mind. "So, you're the artist?"

"Yup," he said as we both turned back to the picture.
"I hardly ever sketch anyone I know, but there was so
much about my grandmother that was just in her being. The only way I could capture her essence was by
doing this drawing. I felt like her face told her life's
story."

"That's exactly what I was just thinking," I told him.

He nodded. "Every line in her face was more than
just her aging. Each line was about the passage of time
. . . her journey through the decades, revealing everything that was old and showing us all that was new."

"That's exactly what I was just thinking," I repeated.

He continued, "But even though she'd been through
so much in her life, she still had a peace, a joy that I
wanted to capture."

Okay, I wasn't about to tell him that I'd been thinking that, too, even though that was exactly what had
been in my mind. So, all I did was smile at that last
part, though as I looked up at him, I couldn't believe
that my thoughts could be so connected to a stranger.
It was the same connection that I had with his grandmother. What was that about?

"Well, whatever you were trying to do in this sketch,
you did that . . . and a whole lot more. This has got to be
the best piece in the exhibit."

He laughed; it was a joyful sound, deep and rich and
full of wonder.

He'd make a great Santa Claus for our children.

What? I coughed and coughed and coughed to get
that ridiculous thought out of my head. Where did that
come from?

He placed his hand on my shoulder—just as he'd
done yesterday. And the concern and caring were back

in his eyes. "Are you all right?" he asked when my coughing went on and on.

I nodded, glad that I had wiped away stupid thoughts. "Just had a little something in my throat."

He nodded as if he understood. "So, would you like me to show you around the exhibit? This was my featured piece. That's why it's up front. But I have a few other pieces here."

"I'd definitely like to see them."

When I turned around, he placed his hand gently on the small of my back, as if he knew me, though his touch wasn't intrusive in any way. In fact, it felt like the most natural thing in the world for me to be walking beside him, through this grand ballroom. The crowd had thickened and we had to navigate through, but I kept up with my man.

My man! Once again, I coughed away that thought. How could I call Mr. Locks and Lips my man when I didn't even know his name? I was just about to ask him, but then we stopped in front of a large wall.

Dozens of sketches, black and white, charcoal drawings—all took my breath away. These were clearly drawings, but again, the exactness of the lines, the attention to the details made the pictures look like photographs, made the people come alive.

What I loved most was the way each rendition had a different focus. There was an old man with his hands resting on a cane, but his fingers were so long and elegant, I was sure that at some time in his life he'd been a pianist. Then there was a girl, a dancer with a neck as long and as graceful as a swan's. And then the little boy with ears that were the largest things on him. But the sketches were all so beautiful; every person was portrayed with love.

"These are amazing!" I said half to myself and half to him.

"Thank you."

Slowly, I walked past the wall, trying to savor each sketch. Mr. Locks and Lips moved behind me, smart enough to be silent. Smart enough to let me interpret and appreciate on my own. I was glad for the moments of privacy—even though I was standing in the middle of hundreds of folks, I felt alone and lost in this fabulous world of black and white.

I have no idea how long I stood before those sketches, but when I faced Mr. Locks and Lips, I wanted to ask, "Who in the world are you?"

As if he could read my mind, he gently took my hand. I followed him, loving his leading, and after a stop at the bar, we settled on an upholstered bench right outside of the ballroom.

"All I can say is, 'Wow!'"

He smiled and took a sip of his ginger ale. "And all I can say is, 'Thank you.'"

"Where does that come from? I mean, your inspiration?"

After a pause, he said, "Believe it or not, I didn't really start doing this until I was in college."

"You studied art? Where?"

He shook his head. "Never studied art. My major was psychology. I studied human behavior, and that's when all of this stuff"—he waved his hand back toward the exhibit—"came out of me."

"You know that's incredible, right?" I took a sip of my soda. "Most artists knew what they'd be doing from the time they were children."

His eyes roamed over me, but not in a leering kind of way. I felt comfortable as he took in the sight of me, and I was so glad that I'd worn my favorite champagne cocktail dress. He said, "You talk as if you're speaking from experience."

I nodded. "Yeah, I'm an artist . . . in a way. I'm a fashion designer."

"Ah, that's what you were doing on Seventh Avenue."

I nodded. "Yup, the fashion district."

"So, you're a designer. Is that what brought you to the show?"

Tilting my head, I said, "Yeah, I look for inspiration everywhere—especially from other artists."

"An artist knows that inspiration can come from anywhere, at any moment—even from a collision on a sidewalk."

I laughed as we both leaned back on the bench and exchanged stories of our love for our art—how we'd both gotten started, how we were both in the early parts of our careers, and our hopes for what the years would bring. Around us, the chatter continued as art enthusiasts entered the show, while others left. Droves of people flowed back and forth in front of us, but we stayed in each other's space—as if we were the only two people in the hotel.

It wasn't until I felt someone standing over me that I broke my eyes away from the man who had totally captured me.

"I've been looking all over for you." Devin stood with his arms crossed and his lips a little poked out. But I could tell that he wasn't mad. More like amused . . . and curious. "I thought you wanted to look around the show," he said as his eyes looked over the man sitting next to me.

"I did." I stood up and faced him.

"Doesn't look like you're doing too much art appreciating right now. Looks more to me like you're appreciating—"

"Devin!" I said, cutting off my friend before he went totally inappropriate on me. "This is one of the artists." I turned to Mr. Locks and Lips and once again remembered I didn't know his name. Dang, we had been talking for over an hour and hadn't even gotten to that part.

As if he knew what I was thinking, Mr. Locks and Lips stood up, extended his hand toward Devin, and said, "I'm Noah Calhoun."

Devin grinned as he shook his hand. "Ooohhh! Fine and polite."

I rolled my eyes. Sometimes, it was hard having a gay friend. I mean, there were times when I wondered if we would ever end up competing for the same guy—though anyone who couldn't choose between me and Devin certainly didn't deserve me.

Devin introduced himself, and then I did the same.

"We've been talking for all this time, and I didn't tell you my name, either. I'm Skye. Skye Davenport."

"A beautiful name for a beautiful woman," Noah said, taking my hand.

"So, Skye, you ready to blow this joint?" Devin asked.

Huh? Did he want to leave already?

Then Devin explained, "The show is getting ready to close."

"Oh. Wow. Didn't realize we'd been out here talking that long."

"Well, you have," Devin said as if he was in charge of me. "So . . ."

I tried to give Devin that look—that "let me be" look. But he just stood there as if he didn't plan on going anywhere without me. Dang!

I turned to Noah. "Well, it was really nice meeting you," I said, while trying to figure out a way to give him my card or ask for his.

"Yeah, thanks for making the hours go by so fast."

I nodded and shifted from one foot to the other, trying to buy some time. When Noah didn't say anything more, I said, "Okay . . ."

"Okay," he said.

My heart dropped. Usually, the first thing a guy did was ask for my number, whether I wanted to give it to him or not. So, what was up with Mr. Locks and Lips? I thought we'd had such a good time talking.

Oh, well. I'd vowed off dating for a little while, anyway, right?

But then, before Devin and I had taken two steps away, Noah called out to me. "I know we just met," he said when he caught up to me, "but do you wanna hang out a little bit tomorrow? Maybe go for a walk in the park?"

I guessed he was talking about Central Park, though it really didn't matter to me. I couldn't say yes fast enough. I gave him my card, jotted my cell phone on the back, and he promised to call me in the morning.

This time, he gave me a hug before I walked away, and I swear, when I turned around and followed Devin, my feet didn't hit the ground.

Chapter 7

Devin

I couldn't remember the last time I'd kept a secret from my girls, but I had to do it this time. I mean, we were all so busy—there was no need for false alarms. That was why I hadn't called one of our Code Reds. No need to get my girls excited until I was sure there was something to get excited about.

And, anyway, right now I had enough excitement for all three of us. I couldn't remember the last time I went on a date, and what made tonight's date so much better—and so exciting—was that it was so unexpected.

I really had to thank Leigh for the heads-up about that art show. If it weren't for her, I would've never met Tony. I know, I know, I was supposed to hook up with Clarke. But that was Leigh's idea, and I did try. Clarke was nice and all. He was so well dressed, so polite, and there wasn't a more intelligent man on earth—at least not one who knew more than Clarke did about the history of Eastern art and Western art and every art in between.

But Clarke was so stuffy. He talked through his nose, walked like he had to go to the bathroom, and he didn't find a thing I said to be funny. What was up with that?

But Tony, or Antonio, which was the name I loved to call him, laughed from the moment I said hello. And it was his laugh, which exposed two huge dimples in each cheek, that captured me. Not that he fell short in any other part of the game. Boyfriend had it going on for real; he looked good! His black turtleneck and black leather pants might have been a bit cliché, but Antonio wore them as if that outfit was a new idea—his idea—an outfit that had been made just for his hips and his butt and his chest.

Hmph. Hmph. Hmph.

Just thinking about meeting him had me going. From the moment he walked up on my little rendez-vous with Clarke at the art show, inquiring about a painting we were standing next to, until now, seven days later, Antonio and I had been just about insepa-rable—at least in the virtual world. It was my luck that Clarke had to step away to take a phone call, and by the time he finished, I was long gone—and so was Antonio. We hid out in the hotel restaurant, far away from the exhibit, and just talked and talked and talked—about everything that didn't have to do with art. I told Anto-nio about my business, and he told me how he had a passion for sports. He had had an opportunity to play professional football but injured his knee, and now he worked for a company that provided insurance for pro-fessional athletes.

"Well, it seems like you made the best out of a dis-appointing situation." I admired the fact that Antonio hadn't fallen into a depression after his injury shattered his dream and had still found a way to work within the industry. I could tell he was a real go-getter, and that was very attractive to me since I saw it in myself.

I knew Skye and Chyanne would really like him. I could just see them all getting along really well, espe-cially since I hadn't brought a man around them in who knows how long.

But before any of that happened, Antonio had to first pass my test, though, on the real, I wasn't a bit worried about that. With the way we'd been going at it all week, neither one of us could wait to get together. I had a feeling that Antonio was going to pass my test with flying colors.

I'd decided to do it up right for the first date I'd had in I didn't know how long. I thought it would look much better if I grabbed a cab instead of riding the train into a part of Lower Manhattan I'd never been to. But when the cab rolled to a stop and I caught a glimpse of the meter, I wished I'd walked instead. Not that twenty-five dollars was all that bad, but it wasn't like I was rolling in it, like Skye, Chyanne, and Leigh.

"Devin?"

Just the sound of his voice made me stop thinking about money. And when I turned and looked at him, I stopped thinking about everything else, too. The only thing that was on my mind was this fine-ass, half-Black, half-Latino man with that long black braid down his back

"What's up, Antonio?" I said all nonchalantly, even though I was taking in every inch of him, once again dressed in all black.

He laughed. "I told you . . . only my mother calls me Antonio."

"Well, just call me Mama," I kidded.

He laughed again as he led me past the line of folks who waited outside of Club Reggae. He nodded at the guy at the door, who nodded back, but not before he looked me up and down.

"He's cool," Antonio said, vouching for me.

I glared back at the bouncer, as if I was hard or something, but the way he broke out in a grin let me know I wasn't fooling anyone. It was all over me. I was a lover,

not a fighter, and if anything went down, I was probably going to be heading the other way unless you were
messing with one of my girls. If something jumped off
with them, I had their back. Oh no, don't mess with my
crew. Devin didn't play that.

We showed our IDs to the cashier, paid our little
twenty-dollar fee, and headed into the club. The music
was bumping, and already I wanted to move. The way
Antonio's head was bopping and his hips were sway-
ing, I knew he felt the same way. But he led me to one
of the countertop-height tables for two and sat down.

I eyed the RESERVED sign that was at the center of the
table, but before I could say anything about it, this fe-
male who looked barely out of high school came over,
balancing a tray in one hand.

"What's up, Tony?" the petite little thing said so
sweetly I thought she was made out of sugar.

"Just you, Van."

The way she grinned at Antonio made me frown. I
didn't like the way she was looking at him—like he was
a tall glass of pink lemonade and she lived somewhere
in the Mojave Desert. I mean, I wasn't jealous or anything. I didn't know Antonio like that. But if he wanted
to roll with her, then he couldn't roll with me.

Then I had to watch Little Miss Barely Legal bat her
eyes and lick her lips, though none of that seemed to
get a rise out of my boy. That worked for me—I was
cool again.

We gave our orders for a platter of wings and two
beers, and once the waitress disappeared, I sat back
and took in the view. The lights were really dim, so
there wasn't a lot to see. But from what I could make
out, I knew this place was tight. This place looked like it
was an old warehouse with all the exposed brick. There
were dozens of counter-high tables surrounding the

parquet dance floor, and in the center was a glass-encased DJ booth. I'd never seen that before, but I guess that gave the music master a full 360-degree view of what his music was doing to the crowd.

Already, the dance floor was packed—with men and women, women and women, and men with men. Yeah, this place was mad cool, exactly like the world should be.

People were jammin' to Damian Marley, and it was hard to sit still.

Antonio and I watched the dance crowd sway and swing and sing along. Then, finally, over the music he asked, "So, are you out?"

I raised my eyebrows and made a big deal of looking around the club. "Oh yeah, I'm out," I said. "I'm out with you."

Antonio chuckled as if he got my joke. But then he stopped, stared at me, and asked, "Do you know what I mean?"

What? Did he think I was stupid? Of course I knew what he meant, and I told him so. "I've been out since I was born. Because I came out of my mama's womb this way. All I'm trying to do is live my life. Just do me and I let everyone else do them."

Antonio nodded with a smile, as if he was pleased by what I said. And I was pleased because he smiled and showed me those two gorgeous, deep dimples.

"Cool. I'm all the way out, too."

I didn't know what he wanted me to say to that. I mean, I knew he was out. Though neither one of us had said a thing about being gay, gay men knew gay men. And I never got involved in any kind of way with those down-low brothers. I didn't want to have any kind of relationship with anyone who couldn't be honest about their sexuality. Because if you'd lie about that, what else would you lie about?

Antonio said, "So, thank you for coming out here tonight."

"No problem. This place seems cool, and I've never been down to this part of the city."

"I just wanted to show you a little bit of my world."

"So, do you live near here?"

"Yeah, not too far away from here. In SoHo."

I laughed every time I heard that name. "That sure is a funny name for a city."

"It's not a city, just an area in Manhattan. Stands for South of Houston."

"Oh! No one ever told me that. I'm still trying to figure this city out. I mean, there's New York City and New York State, but then some people, when they say 'New York,' they're just talking about Manhattan. But there's more to the city than Manhattan, because there are five boroughs . . . and, anyway, what the heck is a borough?"

Antonio laughed at my analysis. "So, what brought you to all this confusion that's New York?"

"Well if you're serious about being a hairstylist, New York or L.A. is the place to be. Not that I have anything against my hometown of Atlanta, but you know what I'm saying."

"Yeah."

"And then I have some friends who came up here with me from the ATL. All three of us want to make it big, and we know there ain't no place better than the concrete jungle."

Antonio frowned when I said that—like now he was jealous.

I couldn't help myself. I chuckled and decided to play with Antonio a little. "Oh, yeah, my friends. We're real close." When his frown deepened, I said, "Yeah, Skye and Chyanne. Two girls. Two very heterosexual girls."

And just like I'd done a moment ago, Antonio grinned and relaxed.

Just then Little Miss Thang came swishing back to the table with our platter of wings and beers in her hands. After arranging our plates, she left us alone, and as the music played and the people did their thing to the reggae jams, we ate and chatted and people-watched the night away.

Antonio, the native New Yorker, told me about all the hot spots. "I don't hang out at too many gay clubs. That's not my scene."

I was glad to hear that, 'cause I wasn't into that, either.

"I like places like this—where everyone mixes together."

I let Antonio do most of the talking, and as he talked, I just watched . . . those dimples. I could get lost in there.

"Devin?"

"Huh?"

The way Antonio was looking at me, it was like he had already called my name a couple of times. "I was just thinking . . . You wanna go do a little somethin' to work these wings and this beer off?" He pointed toward the dance floor.

"You know how to do a little something?"

"I can show you better than I can tell you." Antonio laughed.

Oh, it was on now. I let Antonio lead the way. Not only because this was his spot, but I could sure tell a lot about a man from behind. So, I watched Antonio sashay and sway onto the dance floor, and I was beyond pleased.

And that man just continued to move his groove thang for the rest of the night. I couldn't believe the way we danced to song after song, changing partners sometimes, but always ending up back together.

It was just a regular Saturday night, but the folks in Club Reggae were partying like this was a major celebration. I could get used to a place like this.

By the time we finally sat down, my little 160-pound frame was at least ten pounds lighter. And by the time I told Antonio that I was ready to go, it was two o'clock in the morning. The folks were still going strong, but this dude was ready to go home and find that soft spot in my bed. Not that I wasn't having a good time—I just needed to crash.

"You can stay if you want to," I told Antonio. "But I'm gonna head back to Brooklyn."

"Nah, I'm ready, too. We'll walk out together."

We were still moving as if we were dancing, but when we stepped out into that brisk April wind, all the good times went away. I was already dreading the long trek back to Brooklyn. It was probably going to take over an hour—most of it spent waiting for a cab.

But we weren't out there for a minute before a cab stopped in front of the club.

"Dang!" I said.

As if he knew what I was thinking, Antonio said, "This is New York." He opened the cab's door for me. "Thanks again for coming. I had a great time."

"I did too," I said, then paused. So, what was I supposed to do now? You see, for all my big talk, I hadn't really done this thing seriously with guys. Most of the time in high school, it was all about curiosity. And after I graduated, I was so into learning my craft that I didn't have time for building any kind of relationship.

So, really, I didn't know how Antonio and I were supposed to say good-bye. But he took over and just hugged me. I can't tell you how relieved I was. Not only because Antonio handled this, but there was no pressure for anything else.

He said, "So, we'll talk tomorrow."

"Definitely."

I slipped into the cab and waved as the driver maneuvered away from the curb.

When the car made a right at the corner, I leaned back and smiled.

Oh, yeah. I thought I was really gonna love New York.

Chapter 8

Chyanne

God is gooder than good!

I know, I know . . . *gooder* is not a word. Well, it was definitely not a word for someone with eighteen years of education. And it was not a word that a first chair should be using on this *Ferguson v. Household's Best* case.

That's right—you heard it. I was the first chair . . . for the first time; I was leading the legal team. Now, I'd been on lots of important cases before, but now that I was the lead, it was a must that I made a great first impression. And that meant I had to win.

That was why I'd been working mad-crazy hours over the last three weeks. So many hours that I hadn't had a chance to hang out with my crew. Though that seemed to be okay with Skye and Devin. Seemed like they were caught up in their own little New York world, too. Skye—with some guy that she'd met at the art show. And then Devin was doing God knows what. But we'd promised that we would all get together soon.

This case, though, was even affecting my relationship with Malcolm. I still saw him on the regular at the firm, but the two of us hadn't had much alone time. It was impossible to get together in the office, of course. And now our lunch dates were all about business. Malcolm had appointed himself the coach for my case.

Now, don't get me wrong. . . . I was not complaining. Someone who really loved me was preparing me for my first battle, and I was really happy about that. I just missed the little bit of time Malcolm and I used to have for just each other. It was hard sneaking a quick hug here or a quick kiss there. But once this case was over, it would be on. Malcolm and I would be back to doing our thing.

I was so deep into my thoughts that the knock on the door startled me.

"Hey, you got a sec?" Nicole West sauntered into my office.

Nicole was another junior associate, though she'd joined the firm a year behind me. But she was already building up quite a reputation. Many called her "the Gopher," because she could dig up information that no one else could find. And the thing was, she helped you win. Even though she'd never been first chair—at least not yet—she'd never been on a losing team. Many attributed that to her, and because of that, even the senior associates clamored to get her.

And for my first case, she'd been assigned to my team!

See what I mean? God is gooder than good!

"What's up?" I asked her. If Nicole was knocking on my door, then I was sure that she'd come bearing some news. And the smile on her face let me know that it had to be good news. "You have something about the case!"

My eyes searched her hands, but she held nothing.

Slowly, she sauntered toward my desk, took a seat in one of the leather chairs, and grinned even wider.

"What's wrong?"

"Nothing. In fact, everything is right. I just heard Tyler Paxton talking."

Tyler Paxton—one of the partners.

She continued, "I was in the elevator, but you know how they are. They barely notice us younguns. Anyway, he was talking to someone on his cell, and he said the partners are really interested in this case because some legal precedent could be set."

Oh, God. My stomach began to rumble.

Nicole said, "The way he was talking, this is big, Chyanne. We win this thing and there will be nothing but good things ahead . . . for both of us."

Part of me wanted to get up and dance a jig. I mean, the partners' eyes were on me. But I couldn't stand up—because I was sick to my stomach with that thought.

"You don't look so well," Nicole said.

"No, I'm fine. You know, just nerves."

Nicole pushed herself up from the chair. "Girl, don't worry about this," she said. "You got this. I'm on your team, right?" She always spoke with such confidence. I just prayed that she was right.

When I was alone, I replayed Nicole's words in my head. The partners were watching me? Oh, God!

That was when I decided, I wasn't even going to go home. I was going to stay right here in the office and work through the night.

Chapter 9

Skye

Smart, sweet, kind, fine! Was there anything else? Oh, yeah . . . fine! I'm talking about the kind of fine that comes only once every hundred years or so. The kind of fine that was as rare as a solar eclipse. The kind of fine that you saw only in movies or in your dreams. And the kind of fine that was all mine.

Not that I was being superficial about Noah. His kind of fineness was more than his juicy lips and thick eyebrows. His kind of fineness was more than the way his locks swayed when he laughed or when he talked with such passion. Noah's fineness was wrapped up in his being. It was in his swagger and went right down to his bones.

I had hit the fine-man jackpot!

They say it takes twenty-one days to create a habit. Well, Noah Calhoun was my habit for real. It had been three weeks since I'd met him at the art show, and from that moment, we'd been just about inseparable. We weren't able to see each other every day—even though we wanted to. But we didn't let many hours pass between our phone calls. Many nights I stayed up well beyond midnight just so that his voice would be the last thing that I would hear. And he'd wake me up early in the morning so that he could greet me with the sun.

It was official. Noah and I were definitely having a relationship.

What was best about my man was that he made every minute of our time together count. Our dates were never over the top. Of course, Noah—as an artist—wasn't working with the Benjamins that some of the other guys I'd gone out with had. But that didn't matter, because Noah made our time together all about us. Wherever we went was the backdrop. We were the main attraction. Like the very first time we went out for that stroll through Central Park. The park was magnificent, with the joggers and the bikers and the rollerbladers mixing with all the pedestrians. But it was all about Noah showing me a good time. He took his time pointing out all famous park landmarks; the Loeb Boathouse and the carriage houses, the zoo, and both lakes. It was a beautiful sight on a beautiful day shared with the most beautiful man.

Three days later Noah took me to a club called Basement Groove, which was literally a basement—a small club in the bottom of a brownstone up in Harlem. But it was one of the best places I'd ever been, not only because it was an open-mic spot where lots of creative types hung out—musicians, designers, artists like Noah. But the best part was that half of the people in there were Noah's friends. It was only our second date, but Noah was ready to introduce me to his friends.

It was a great place for me to be. Not only did I get to meet the people who were important to Noah, but just being around those kinds of people boosted my own creativity. We jammed that night, listening to what had to be some of the most talented poets in the country.

Tonight, though, was the best date of all. Twenty-one days after our first meeting and I was having dinner at Noah's studio loft. And Noah was cooking for me!

Like I said, jackpot.

This was the first time I'd visited Noah's home, and being here was a full-on assault on my senses. The naked brick walls were amazing; the artifacts that represented the countries of the world were beautiful; the soft beat of the African drums that played through the speakers that sat in every corner was almost hypnotizing.

And then there was the scent of the jasmine incense that burned throughout the space and mixed with the aromas of the pots that simmered on his stove. Was there anything else?

"Here, taste this." Noah handed me a flute filled with a yellow liquid.

"What's this?"

"Trust me. Taste."

I took a sip, closed my eyes, and savored the ginger. "Is this wine?"

He nodded. "Something like that. A drink from my native land."

"Ah, Jamaica," I said before I took a bigger sip this time. "I like it."

He smiled and returned to the kitchen area of the loft. The space wasn't very big—Noah was only about five giant steps away from me.

"Do you want me to help with anything?"

"Oh, no!" he said. "Tonight is all about me serving you."

See what I mean? There was never a moment when Noah didn't say or do something that was absolutely wonderful.

I curled up on the couch and wrapped my fingers around the glass. "So," I began as I kept my eyes on him, "where did you learn to cook like this?"

"My mother. I was blessed with the best of both of my parents. I got my mother's love for serving her family, and I got my father's work ethic." He chuckled a little. "You know what they say about Jamaicans, right?"

I shook my head.

"Jamaicans work fifteen jobs each beginning when we're in kindergarten." He laughed as if he'd just told the best joke. "In fact, most in my country would consider me lazy."

I laughed, not so much because I thought what he'd said was funny, but because he was just so tickled by what he'd just said. "So, what are we having?"

"Ah . . . something, I think, that you probably haven't tasted before . . . a lamb stew . . . Jamaican style."

I smiled, but to be honest, that didn't sound too appetizing to me. I mean, I hadn't had that many lamb dishes . . . and a stew? Wasn't that something that retirees ate?

"Trust me," Noah said as if he heard my thoughts. "You will like."

Twenty minutes later he served me dinner in beautiful bowls that looked like coconut halves. I opened my mouth, and the first spoonful of stew passed from my lips to my tongue and melted.

"Oh my God!" I exclaimed as I took another taste. Surely, this was the type of food we'd have in heaven. "This is wonderful."

"I told you that you'd like it," he said, full of confidence.

"You were right. So, this is Jamaican stew?"

"Yes, you can taste the curry, right?"

I nodded.

"And the cayenne pepper. You know we like things hot in Jamaica."

I laughed.

He added, "And of course the wine."

"In stew?"

"We use wine in everything."

"And I'm glad that you do."

We both laughed. As I relished each bite of my dinner, with the beat of the drums still filling the air, Noah told me about his native land. I hated to admit it, but I didn't know a lot about Jamaica beyond hedonism. And, I wasn't about to go anywhere and take off my clothes.

However, Noah painted a totally different picture of the home that he loved. Through his eyes, I saw the lush island that sat in the center of the Caribbean Sea, with full trees as tall as skyscrapers and beaches that framed the crystal clear ocean. I met the hospitality of the natives and the love and loyalty of the families that inhabited the island. He took me to his home with his words, describing a place that I couldn't wait to visit, a place that I hoped to visit with him.

Noah cleared the table of our bowls, then took my hand and led me to the couch. Now a different music, some kind of flute, accompanied us as we sat next to each other, staring at the paintings that hung on the wall opposite us.

"So, tell me about yourself, Skye," Noah whispered in my ear.

I squinted a little. What else did he want to know? We'd talked about me a million times. "I've told you everything."

"Oh, no," he said. "You've told me everything that you wanted me to hear. But now tell me those things that you don't."

"What do you mean?"

"The essence of a person"—he rested his hand against my chest and I shivered—"is right here. Inside that place in your heart is where you keep your secrets . . . the things that are difficult to share. That's what I want to hear from you."

I stayed quiet for a moment, until he lifted my hand and kissed the inside of my palm, sending more tremors through me.

"Tell me, Skye, what is it that you don't want anyone to know?"

The seconds that passed were filled with my thoughts and the realization that there were many things that I hadn't told Noah, many things that I hadn't said to anyone. Yet this man gave me a safe space to speak, so I began with my family, and how I'd never been able to please my father.

"The first memories I have are of him looking at me in some kind of displeasing way. And as I got older, it got worse. He was never happy with me, never proud of my choices." I held nothing back as I told Noah about how a couple of years had passed when my father wouldn't even talk to me. "All communication came through my mother. As far as my father was concerned, I was not a part of his family."

As I talked, Noah stayed silent, moving only to nod whenever I needed affirmation, whenever I needed encouragement to continue. I kept on, telling him my story of how I continued to fall short in Pastor Davenport's eyes.

"It's this designer thing," I finally said, ready to close out my soliloquy. "My passion was to the detriment of my relationship with my father. He wanted me to follow him into the ministry, and I never had any desire to do it."

After a moment Noah said, "Still, it's better now, right?"

I nodded. "He's come around a bit because of my sister."

"The singer."

"Yes, it's just the two of us. When my dad realized that he was about to lose Simone, too, I think it made him take inventory of the entire situation. Since then, he's learned to let go."

"That's good."

"Also, I'm learning to forgive him for not loving me the way I needed to be loved."

Wow! I could not believe that I'd said that out loud. In fact, I couldn't even be sure that I was aware that those feelings were in my heart, not until this very moment. Even so, for some reason I felt so relieved speaking that truth.

Noah wrapped his fingers through mine, lifted my hand, and once again rested his lips in the center of my palm. This time his lips lingered, and I sighed. Finally, he looked up. "You're a brave woman."

"I don't know about that," I whispered.

"You are." His voice matched mine. "Brave for standing up for your dreams and brave for releasing your secrets . . . to me."

I nodded, and my eyes wandered to the clock encased inside an African mask that hung on the wall. Noah's eyes followed my glance, and I knew he was thinking what I was, that I couldn't believe that it was already past midnight. I had to get up early in the morning for a Saturday photo shoot.

But I didn't want to leave this place. Not just physically. I didn't want to leave the soft, safe place that Noah had made for me emotionally. The way Noah pulled me into his arms, I could tell that he didn't want me to leave, either.

Was this the moment of our truth?

When I'd accepted his invitation to visit his home tonight, I knew it was safe, a Friday night when I had to work the next morning. Even though I was feeling Noah something fierce, I wasn't ready to go to the next level, and the way Noah had been treating me, like an absolute gentleman, made me believe that he wasn't ready to go there, either.

Of course, that was before the wine, the dinner, the music, and my confession.

Was I supposed to stay? Or should I leave?

Noah lifted me from the couch. Our eyes held each other for the longest minutes before he leaned forward and pressed his lips upon mine for the first time. The lips that I'd dreamed about for twenty-one days felt as soft as a cloud, and were sweeter than any nectar.

It was way too short for me, but the fact that it was filled with a passion that I'd never felt before made the kiss complete.

We pulled apart. "Come on," Noah said huskily. "Let's go. I've got to get you home."

We were silent as I slipped on my sweater and Noah grabbed his keys. Outside of his building Noah did what he always did: he stopped a cab, then slipped inside with me. Even though women took cabs in the city all the time, that didn't matter to Noah. He never just put me in a cab; he always rode with me.

This time we didn't talk the way we normally did. This time all we did was hold each other—all the way uptown. He paid the driver the first part of the fare, told him to wait for two minutes, then escorted me to my apartment.

This time when he kissed my cheek, tucked me behind my closed door, and left me, I wished to God that he had stayed all night long.

Chapter 10

Devin

Retail therapy. That was what this was all about for me.

I grabbed Leigh's hand and pulled her into Fashionista, the fabulous Fifth Avenue boutique that I'd discovered my first week in the city. I was just thrilled to be getting out of the shop—and on a Friday at that. And hanging with my girl was the cherry on top 'cause I wanted to thank a sista for giving me the ultimate hookup.

"So you ready to do some damage?" I asked Leigh.

She nodded but didn't have the attitude that she normally had when we were about to storm this place and say, "Charge it!" to everything.

It might have been the middle of the afternoon on a workday, but this was New York City, where nothing was like the rest of the world. Fashionista was overflowing with folks, as if it was the day before Christmas.

"So . . ." I spun around in the center of the store, taking in every corner. "Where should we begin?" I didn't give Leigh a chance to respond. Not when I peeped my favorite part of the store. "Let's hit the shoes."

I led the way to the stacks of styles that had just been shipped in for the summer season. As we browsed through the shoes, I couldn't keep that big ole grin off my face.

Leigh picked up one of the new Chanel sandals. "So what are you beaming about?" But before I could tell her, she said, "Oh, you don't have to tell me. I know. And you don't have to thank me, either, for introducing you to Clarke."

"Oh, yes, I really do have to thank you for the intro to Clarke, because if I hadn't met him, I wouldn't have met Tony. And Tony . . ." I tried to think of some words to describe my man, but all that came out was, "Hmph . . . hmph . . . hmph!"

Leigh frowned. "Who the heck is Tony?"

"Tony is my new boo."

She dropped the shoe she'd been holding back onto the display stand. "What?"

"Oh, yeah," I said and then filled her in on the details of what had happened at the art show. "Look, Clarke was a nice guy and all, but Antonio . . ." I shook my head. "There's a reason why I call him Mr. Dark and Lovely."

Leigh laughed, but I could tell that she was disappointed. "I'm sorry that it didn't work out with you and Clarke. I was sure that you two would've been good for each other."

"Now, don't get me wrong. Clarke is a nice guy, but he wasn't my type. Not really."

"Okay," she said, picking up a new shoe this time.

"Come on, now. Don't be like that. The point of the whole introduction was to get me hooked up, right?"

She nodded.

"Well, girl, I'm hooked up."

"So, it's that serious with . . .What did you call him? Mr. Dark and Lovely?"

I went on to tell her about the last three weeks of my life. How Antonio and I talked every night, had been out together on the regular, and had turned this into a relationship. "It's still at the beginning stages," I said. "You know, we're both still on our best behavior, still determining if this is really going to work, still doing that new relationship dance. But I'm telling you . . . I have a feeling this is it for me."

"Wow!" She paused. "Well, I'm glad to hear that, Devin. That's all I wanted for you. Congratulations."

Leigh was saying all the right words, but her tone, her facial expression said something totally different. I grabbed the shoe she was holding, dropped it back onto the display, took her hand, and led her over to the dressing room area, where there were fewer people milling about.

"Okay, fess up," I said. "What's wrong with you?"

She shrugged. "Nothing."

I sucked my teeth. "Please don't make me stand here for the next hour and ask you over and over until you finally tell me, because you know that's what I'll do."

She sighed.

"Come on!" I whined. "I am so ready to start spending my way into serious debt, but I'm not gonna make a move from here until you tell me what's up."

"I don't know." She shrugged. "Hearing about how great things are for you right now made me think about what's going on with me . . . at home . . . with Michael." She paused for a minute, as if she really thought that was going to be enough for me. But when I folded my arms and started tapping my foot, she kept on. "You know, I'm really busy with my business right now, but whenever I get home and I'm dying to see Michael . . . he's not there."

"Where is he?"

"Working, too. I mean, we've talked about this. How our paths are crossing and nothing seems to be happening with us, but Michael feels like I am the one that should make the change. He thinks that it's a problem that we both have such demanding careers, but he's certainly not going to give his up."

"Well, you can't blame Michael for that. I wouldn't give up being the agent to all those fine NBA players."

"I have my own business, too!" Leigh snapped.

"Whoa!" I held up my hands. "I didn't mean nothing by that."

"I know." She sighed. "I'm sorry. It's just that you sound like my husband, and what would you expect me to do? I don't want to give up my career. I don't want to sit at home just waiting for him. And, I'm not ready to have children."

"Is that what he wants you to do?"

"No. I'm just saying that we both have challenging careers and we should both make sacrifices."

I waved away her words. "Girl, Michael knows that. You guys are just going through the second phase of marriage, the part where the honeymoon is over."

"It's been this way for a while."

"So? Who said there's a time limit on the phases of marriage?"

She frowned at me. "What do you know about marriage?"

"Please. I know a lot. My parents were married. My aunts and uncles were married. Shoot, there are even a few married people on TV. Hmph, I know a lot about marriage."

Leigh couldn't help it—she laughed. Just like I wanted her to.

"Look," I said, being serious again, "you guys have only been married a couple of years, and this is just your first dip in the marriage. You're supposed to have dips—that's why you have to take vows . . . for better or for dips."

She laughed again.

"Don't even trip," I said, really wanting to encourage my friend. "You and Michael were made for each other. You guys are gonna be all right." I paused for just a second to give her a chance to breathe. But then I said, "Now, can we get back to what we're supposed to be doing?"

"Definitely," she said, sounding better. "'Cause, you know, I really do need something to wear for next Saturday."

"What's up next Saturday?"

"I'm hosting the launch party for Perry Danville."

"Get out!" I said so loud a couple of these uptight Fifth Avenue types put down their credit cards for a minute to stare at me. But I couldn't help it. Perry D was this up-and-coming fine singer and word on the street was that he was gay. "Oh, you are gonna have to take me with you," I said. "Leave Michael at home!"

"No worries about my husband. Michael isn't going. He's going to be out of town on business."

"Well, then, you've got yourself a date! Hmph, hmph, hmph. Perry D?"

Leigh cracked up. "I thought you were booed up. What are you doing pining after Perry? You need to stay focused on your Mr. Dark and Lovely."

"Shoot! Ain't a damn thing written in concrete yet, chile. And, anyway, you know my motto. . . ."

Leigh recited it with me. "Date cute, marry rich!"

And while she stood there laughing, I said, "And my Dark and Lovely is certainly cute, but Mr. Perry D . . . his potential is all about rich! So, I've got to keep my options open." I hooked my arm through Leigh's and led her right back to the shoe department.

Chapter 11

Chyanne

It had been four days. Four days of pure torture. Four days of being physically sick . . . except for when I sat in that first chair in front of the judge.

Inside that courtroom I had found my heaven. It was the first time I was the one in charge. Standing in front of the jury, the judge, the plaintiffs, and their attorneys, I was the one calling the shots.

But now, as I sat in my office, waiting, my stomach was back to doing those anxiety flip-flops. The nervousness came from the fact that the jury had been out for two days, giving me nothing but time to question every move I'd made during the four days of the trial.

It wasn't that I was questioning my abilities; the truth was, I knew we had nailed it. We had proven beyond anybody's reasonable doubt that Household's Best Corporation was not at all liable for what had happened to the Ferguson family when their son ingested the lemon-scented dishwasher detergent. Yes, there were lemons all over the label, and yes, their nine-year-old son was autistic, but it was a parent's responsibility to keep a child safe—not some multibillion-dollar corporation.

The Fergusons' attorneys had argued that Household's Best purposefully misled customers with their enticing packaging, saying that the detergent bottle's shape, as well as the labeling, would lead many to believe that it was a product that could be ingested.

The first time I read the legal complaint, I'd wondered if I was in the middle of some kind of test, or firm hazing. Because, surely, this wasn't real; there was not a court in this country that would entertain such a lawsuit.

But during our preparation for the case, I discovered that there were many complaints like this. What was even more amazing was that most of the time juries found for the plaintiffs—handing over large cash settlements from companies who in the minds of jurors looked too much like the big, bad wolf.

And in this instance, there was a huge strike against us—a little boy who'd been hurt, a *special* little boy who'd had complications from the potassium carbonate, which had done damage to his organs.

Household's Best had offered—without any admittance of wrongdoing—to pay the Fergusons' medical expenses. But the family wanted more—twenty million dollars.

So, we'd gone to trial, arguing that, while we all felt sorry for the young boy, Household's Best was not responsible for what went on inside the homes of their consumers. It was up to parents to keep products away from their children, and the instructions made it clear that this product was not to be ingested.

But the best part of our case was our secret weapon—Nicole. She'd discovered that the Fergusons had lived in five different states in ten years. Anyone else would have ignored that. After all, what did dishwashing detergent poisoning have to do with where the Fergusons lived or how many times they'd moved? But Nicole and our investigative team were no ordinary people. Twenty-four hours after Nicole had asked why the Fergusons moved so much, she had her answer. This family had a legacy of litigation, suing companies from coast to coast. They'd sued fast-food chains, hospitals, even the schools their son attended. And they'd had good attorneys, who'd pushed the corporations to settle before the cases went to trial.

I was able to present the Fergusons for what they really were—corporate extortionists. I'd even left some doubt in everyone's minds: had the Fergusons done this to their son on purpose just to get some money?

Although it was clear to me, I wasn't sure now if I'd made it clear to the jurors. Even if it was clear, would the jury care that this was how the Fergusons made their living when there was a little boy who had been hurt?

I was sure that I'd answered those questions; but now, two days later, I just didn't know. I'd been on the losing end of too many cases that we should have won. Juries were totally unpredictable.

What made this worse was that without knowing it, the jury had more than the fate of the Fergusons and Household's Best in their hands. What would happen to me and my future was at the feet of those twelve people as well. The partners were watching . . . and that meant I had to win.

Oh, God! That thought made my stomach rumble some more, and the Mediterranean salad that sat in the center of my desk, right under my nose, smelled as if it had spoiled—even though my assistant had just brought it to me less than ten minutes ago. I pushed the salad to the edge of my desk, far away from me, before I rested my head in my hands.

This was ridiculous. I had to get my nerves under control.

But then the knock came, and I almost fell out of my chair.

Nicole opened the door before I had a chance to tell her to come in. She didn't step inside; she just peeked in. "We've got an hour to get to the courthouse. The verdict is in."

"Okay," I said, as if my life didn't depend on what was now happening. "I'll come down to your office when I'm ready. It'll only be a minute."

She nodded, left me alone, and I sat there silently for a moment, trying to prepare myself for all that was about to happen.

Then I slowly pushed myself from my chair, stepped around my desk, but then rushed from my office, straight to the bathroom. I was about to barf again—for the third time today.

But once I was finished and had washed my mouth out, I'd be ready.

I'd be ready to face my fate!

I sat as still as stone. I had not moved since the judge had entered. I had not moved when he asked the jury for a verdict, nor did I move when the jury announced their decision.

"Our decision is for the defendant, Household's Best."

Not only did I not move, but I couldn't really say that too many of my bodily functions were working. 'Cause I didn't even hear the monetary decision that Household's Best owed nothing to the Fergusons—not even their legal fees.

The bottom line was my client was not liable for anything and I had won my first case!

It was the cheers that knocked me out of my stupor. Nicole hugged me as if I'd just given her the ultimate gift, and Jason, the researcher on the case, tried to give me a high five, but it was hard for me to even lift my hand.

Finally, I got myself together when we were given the "All rise" for the judge to leave the courtroom. Once he exited to the left, I turned to Nicole and hugged her back.

"We did it!" she exclaimed. "You did it. You won your first case."

I already knew that fact, but having her say it made it even more real. "I know. Isn't it amazing?" I paused before I hugged her again. "We did it together. This would have never happened without you."

Nicole laughed. "You're right about that," she kidded, though we both knew her words were the truth.

There was no way this would have been such a slam dunk without Nicole on my team. I was going to have to speak to Malcolm about how I could always have the Nicole West hookup.

OMG! Malcolm!

How had I forgotten about the most important man in my life?

Now I was in serious moving mode. I couldn't wait to tell Malcolm. We rushed out of the courtroom, and as we made it outside, I grabbed my cell phone from my purse. There was no way I was going to be able to wait to tell Malcolm.

"We need to celebrate this one," Jason said. "I'm not even going back to the office."

"No need to do that," Nicole agreed. "Let's party! Where should we go? Any ideas, Chyanne?"

I glanced up from my cell. "It doesn't matter to me. You guys can choose. But wherever we go, I'll meet you there. I want to run back to the office for just a sec."

Jason groaned. "Don't tell me you're going to work? Come on. This is huge. We have to celebrate."

"And I want to. Really, I'm not going to be long. Just want to make a few calls," I said, glancing down at my cell. Malcolm's number was right there, and I couldn't wait to tell my man this great news.

"Oh, yeah," Jason said. "I guess you gotta call your friends, especially your man."

My eyes widened, and I dropped my cell back into my purse. "What do you mean?" I demanded to know. My heart was already pounding. Did people know that Malcolm and I were an item, after we'd been so careful?

"Whoa!" Jason stepped back. "I didn't mean a thing."

"You said my man," I barked, as if I was interrogating him.

"I was just sayin'. I mean, a girl as fine as you gotta have a man."

"Uh," Nicole said, stepping in, "we won't even begin to talk about how sexist that remark is."

"Look, ladies, I'm not about to get into a fight with the two who just won this case. All I'm gonna do for the rest of the night is drink!"

"That's more like it." Nicole laughed.

But I didn't find a thing funny. There was no way anyone could ever find out about me and Malcolm. Malcolm had made it perfectly clear that our relationship could jeopardize both of our careers at Bailey, Booker, and Smith. And I wasn't about to put Malcolm in that kind of situation.

Though I did wonder what was going to happen in the future. I mean, it was clear that our relationship could be categorized as serious and was heading toward the next level. But if I kept winning cases like this, it would be a nonissue. The firm would be crazy not to want to keep both of us.

But until that happened, I had no problem keeping our relationship on the down low. It was easy here; unlike many other places I'd worked, there wasn't any gossip, no talk of the partners at all, at least not with the crew I hung out with. That made it all the easier for me. No one asked about my private life, and I didn't ask about theirs.

"Okay," I said, getting my regular voice back. "I'll meet you guys over at Chelsea's. Give me about an hour," I said as I hailed a cab right in front of the courthouse.

After I gave the driver the address, I called Malcolm, but the call went straight to voice mail. That was okay—I was sure that he was in the office and would hear the news soon. And now I could just use this short ride uptown to bask for a few minutes in this victory. Even though this was the outcome that I'd worked eighteen hours a day to achieve, I still couldn't believe it had happened for me.

Inside the office my assistant met me at the elevator. With the way she was beaming, I knew she had already heard. "Congratulations," she sang before I could say a word.

"Wow! I guess what they say about good news traveling fast is true."

"Yeah! Everyone in the office already knows."

I stepped through the hall and into my office with my three-inch pumps hardly touching the floor. Closing the door behind me, I inhaled the air.

Ah, victory smelled so sweet.

Rushing to my desk, I picked up the phone and tried Malcolm once more. Voice mail again. But I didn't dwell on that. There were some other folks I had to contact to tell this fantastic news.

I dialed another number.

"Hey, girl," Skye said the moment she answered the phone. "What's up?"

"Just hold on," I said, without even saying hello. "Hold, hold, hold!" I clicked over, dialed Devin's number, and when he picked up, I connected the three of us.

"Okay, we're all here?"

"Yes," my crew sang, as if they were in a chorus.

Devin said, "What's up, Ms. Chyanne?"

"I have some news for you guys. I won . . . I won my first case!"

My crew cheered, just like I knew they would. The three of us always had each other's backs that way.

"You won?" Devin asked. "You actually won?"

"Yeah, you sound surprised."

"Well, I am. I mean, I'm not, really. But . . . this is big!" Devin exclaimed. "Chyanne, do you know how big this is?"

Skye and I laughed at Devin's silliness.

"We have got to get together and celebrate," Skye said.

"For real," Devin agreed. "Let's set it up for tomorrow night. Right after work. And nobody can cancel, Ms. Chyanne. And nobody can be late, Ms. Skye."

"What you trying to say?" Skye and I said together, and then all three of us laughed.

"Okay, tomorrow it is," I said. But before I could say anything else, there was a quick knock on my door. Three men entered, and I gave my friends a quick good-bye before I stood in front of three of the partners of the firm—Calvin Bailey III, Patrick Henderson, and my man, Malcolm.

But even though Malcolm was there, I was still intimidated by the presence of the other two, who were actually there, in my little office. It wasn't that I didn't feel worthy. I did. . . . I'd just won this case. It was just that I was in the presence of legal royalty. Calvin Bailey was the grandson of the man who'd founded the firm. He was from a long line of wealth and influence, and his entire bearing—the way he walked with his head high and his back so straight—told that story. Next to him was the man whom the firm had stolen away from another top firm ten years ago, and Patrick Henderson had lost only five cases in his thirty-year career!

And now these two stood in my office, just staring at me, and all I kept thinking was, Thank God I'd won the case. The silence was so long and so loud that it was driving me crazy—and I just wanted them to say something, anything.

It was Mr. Bailey who finally spoke first. "Well, young lady, we just wanted to officially congratulate you on a terrific win. We are aware that you have worked on several high-profile cases, and to win a case like this as a first chair is a big accomplishment for a younger attorney. Definitely the kind of things this firm needs."

"Thank you," I said.

Mr. Henderson added, "We are proud of you and glad that you're a part of Bailey, Booker, and Smith."

I wanted to think of something intellectual or at least clever to say, and all I could come up with was, "Thank you," again. I was sure it was Malcolm's turn to say something, but all he did was smile.

Mr. Bailey said, "We're here to not only offer our congratulations, but we'd like you to come to the firm's gala."

Okay, now I had something else to say. "Really?" OMG! This was a big deal. The summer gala was for the most senior of associates, and it was kind of a midyear celebration. I had never heard of a junior associate being invited.

"Thank you," I said to all three of them, though Malcolm looked like he was a little surprised by the invitation. "I would love to attend."

"Good. My secretary will get the invitation to you, and I just want you to know, Chyanne, that we expect to see lots of good things from you."

"Yes. Definitely."

Mr. Bailey and Mr. Henderson turned to leave, but Malcolm lingered behind. When we were alone, he closed the door, and it didn't take two seconds for me to be in his arms. He kissed me with a passion that we normally reserved for the bedroom, and when we stepped away from each other, I was breathless.

"I am so proud of you," he said.

"Thanks! I can't believe I did it."

"You were well prepared."

"Because of you. Thank you for all you did for me."

"You're welcome—not that I had to do much. You had it under control the whole time."

Yeah, right! If he only knew that for the last week I'd spent half my life on my knees, hugging the toilet bowl. "Thanks, but I'm telling you, I wouldn't have been able to do it without you. And can you believe that I was invited to the gala?"

The smile that was on Malcolm's face dimmed just a little. "Yeah, they didn't tell me about that. It's nice. . . . It's just that . . ."

I frowned. "What?" But before he answered, I said, "Oh, I know we won't be able to go together."

"Yeah," he said. "And that might be awkward."

"Why?" I smiled. "You don't think I'll be able to keep my hands off of you?"

"Actually . . . I was thinking it was the other way around." He pulled me into his arms. "How will I keep my hands off of you?"

We both laughed.

"We'll talk about this some more later," he said. "So, I take it that you're going to go out to celebrate with Nicole and Jason."

I nodded. "But you know I want to celebrate with you."

He kissed me again, and I hoped that was his answer. He said, "I have some work I have to finish up here, but I'll call you and we can hook up at your place."

That was not exactly the celebration I wanted—I was hoping that he would sweep me away and take me out to a fabulous dinner. Because of our positions at the firm, I knew we had to be careful but we could go any-where and not run into anyone. I wasn't all that excited about just being in my apartment . . . once again.

But did that matter? It really was all about the two of us being together—no matter where we were.

"Okay," I said, already shivering at the thought of all that we would do tonight in my bed.

When he kissed me again, I sighed. If he didn't get out of here, I was going to tear this man's clothes off of him right here in this office.

Finally, he left me alone, to bask in the wonderful-ness of my life.

Chapter 12

Skye

My life was a whirlwind of wonder.

First there was work. My boss was so excited about some of the new designs I'd come up with in the past week . . . my black-and-white collection, I called it. She had decided to include three of my dresses in her next spring line, and can I tell you . . . I was ecstatic!

Of course, this collection had been inspired by the man in my life. OMG! I was totally and completely smitten by Noah! I laughed at that word—*smitten*. It sounded old like lamb stew. And we all know how that turned out: absolutely wonderful.

Noah was everything that I expected a man to be. He was still smart, sweet, kind and fine. But I was beginning to know this man on another level—through his passion. Of course, I'd already seen his passion in his work, when he created and when he just talked about his art. But I had also now been introduced to his passion . . . as a man . . . with a woman.

No, we had not yet taken our relationship to the ultimate level. But we had progressed from just kissing. And the way he kissed me and touched me and held me, trust me, it was hard not to go all the way.

I was glad that Noah and I were taking it slow, although in my heart, I knew what we had together was real. I didn't want to get too excited about this, though, didn't want to get all ahead of myself and start thinking about matching monogrammed towels in our master bedroom. But there were just some things that a girl knew—and what this girl knew was that Noah Calhoun was the man for me.

That was why I couldn't wait to see my crew. It had been too long since we'd gotten together, and tonight we would be celebrating more than Chyanne's big win. When I told Chyanne and Devin about Noah, I knew for sure that they were going to be just as happy for me.

I slipped into the jacket I'd designed, even though New York was having one of those summer days in May. But a fashionista like me still had to be cute at all times. And this dress needed this little cropped jacket.

I took two steps to the door, and it happened. . . . It always happened. My phone rang. This time, though, when I glanced at the caller ID, I didn't do anything but grin and then grab that phone.

"Hey, babe," I said.

His voice was low, seductive. "What you doing?"

"Thinking about you."

"Good answer." He laughed.

I chuckled, too. "No, really, I was just thinking about you."

"Good thoughts?"

"Are there any other kind when it comes to you . . . and me?"

"Absolutely not," he answered. "So, what time can I see you tonight?"

I slumped down into my chair. "Oh, babe. I can't. I forgot to tell you when we talked last night that I was meeting up with Chyanne and Devin for dinner."

He chuckled a little. "Well, I can understand you forgetting. We weren't exactly, uh, having a normal conversation."

Noah had that right! Our talk had gotten so hot and heavy that after I hung up, I dreamed about him all night long. Dang, I needed to be with my man tonight. "It's just that I haven't hooked up with Chyanne and Devin in a month, and if I cancel . . ."

"No, no, no, no, no! Don't cancel," he said. "I understand."

Even though those were his words, I could hear the disappointment in his voice. I recognized it instantly because it was exactly what I was feeling. I said, "But tomorrow . . ."

"Oh, yeah, babe. We have a lifetime of tomorrows."

See? This is what I was talking about.

"But definitely tomorrow," he said, "because there's something I want to give you."

I sat up straight. "Really? What is it?"

"Tomorrow," was all he said.

"No, please," I whined. "Tell me now."

"Okay, I can tell that we haven't known each other long enough, or else you would know there ain't no way I'm giving up any information. No matter how much pleading, no matter how many pretty pleases it ain't gonna happen till tomorrow."

I laughed. "All right," I said, as if I was pouting, though I was grinning so hard, my face was starting to hurt.

We said our good-byes, and I almost skipped out of the office. It was only five, and I wasn't hooking up with Chyanne and Devin until seven. There were a couple of errands I wanted to run before I caught up with my crew, but first, I needed my second daily dose of java. I hadn't had any coffee since this morning; I'd worked through lunch and even my normal mid-afternoon break since I knew I was going to be leaving early.

So that was going to be my first stop. Except the Starbucks on the corner had a line of people ten deep. Dang. Had everyone missed their midday coffee break? I wasn't about to stand on this line.

Then I thought, *Why not?* I had time. But waiting for me was not going to be pretty. I glanced at my watch, crossed my arms, started tapping my foot, and tried to pretend that I had some semblance of patience.

Of course, patience wasn't a virtue that I'd been given, but I wasn't alone. The man in front of me seemed to have even less than I did.

He was on his cell phone, barking orders to someone about making sure he "got that bid"—whatever that meant. But every couple of seconds he inserted something into his conversation like, "Why the hell don't they have more people working here?"

The line was long, and I didn't want to wait, but at least I wasn't about to curse anyone out.

Finally, he clicked off his phone, said, "I can't believe I'm standing in a doggone coffee line."

He kinda said that into the air, not talking to anyone in particular. But even though I couldn't see his face, I could tell that he was pissed. He stood with his back still to me, shifting from one leg to the other. He towered over my five-foot-five-inch frame by almost a foot. But what really caught my eye was the classic, custom-made deep olive suit he was wearing. How did I know it was tailor-made? First of all, it fit his body better than any leather glove would fit his hand. And remember, I knew fashion. I knew a tailored suit when I saw one.

"I'm outta here," he said before he suddenly spun around so fast that he bumped right into me, almost toppling me over.

Dang.

"Oh! Oh, my bad." He grabbed me by the shoulders and held me until I was once again steady on my feet.

Dang, I thought again. What was it about me that had all these men almost knocking me over? Not that I minded—because now that he faced me, I got a full frontal view of this man, who was as good-looking as anyone I'd seen in New York.

My goodness. Fineness was running rampant in New York City!

This dude had hazel eyes, caramel-colored skin, and what I loved best was the facial hair that covered a good portion of his face. No, it wasn't a full-fledged beard. He had more of a shadow, which just added an air of mystery to this stranger.

"I'm so sorry," he said. "Are you all right?"

How many weeks had passed since Noah had said those same words to me?

I chuckled. "I'm fine," I said to the stranger. "You're okay."

"I really am sorry," he said. But the man, who was in such a hurry just seconds ago, didn't make a move to leave now. Instead, he gazed at me . . . his eyes giving me the once-over.

Oh, he tried to be subtle about it; he looked me up and down with class.

It did make me a little bit uncomfortable, though, the way he stared at me, so I said, "Really, you can go. I'm fine."

"You sure are." He shook his head. "I didn't know they sold lottery tickets in here."

I frowned.

He kept on. "'Cause I just hit the jackpot."

Oh, that was cute. Corny, but cute.

He reached his hand toward me. "Trent Hamilton."

I took his hand. "Skye Davenport."

"A beautiful name for a beautiful woman."

Dang! Couldn't guys come up with anything more original?

"So, do you come here often?" he asked, as if this were Club Starbucks.

"Not if I can help it," I said as the line inched up just a little and the stranger moved, too, right alongside me. Well, since he wasn't going anywhere, I decided to get my little flirt on, too. So, I said, "What about you? Do you come here often?"

He said, "I haven't in the past, but if I would get the chance to see you every day, I'd be here from sunup to sundown."

Okay, someone needed to help this brother with his lines. Though I guessed when you looked like him, it didn't matter what you were saying. Well, he kept on talking until I was the second person in line. That was when he reached into his jacket and pulled out a card. He leaned over onto the counter, jotted something on the back, and then handed the linen card to me.

"On this card is every telephone number that I have—work, home, and my cell. I want you to use this," he said, tucking the card into my palm. "I want you to use this soon and use this often."

I couldn't help it now. I laughed. This brother had some lines!

"Thank you," was all I said.

Then the barista said, "Can I help you?"

But Trent just pointed to me before he spun around again—this time not hitting anyone—and rushed out the door. Without ordering a cup of coffee. After all of that.

I shook my head and gave my order to the cashier. Standing to the side, waiting for my drink, I glanced at the business card. Just like he said, his name was Trent Hamilton. Real estate investor.

I thought back to what he was saying on the phone. Maybe he'd been in the middle of a deal.

Ah, fine and probably rich. Too bad, 'cause it didn't matter to me. I already had my knight. Noah was all that I wanted or needed.

I glanced toward the garbage pail, but I thought that would be rude—especially if someone saw Trent give me his card. So, I opened my purse and tucked Mr. Hamilton's card inside one of the pockets.

I'd get rid of it later.

Chapter 13

Devin

B. Smith's was the place to be. Especially tonight, because this was where my girls and I were going to hang out and catch up. Since getting together was my idea, I got to choose the place. And who didn't love some real good down-home cooking especially in the heart of Harlem?

I had a feeling this night was going to be full of surprises—especially when we got to the part about what I'd been doing in the past weeks. I couldn't wait to tell my girls my news. But the first surprise came when I got to the restaurant and I was the first one there.

What? Ms. Always On Time Chyanne wasn't sitting here, waiting for me?

But I let the hostess seat me, anyway. No need to wait—my crew would be right behind me. Even though Skye was always running late, I had a feeling she was going to be on time tonight. I knew she couldn't wait to hear about Chyanne's win; Skye was nosy like that. And I wasn't really talking about my girl . . . not at all, because I was the same way, and nosy people knew nosy people.

And, anyway, I was right, because I hadn't even sat down when Skye rushed to the table.

"Devin!"

"Skye!" I cried right back at her.

In the center of that high-class place, we acted a fool, hugging and kissing like one of us was coming home from war.

Finally, she stepped back. "Boy, look at you!"

"Uh-huh," I said, spinning around so that she could get the full effect of one of those new unisex jackets that I'd gotten at Fashionista when I shopped there with Leigh. The sunrise orange color was perfect for my complexion, and I knew I was looking hot. "What do you think?"

"As fine as wine," Skye said to me.

"And you don't look too bad yourself," I said, giving her a half compliment, knowing that I was the star of this fashion party. But, my girl did look good wearing one of her Skye originals.

But the moment we sat down, Chyanne bounced over to our table, and we were back on our feet, doing that hug fest thing all over again. When we finally stepped back, I held Chyanne at arm's length and announced, "Here is the lady of the hour!"

The people at other tables looked at us; some glared at us. Not that we cared. We didn't mind being young and dumb when it came to this sort of thing. We weren't into that whole image thing yet . . . at least not when we were out just hanging.

We must've stood there hugging and laughing for fifteen minutes before we sat down. I snapped my fingers, and the waiter came over to take our orders of fried chicken, fried catfish, and pork chops with a bunch of sides . . . though, he didn't move fast enough for me. I couldn't wait for us to get our talk on.

"Okay," I said, taking charge once the waiter went away. "So, Chyanne, you go first, because this is really your party."

Skye and I leaned forward on the table, and Chyanne told us everything that she'd been going through over the past few weeks. From how she had worked the case to how she had won the case. It all sounded pretty exciting to me, and as I sat there, I realized that Chyanne was going to be an important lawyer, probably a real New York City mover and shaker, in a couple of years. And it was a good thing that I had her number sitting right up in my iPhone.

"So, did you celebrate with Malcolm last night?" Skye asked right after the waiter sat all of that food down on the table.

We were all smiles, ready to get our grub on, but for some reason, all the excitement that had been in Chyanne's eyes faded when Skye asked that question.

Chyanne picked up her fork and shrugged a little. "We didn't have a chance to go out last night."

"He didn't take you out to celebrate?" I asked. What was that about?

"Well . . . he wanted to but, you know, I wanted to celebrate with my team. And afterward, it was too late for us to get together to do anything."

"Oh," Skye said as she broke off a piece of catfish. "That makes sense."

I'm glad it made sense to her, because it didn't make a bit of sense to me. If that was her man and if they were so close, why wasn't he number one? Why did her team come first?

Chyanne said, "But he was real excited and we're going to celebrate tomorrow." Then she took a sip of her water, as if that was a good enough reason for her to stop talking about her guy.

Hmm. Umm. Something was going on with our girl, and now I was even more curious about this Mr. Malcolm. Skye and I had yet to meet him, even though he and Chyanne had been hot and heavy for close to a year. I was going to have to fix that. We needed to check out this Mr. Malcolm to make sure that he was treating our girl right.

But, I wasn't going to bring that up right now. I didn't want anything to spoil the festivities.

"Okay, okay," I said, getting all excited again. "Now, you go, Ms. Skye." I wanted my news to be the finale! "I remember that tall glass of water you were drooling over at the art show. As a matter of fact, don't you owe me something?"

"For what?"

I pointed my fork at her. "For introducing you to your new boo."

"You didn't introduce me. You weren't anywhere around when I met him."

I waved my hand in the air. "I cannot stand people who are unappreciative." Then I turned to Chyanne, as if Skye wasn't even at the table. "She is so wrong. If I hadn't bugged Leigh for the tickets, then bugged her to go with me, Skye would have never met that man."

"Okay." Skye laughed. "You're right. If it wasn't for you, I wouldn't be . . . on the verge of in love!"

"The verge of in love?" Chyanne and I squealed together.

Chyanne said, "Dang! I didn't know it was that serious. That was fast!"

Skye nodded. "Yeah, fast, but right, you know?"

"Yeah, I know," Chyanne said.

"I really like Noah." Skye spoke with a sincerity in her voice that I'd never heard from her before.

I looked at Skye and then at Chyanne. Oh, my! My girls were doing it—in the boardroom and the bedroom! They were taking New York City by storm.

And, I was about to join them in this mix!

I waited for the waiter to clear the table before I sat back in my chair and said, "So, is anyone going to ask me if I have any news?"

Chyanne and Skye looked at me as if I had the most boring life.

"What? You got something to tell us about the shop?" Skye asked.

Now see? If she wasn't my girl, I would've smacked her, minimizing my life like that. Though how could I really be mad? I'd told my girls, I'd told everyone that coming to New York was going to be all about work for me. I was using my twenties to build my career. After I got settled and had stacked up some serious paper, then I could go out and have fun.

But fate had changed all that.

Now Mr. Dark and Lovely was all up in my life.

"Well . . . I do have some news," I said. I took my time filling them in on Mr. An-to-n-i-o! By the time I finished, I had them sweating, too!

"Get out of here!" Chyanne said. "So, you really like . . . like this guy?"

"Oh, yes! Oh, yes! Oh, yes!"

Skye and Chyanne cracked up, but I didn't know why. I was telling the truth.

"Would you look at the three of us?" Skye said. She reached her hands forward, grabbing my hand on her left and Chyanne's on her right. "The three of us are living in New York. We're living our dreams—of careers and love. This is amazing."

"Yeah, amazing," Chyanne agreed.

All I could do was nod my head, 'cause truly I wanted to cry. This was the life. And I had a feeling that everything was just going to get better and better for all of us from this point on.

Chapter 14

Chyanne

I stared at the stack of papers on my desk, and I knew for sure that my world was out of whack. It felt as if the planet had tilted and there were seven full moons all out at once.

I'd felt this way for the past two weeks, since I'd won the Ferguson case. I don't know why, but I'd thought that after that big win, my life would be easy, all wonderful. But it was far from that.

It had started right here at work. The congratulations were still coming, but I'd been given another case right away. I wasn't complaining—I certainly wanted to show the partners that my winning had not been a fluke. I just didn't expect to get another heavy case so soon.

This time my team included six other attorneys—without Nicole—and I wasn't up against an individual. I was defending our client, Mastex, from trademark infringement against Master Pro, a much larger corporation. Just thinking about what I was facing had my stomach doing hourly somersaults.

And this time Malcolm wasn't here to help me. Not that I expected him to hold my hand on every case. But I did expect him to be there for me personally, and since I'd won the Ferguson case, it didn't seem like Malcolm was here at all, even though it hadn't started out that way.

The night after I'd had dinner with Skye and Devin, Malcolm had shown up at my apartment and told me to grab my purse.

"Where are we going?" I'd asked him.

"On an adventure."

Before we even stepped outside of my building, I saw the sleek limousine parked in front. Malcolm helped me inside, and once the driver took off, I asked my man once again where we were going.

"It's a surprise," he said as he took my hand. "A celebration."

I couldn't imagine which restaurant he was taking me to, and once the car crossed over the Triborough Bridge, I was wondering even more. But my heart started bumping hard against my chest when the car edged into LaGuardia Airport.

"You have to tell me now," I squealed.

Malcolm played like he didn't hear me before he whisked me into the terminal. It wasn't until we were at the counter that I found out we were going to Florida.

"Miami?" I said, shocked. "For dinner?"

He shook his head. "South Beach. For the weekend."

"But . . . but . . . but . . . I don't have any clothes."

He grinned. "Exactly. And you won't need any."

OMG! This was why I loved this man.

The whirlwind continued—from our first-class seats to the W Hotel with our penthouse view of the Atlantic Ocean. The hotel was both beautiful and trendy, and after checking in way after midnight, I still had more than enough energy to make love all night long to the man who owned my heart.

The next morning we had breakfast in bed, then just relaxed on the most luxurious Egyptian cotton sheets I'd ever felt against my skin. I never wanted to get up—especially since I didn't have any clothes. But at noon a woman arrived with a trunk load of outfits.

"Choose anything, everything you want," Malcolm told me.

It was Christmas in June for this Southern belle.

The weekend was the most fabulous two days of my life. It was the first time ever that I'd got to spend not only an entire night, but two nights, with the man I loved.

And the wonder continued until Monday morning, when we got up to catch our early flight back to New York.

We were in the shower when Malcolm said, "About the firm's gala. I don't think you should go."

I stepped out of the shower and wrapped a towel around myself. "Why? You really don't think we can handle this?"

He climbed out of the shower right behind me. "No."

Inside the bedroom, as we dressed, I kept silent. But once we were in the cab, heading to the airport, I broached the subject again.

"Malcolm, I know the risk of our relationship, but I know how to behave. I know how to handle this. I've done a great job in the office. No one has any clue."

"But this is different. We'll be together for several hours in front of some pretty sharp people who are paid a lot of money to be perceptive." He took my hand and kissed my fingers. "And you and I have this chemistry," he added, as if those words would make what he was saying sound better. "We have a chemistry that people are going to see. We just can't help it. I just don't think you should go."

"But that invitation is my reward for what I did on the Ferguson case."

"Exactly! The reward is the invitation—not actually attending the gala."

When the cab rolled to a stop in front of the airline terminal, Malcolm added, "Look, you just don't need to go. Period." He said it as if it was a demand. As if the subject was closed.

And that was the end of the most perfect weekend of my life.

I was so upset by it all that the moment we landed and Malcolm put me in a cab to go back to my place to get ready for work, I called Skye.

"This better be good," Skye had said. I could tell that she was still asleep. She never got up before eight.

"Hey, it's me," I said, and then, without another pause, I told her about my whole weekend.

"Girl, get out," she said. "The W? In South Beach? When am I going to meet this man and shake his hand?" Skye laughed.

"But wait," I said, not feeling anywhere as good as she did. "There's more." I told her about the invitation to the gala and how Malcolm didn't want me to go now. "He is so sure that one of the other partners is going to figure out that he's sleeping with one of his junior associates and—"

"Hold up! Hold up! Hold up!"

I frowned, wondering what had Skye all wound up. And then my eyes got big. Oh, no! I was so caught up that I'd told Skye what I had never revealed to her or Devin—that Malcolm was my boss.

"He's one of the partners? Where you work? Why didn't you tell me?"

"Yeah," I said, dragging the word out because I needed some time to figure out what I was going to say now. But what was the point? The secret was out, and I needed my girl to help me figure this whole gala thing out.

"So, that's why he doesn't want you to go? Because he's one of the partners?"

"Yeah. Because he's one of the partners and no one knows about us. No one *can* know about us, and he thinks if people see us there together, they'll figure it out." I sighed. "And, it's not like I want either of us to lose our job."

"Well, if he's one of the partners, that's not going to happen. Neither one of you is going to lose your job. And you can trust and believe, this is not the first time two people in the firm have hooked up. No!"

The way she said that, I could almost see Skye shaking her head.

She said, "You should go."

"You think so?"

"Definitely. The gala will be a great time and place for you to prove to Malcolm that you *can* handle it. That you can handle any situation. And once he sees that, Chy, it will bring the two of you closer together."

It was the part about Malcolm and me getting closer that had my attention. That was what I wanted. And what Skye said made a lot of sense.

I'd been thinking about Skye's words for the past two weeks. And there'd been so many times when I'd wanted to talk to Malcolm about it . . . just one more time. But he'd been so unavailable. I knew, of course, he was working on one of the biggest cases of his life, but even at night he didn't answer his phone. And he didn't call me.

I saw him a few times in the hall, but there was never a moment to sneak a kiss or even a hug. Something was wrong and I had to do something about it.

The ringing phone startled me out of my thoughts.

"Hey, girl," Skye said once I answered. "Have you gotten your gown for the gala yet?"

Even though she couldn't see me, I shook my head. "No. I haven't had a chance to talk to Malcolm again."

"Don't talk to him. Surprise him."

"I don't know." I wasn't sure I wanted to do that. I mean, I wasn't into playing any games.

Skye said, "Look, just bringing it up again will only stress both of you out. Malcolm has to see that not only can you handle this, but that you're serious about your relationship." When I didn't say anything, Skye sighed. "It's not like you're crashing a party or something. You were invited. And what will the other partners say if you don't go?"

Skye had a point.

She said, "So you're going to go, and I have the perfect gown for you."

"You don't do gowns."

"Aha! But you have forgotten who your best friend is and who I know."

She went on to tell me about an acquaintance of hers, another designer—Mona—who went by just her first name.

"Meet me there in an hour."

I looked down at the pile of paperwork on my desk. I hadn't made my way through half of the depositions. But while I loved my work, I loved Malcolm even more.

"Okay, give me the address."

After I hung up, I sat back. Skye was right. This would make an impression on Malcolm—in every way. I needed to walk into that gala and make his jaw drop. I needed to have confidence, to be beautiful, and totally aloof.

I smiled at that thought. I was getting excited. Malcolm would enjoy the aloof part.

Oh, yeah. This was the right thing to do. And now I couldn't wait.

Chapter 15

Skye

My friend looked sick. And I didn't mean that in a good way.

Chyanne, the beautiful one, looked pale—even paler than normal with her already fair-skinned complexion. To top it off, she looked like she'd lost a couple of pounds since I'd last seen her, and that was only two weeks ago.

But at least she was smiling, though her eyes looked sad.

"Hey, girl!" I said, keeping my voice light. I didn't want Chyanne to see that I was worried. Really, there probably wasn't a thing for me to worry about. It was probably that she was working too much just like I was. Right then and there, I made a vow that I was going to start spending more time with my friends. Because work wasn't worth as much as friendship.

"So, let's get on in here." I grabbed Chyanne's hand and led the way.

Mona met us at the front door of her studio/work space/living quarters loft, and she hugged me. "I haven't seen you in months," she said.

"I know. We have to do better."

I introduced Mona to Chyanne, and they hugged as if they were old friends.

"Come on in," Mona said. "I've got lots for you to see. Six gorgeous gowns."

"Really?" Chyanne said, her face brightening up.

That made me feel good.

But if Chyanne had started to look better before, she looked even better after Mona pulled the rack in with the gowns.

"Oh my God!" Chyanne and I said together.

I didn't have any words for the gowns that my friend had picked out for Chyanne. Any of these could have been on the runway, and what I loved best was that there was only one black dress among them. The others were all colors that would light up any red carpet: fuchsia, emerald, lavender, red and my favorite, sky blue.

"I don't know what to say," Chyanne said.

"Don't say anything yet," Mona responded. "Let's get you into these things and see which one will be best."

I stayed back as Mona picked up the first one—the black one, with the tan underlay—and led Chyanne toward the dressing area.

"Would you mind if I used the restroom first?" Chyanne asked.

"Over there." Mona pointed. "Then, when you're finished, I'll help you get into this dress over here."

Chyanne moved with slow steps toward the restroom, and I stared at my friend. Something was up with her—maybe it was just work, or maybe it was this thing with the gala and Malcolm. But whatever it was, I was going to find out and help her fix it.

As we waited for Chyanne, Mona and I chatted away, and I was thrilled to hear that Mona had heard my name mentioned in a couple of fashion circles.

"Everyone is talking about the new girl at Zora Davis," Mona said. "Nothing but good things."

"Are you kidding me? Oh, my God! That's wonderful. I just want to be where you are one day."

Mona laughed. "Please. You'll make it to here and beyond."

I was just about to go into the restroom to see what was taking Chyanne so long when she came out. But now she looked even paler than before.

This time I couldn't keep my concern to myself. "Are you okay?"

Chyanne kind of nodded her head, as if it took much effort for her to move. "Yeah, I'm fine. I just haven't been feeling well. It's the pressure of work and this new case and . . ."

I waved Chyanne's words about work away before she had me and Mona as stressed as she was. "We are not talking about work right now. We are just here to get you beautiful."

Mona agreed. "Come on, Chyanne. Let's make this happen."

As they disappeared into the dressing room, I lingered behind in the studio, strolling through, checking out some of the other dresses that Mona had hanging around. But my thoughts were on my friend. We really hadn't stayed in touch the way we did when we were growing up in Atlanta. I'd known her from my first days in school, but we'd really become close when she'd lost her father in an automobile accident when she was just seven. Chyanne had been in the car, too, but had not been hurt.

From that day, she'd been like my sister, and we did everything together—even coming to New York. So, that couldn't change now. Weeks couldn't go by without me knowing what was going on with her—and Devin, too. Dang! He had been all up in a relationship, and I hadn't known a thing about it. No, things had to change between me and my friends, because if they didn't, I had a feeling that we were all going to regret it.

"Here we are."

Mona's voice was behind me. I turned around and gasped. My goodness. There was not a word appropriate enough to completely describe how beautiful Chyanne looked in this Mona original.

The black beaded, lace dress fit Chyanne's form so well, showing all her curves. I really loved the one shoulder strap, as well as the way the dress flared out around her calves, adding a 1920s vintage look.

Mona held Chyanne's hand as she helped her onto the platform in front of the full-length, three-panel mirror. All three of us stared at Chyanne's reflection.

"You look amazing," was all that I could say.

I watched my friend stare at herself. Then, as each second passed, her eyes got smaller and smaller and smaller, until she jumped off of the platform and bolted into the restroom.

Mona and I stared at each other for just a couple of seconds before we dashed in there behind her.

Chyanne was already hugging the toilet bowl, and I slicked back her hair while Mona grabbed a towel and stuffed it under Chyanne's chin, covering the front of the dress. It was mostly dry heaves, thank God, and when she finally finished, with the love of a sister, I cleaned Chyanne up with Mona's towel.

We helped Chyanne move from the floor to the stool, and she sat until she got herself back together.

A couple of minutes passed before I asked, "What is going on with you?"

There were tears in Chyanne's eyes when she looked up at me and shook her head.

I inhaled a deep breath. Neither one of us was stupid . . . or naive. "How long have you been throwing up?"

"I don't know. A couple of weeks now. I thought it was because of work," she said.

"But . . ."

"I . . . I can't be."

It was like she couldn't even say the word. And I understood why. But one of us had to say it. "Have you taken a pregnancy test?"

"No . . . I was hoping that it was just work and stress, maybe."

"We have to go and do that."

I could tell that Chyanne was thinking about work, but she nodded, anyway.

"We'll go to my house," I said. "We'll pick up a kit on the way."

This time, in the dressing room, I helped Mona get Chyanne out of the dress.

"I'm so sorry," she said, apologizing.

"No harm, no foul," Mona said. "The dress is fine."

"Well, I'm going to buy it."

"You don't want to try on the others?" Mona asked. "I mean, not right now."

"No. I'll take this one."

"Okay," Mona agreed. "There are just some things I want to do to the hem, and I'll tighten up the seams a bit."

"That's fine. Just tell me how much it costs and the dress is mine," Chyanne said. But then she put her hand over her stomach and looked down.

I exchanged a sad glance with Mona.

"Okay, sweetie," Mona said before she hugged Chyanne. She hadn't even known my friend for an hour, but what Chyanne was going through right now was a universal scare. Mona understood—even if she didn't know Chyanne well.

"Call me . . . tomorrow," she told Chyanne.

I hugged Mona, too, and thanked her for what she'd done. Then I turned all my attention to Chyanne. Taking over, I led her from the studio, into the street, and hailed a cab right away.

Once we were settled into the cab, I told Chyanne that there was a drugstore on the corner of my block that we would stop at first. She nodded and reached for my hand. No other words were needed. We just held each other—both of us too scared to say anything else.

Stunned! That was the word that kept going through my mind. I had never been more stunned in my life.

Chyanne was pregnant. We had two pregnancy strips to prove it!

I walked back and forth, pacing in front of the couch, where Chyanne sat as stunned as I was. We'd been like this from the moment we found out the results; and after all that we'd been through, after all of our years together, I can honestly say, this was the very first time I didn't have any words.

But I had to find a way to comfort my friend. So, I stopped walking. And sat down next to her, even though I still couldn't think of anything to say.

Chyanne was the one who spoke first. "Nice picture," she said.

I frowned. *What?* "Oh," I said as I followed her eyes to the wall where I'd just hung the picture. It was the portrait that Noah had done of me—in his signature style. "Noah did that."

"Wow, he's talented. I can't wait to meet him."

I had let Chyanne stall long enough. I twisted onto the couch so that I was facing her. "Chyanne, what . . ."

Before I could say anything else, she burst into tears. Dang, I guess that wasn't the right thing to say. But I knew the right thing to do, and I just held my friend. I held her and hugged her until she didn't have any more tears left.

"Do you want to talk about it?" I asked when she pulled away.

She sniffed and shook her head.

"Okay," I said. "But why don't you stay with me tonight? Then, if you want to talk . . ."

"No. I really want to go home. I need the space to think, you know?"

I nodded, even though I didn't really understand. If this was me, I know I wouldn't have wanted to be by myself.

Chyanne pushed herself up and tucked her purse under her arm. "I'm gonna get going."

We walked in silence to my front door. When we faced each other, I asked, "Are you sure you don't wanna stay?"

"I'm sure."

"I don't think you should be by yourself. Are you going to call Malcolm?"

Oh, boy. When I saw the tears that came to her eyes, I decided right then that I wasn't going to say another word.

She nodded. "But I probably won't call him tonight. Tomorrow."

"Okay, sweetie," I said, keeping my words to a minimum. "Call me when you get home, please?" I hugged her, then stood at my door until she got onto the elevator.

Finally in my apartment alone, I released a long breath. "Wow!"

As much as Chyanne and I liked to perpetrate, we were really the good girls in our neighborhood. Of course, we had lost our virginity—but not until college.

And we didn't sleep around. Sex didn't come early and it didn't come easy in a relationship with us. We had to be in love.

I knew Chyanne was in love with Malcolm—she'd been talking that way about him for a couple of months now. And from what she told us about him, I knew he felt the same way about her.

I just prayed that he was ready to take things to the next level.

My apartment felt so empty, so quiet. I turned on my iPod, but that was not enough. I needed to talk to someone.

Devin! I reached for the phone but then pulled my hand back. This was something Chyanne needed to tell—in her own space, in her own time. I was going to have to keep this news to myself.

Still, I needed to talk to someone. I needed to hear a loving voice.

I thought about Noah, but when I picked up the telephone, I called my parents.

Chapter 16

Chyanne

Tonight was the night. For two weeks, I'd held this secret between just me and Skye. But tonight I was going to tell the most important person. Tonight I was going to tell Malcolm.

I hadn't planned to wait for the night of the gala to break this news. It had just worked out that way. He was so busy with the case he'd been working on—a major merger between two corporations—that he hadn't been to my apartment in weeks. In fact, we hadn't been intimate since our weekend in Miami. Just my luck—I stopped having sex after it was too late.

I was pretty sure, though, that tonight we would be together—especially once I stunned him at that gala. I still hadn't told him that I was going, but I knew he would be glad to see me—he always was. I just prayed that the news I had for him tonight would make him smile.

Malcolm and I hadn't talked a lot about marriage, but we were heading that way for sure. We'd been seeing each other exclusively for months now, and the only reason we hadn't talked more about marriage was because of work—and what would the partners would do.

But that was going to change tonight.

I would have to be careful, though. Malcolm was right—these were high-powered attorneys who made big bucks because they could read people. They couldn't see anything in the way Malcolm and I interacted; I was going to make sure of that.

"Would you sit still?" Devin fussed. "I have to get this last curl in place."

I'd spent the last two weeks in hiding—at work, primarily—so that I wouldn't have to talk about this with Skye or reveal it to Devin. Skye had been the ultimate friend, calling every day but leaving the subject of the baby for me to bring up . . . which I hardly did. Not that I didn't want to talk to my friends about this. I really couldn't wait to celebrate with Skye and Devin. It was just that I wanted to see where Malcolm and I were first. He deserved to know before anyone except for Skye, of course.

"All right, you can get up now," Devin said as he waved his hands in a flourish. "And take a look at my masterpiece!"

Behind me, Skye clapped as I stood from the chair at my vanity and glanced at myself in the leaning mirror in my bedroom. Devin had given me what I called Shirley Temple curls—adult style. It was cute, stylish, and elegant all at once.

"Okay, it's time for you to get into this dress." Skye pulled the black gown down from the hanger as I slipped my bathrobe from my shoulders, then stopped.

I looked at Devin. "Are you just gonna stand there?" I asked him.

He waved his hand. "Girl, as long as we've been friends, I've seen it all. And you don't have a thing that I want."

Skye and I laughed at Devin, but he wasn't playing. He stood right where he was as Skye held the gown for me to step in. So, I pushed my robe all the way off and stood there—in just my bra and thong.

"Hmph, hmph, hmph," I heard Devin say behind me as I slipped into the gown. "From that teeny-weeny underwear that you're wearing, it looks like tonight's gonna be a good night."

"I thought I didn't have anything you want?" I joked.

"You don't, but I still like to check out the other side," Devin said as he came over and zipped up the gown for me. Then he took two steps back, snapped his fingers, and said, "Girl, you look something fierce. Mr. Malcolm is gonna be drooling tonight."

That was my hope.

I took a breath as I inspected myself, twisting from the left to the right in the mirror. Then, like I did every time I stood in front of a mirror these days, I let my eyes wander down to my center. My stomach was still as flat as it had always been, and I tried to imagine what I'd look like in a month, and in three months and nine months.

"You so know that you look really amazing," Devin said.

"That is exactly what I told her."

"Thank you," I said to my friends, though I stayed in front of the mirror. By now, I was supposed to be excited. This was my first gala. I was one of only four junior associates invited and I was going to get to be with Malcolm afterward for the first time in weeks.

But there was no excitement in me. Instead, a thunderstorm rumbled in my stomach, but at least now I knew exactly what that feeling was.

"I think your town car is downstairs," Devin said, peeking out the window. "I still can't figure out why Mr. Mysterious isn't here to escort you himself." He shook his head. "Don't men know how to act these days?"

"I told you . . . he's going to meet me there because he had to work." I kept my eyes away from Skye as I said that. Just grabbed my purse and my shawl and headed toward the door.

My friends walked with me all the way to the elevator, then out onto the street. Devin held the door to the town car open, while Skye hugged me.

"Have a great time tonight," she whispered. "And please, call me and let me know how it goes."

I knew she was talking about Malcolm and the baby. I hadn't told her, but somehow, she knew that I was going to tell him tonight. I guess that was what twenty years of friendship got us—she knew me as well as I knew myself.

Once I was inside the car, I rolled down the window and waved until I couldn't see Skye or Devin anymore. Then I sat back and exhaled. There were so many thoughts whirling in my head. Would Malcolm be happy? What would we tell the partners? And then the biggest question, would he want to get married right away?

I prayed that Malcolm was old-fashioned; I prayed that he would want to get married before the baby came. And wouldn't it be something if he proposed to me tonight?

That thought made me smile. Now I could sit back and enjoy the ride uptown. Because inside my head, I allowed that fantasy to play out and it was wonderful.

Tonight was going to be one of the most important nights of my life.

As soon as I walked into the Roosevelt Hotel's grand ballroom, I wished that I'd not come to this gala alone.

Of course, I would be with Malcolm at the end of this night, but still, it was a bit intimidating. All of these people, White people, dressed in tuxedos and ball gowns.

Not that this was the first time I was attending some swanky event. But this was the first time I was attending one for my firm and attending one alone.

Dang! I should have asked Devin to come along with me. Or even Skye. It was too late now, though. I was here—and it really didn't matter. Once I found Malcolm, it would all be better. Even though we wouldn't stand side by side as a couple, we could stand together as colleagues.

And then, tonight . . . at my apartment . . . we would lie together in my bed.

The thought of that made me shiver and smile. Of course, there was the subject of our baby that we had to discuss, but I had a feeling that Malcolm was going to be happy about it. Maybe not thrilled, but he loved me. So, we would work it out.

I pressed my way through the crowd, smiling at the people who glanced my way. I could almost see the questions in their minds—who was this Black girl, and what was she doing here? I guess these were natural questions for them. No one had seen me before, and these people looked and smelled like wealth.

I pushed my shoulders back, held my head up. I wasn't of their kind—they could tell that. But I would be—soon. I was the up-and-coming attorney in one of the largest firms in one of the largest cities in the world. I was sure that at next year's gala everyone here would know my name.

Making my way to one of the bars, I stayed at the edge for a moment, taking in the sight behind me. Two hundred, maybe even three hundred, people milled about. The air was filled with the din of chatter as the men discussed their latest deals on Wall Street and the women dished on what happened at last weekend's social events.

"Hey, beautiful," the bartender said to get my attention.

I looked into the face of a cutie-pie, but I didn't like the fact that he'd addressed me that way. Not at an event like this. He should know better, since I was pretty sure that he hadn't called anyone else anything besides sir or ma'am.

"Whatcha havin'?"

"Just a ginger ale," I said, deciding to keep my opinion of how he was talking to me to myself. I took the glass from him, dropped two dollars into the tip jar, and then turned away. Not that I wanted to be rude, but I couldn't be caught chatting it up with the bartender when I hadn't talked to anyone else yet.

I needed to find Malcolm.

And then, just as I thought that, he appeared. Across the room. At the bar that was on the other side.

Thank God!

I left my glass on the bar, not wanting anything in my hand, not wanting anything to mess up my look. Smoothing out my dress, I tucked my clutch in my hand, then pressed through the crowd once again. My eyes were on Malcolm the entire time as he stood, apparently ordering a drink. I thought about how we hadn't spent much time together lately, but how we would make up for that tonight. I thought about this news I had for him, and knowing him so well, I could already see his reaction. Shocked at first, of course. But then he'd be pleased. With each step I took toward him, my confidence grew.

Finally, I was just a few steps away, and he saw me.

The shock on his face was so apparent, but I smiled, because I knew what that look was all about—he was just surprised to see me . . . and I looked good!

I slowed my stroll and sauntered over to him so that he could get the full effect of my dress. When I stood toe-to-toe with him, I said, "Hey, Malcolm." I reached to give him a hug, but he pushed my arms away before I could even touch him.

"Hey . . . hey . . . ," Malcolm stuttered, then glanced around, as if he was checking out whether anyone had seen us.

Okay, he didn't even want to give me a hug? I mean, didn't people give innocent hugs at events like this? But I had to play this the way Malcolm wanted because he knew best. And really, he didn't even want me to come here, so I had to do it exactly his way.

I stepped back and kept my smile. "It's good to see you," I said.

"I . . . I . . . What are you doing here?" he asked as his eyes still shifted through the room.

Was that the first thing he had to say to me? Okay!

"I decided to come," I said, giving him a little shrug. "I wanted to show you that we could be at these kinds of events together without anyone knowing anything."

He nodded and took a big swallow of whatever he was drinking.

I lowered my voice. "I've missed you, Malcolm." I waited for him to say the same thing to me. But when he didn't, I added, "I need to talk to you about something important. So, can you come over tonight?"

Before he could say a word, a woman pressed her body between us.

"Malcolm, baby? I was waiting for my drink."

My heart was already pounding as I took two steps back and surveyed the woman. She was petite in every way; only about five-two, and probably a size zero. The biggest thing on her was her hair—long, black, hanging down her back, almost to her waist. If I had to guess, she had Indian blood pumping through her veins.

I was shaking by the time I pulled my eyes away from the woman and looked straight at Malcolm. My eyes asked him what my lips could not—to please explain this to me.

"Baby?" she called him again. "Did you get my drink?"

With a little nod, he handed her a martini.

That was when she turned to me and reached out her free hand. "I don't know what's wrong with my husband. I'm Kayla Parks."

Her introduction took my breath away. But there was no way I was going to let her see that. No way I was going to make a scene.

"Hi. I'm Chyanne. I work with . . . your husband."

"Really?" Kayla turned to Malcolm. "You didn't tell me that you had a new associate at the firm." To me, she smiled and said, "Such a beautiful associate at that." She asked me, "Did you just start?"

No, was what I said inside my head. *I've been there . . . at the firm . . . with your husband forever a year!* But since my lips couldn't move, all I did was nod. I had to get away, though. Because if I didn't, I was going to throw up on both of us.

"Excuse me," I said, glancing at Malcolm one last time, praying inside that he had some kind of explanation. But he couldn't seem to keep his eyes on mine.

I spun around as fast as I could—I couldn't let Mrs. Parks see the tears that were already in my eyes. I couldn't let anyone see me fall apart.

Tightening the shawl around my shoulders, I rushed out of the ballroom and then ran down the hallway to the entrance of the hotel. Really, I should have gone to the bathroom, because I could feel the bile rising up in me. But I couldn't stay in the same place with Malcolm and his wife. I couldn't take the chance of seeing him or her.

Malcolm and his wife.

Oh, my God! How could Malcolm do this to me? What was I going to do now?

Chapter 17

Skye

I was almost singing "I Am Woman"!

I mean, really, this was the best of times. I was doing everything. I was working on my new line, I was helping my boss with all the photo shoots . . . and I was managing my man.

The only thing that was bothering me was Chyanne. I hadn't heard from her for three days—not since the gala. I was trying not to worry, though, thinking that she was just spending all her time with Malcolm. After all, they did have lots to talk about. Still, it wasn't like Chyanne to be silent like this, and if I didn't hear from her tonight, I was going to march right over to her apartment and break up whatever lovefest she and Malcolm had going on over there.

The knock on the door stopped me from thinking about Chyanne, and my assistant came in. "Girl, look at these."

Her hands were filled with a bouquet of lilies, and I couldn't help but grin. This was the first time Noah had sent me flowers. Wow!

Taking the bouquet from her hands, I inhaled right at the exact moment that my phone rang, and I grabbed it, praying that it was Chyanne . . . finally.

"Did you get the flowers?"

"Huh?" Now, I know that wasn't the proper way to thank someone, but the thing was, whoever was asking about the flowers wasn't Noah.

"My flowers," the man said again. "They should have arrived a few minutes ago." I grabbed the card from the bouquet: *Nice meeting you.* But there was no name, no signature. Were these from one of the male models I'd worked with?

The man on the phone said, "Don't tell me you've forgotten me already."

"Who is this?" I asked. Since it wasn't Noah, I wasn't interested in playing any games.

"I guess I didn't make much of an impression." He chuckled. "This is Trent Hamilton."

Trent Hamilton?

"We met at Starbucks," he said, as if he knew I had no idea who he was.

Oh, yeah. That fine guy. I would've felt good about the call, except, how in the world did he get my number?

"Let me explain before you think I'm a stalker or something."

"Good," I said, "because that is exactly what I was beginning to think."

He chuckled again. "I Googled you. That's how I found out that you worked for Zora Davis."

Ah! Google!

"So, have I done enough to at least see you again?"

"Well . . ."

"Flowers, my ingenuity, and you're still not impressed? I promise if you have dinner with me, you won't regret it."

"Well . . ." was all that I could manage again.

"Look, Skye, you made quite an impression on me, and I'd like to get to know you better."

I didn't know why I was hesitating. I was in a relationship with Noah. We hadn't completely defined it yet, but I was hoping that we would soon. I was hoping that Noah would want to be committed, exactly the way I wanted to be.

"Trent," I said, "thank you for the flowers, and for tracking me down. But, I'm seeing someone."

"Oh, my bad." He paused. "I'm sorry. I didn't see your ring."

"I'm not married, just . . . committed."

"So, are you committed to the point where you can't even have lunch . . . or dinner? I mean, a woman has to eat. Why should one as beautiful as you have to eat alone?"

I shook my head, even though he couldn't see me. "I'd rather not."

"Fair enough," he said. "I appreciate a woman with integrity. Just one more thing for me to like about you."

Dang! I started thinking about our meeting again. How fine Trent was, how he just looked like money. And now I was finding out that he was a nice guy, too. It was a good thing that Noah and I were solid as a rock.

"I'll keep your number," I said, really wanting to get off the phone before I changed my mind and agreed to go out with him.

"Please do," he said, "because I'm certainly going to keep yours."

I couldn't stop staring at the phone when I hung up. Why hadn't I bumped into Trent before I bumped into Noah? Wait a minute. What was I saying? Noah was a wonderful man. I needed to keep my focus on him and just stay in that lane.

Just as I was setting the lilies on the credenza, my phone rang again. I half expected it to be Trent again, but the moment I heard her voice, my smile went away.

"Chyanne, what's wrong?" I said after she said hello.

"I'm . . . I'm calling a Code Red."

"Where are you?" I asked.

"Home. Home." Then she sobbed, and I told her that I'd be right there. "I'll call Devin. We'll be there in thirty minutes, sweetie. Hang on."

My hands were shaking as I hung up the phone. Code Red—that was our signal for an emergency meeting, and whenever any one of us called that, we all dropped whatever we were doing.

We hadn't had a Code Red since we'd been in New York. In fact, I couldn't really remember when the last time was that we had one. But it didn't matter—we had one now.

I told my assistant that I had an emergency, and I was already out the door when I put in the call to Devin.

Chapter 18

Devin

I was exhausted! Not only had I already had a full day, but I'd just finished up Leigh's hair for some new club opening she had to handle up in Harlem. I loved Leigh, but it was draining to listen to her love life. Not that I was complaining, I knew it was a good thing that Leigh had me to talk to. But she and Michael needed to stop all this foolishness and get it together. It was hard to find true love in this life, and since they had it, they needed to work it out.

I hoped that she would think about my idea for them to take a vacay. That was what the two of them needed—to get away and remember how to be in love again.

Now, if anyone knew anything about that, it was me and Mr. Dark and Lovely. I am telling you, Antonio and I had it going on for real. Hmph hmph hmph. For the first time in my life, I think I was really in love. It was because I was in love with Antonio's mind more than anything else. I loved the way we talked about anything and everything. I loved how he was interested in the world, politics, sports, and everything in between. We were made for each other, and I was even thinking about taking him home with me next time I went down to Atlanta. Now, that would be a big deal if I decided to do it.

Thinking about Antonio made me jump out of my chair. I was ready to clean up my station and head over to my man's place for a little rest, relaxation, and whatever else the two of us could come up with.

When my cell phone rang, I almost didn't pick it up, until I saw that it was Skye.

"Hey, Mz. Thang."

"Code Red," she said.

"What? Who? You or Chyanne?"

"Chyanne. Meet me over there."

"On my way," I said and hung up.

Wow! A Code Red. When was the last time we had one of those? It was with Simone, Skye's sister, a long time ago back in Atlanta. And really, I couldn't remember the last time Chyanne had called a Code Red personally for herself. She was the one out of all of us who always had it together.

Well, that was exactly why I had to be there for her now.

"Carmen," I said to the stylist who was like the assistant manager, "can you close up tonight?"

"Sure."

I gathered my things and headed out of the door. There was no way I could take the train into the city. That would take too long. This called for a cab.

I jumped into the first one that stopped, gave the cabbie Chyanne's address, then called Antonio. I was going to have to put Mr. Dark and Lovely on hold for tonight.

Chapter 19

Chyanne

It had been three days of nothing but depression for me. I just couldn't get it together.

Sunday I'd cried the entire day, and then Monday I'd called in sick before I rushed to my gynecologist and found out that yes, I was seven weeks pregnant. It was a good thing I'd already told my assistant that I wasn't going to be in, because the only thing I'd done was cry for the rest of the afternoon.

My plan was to go to work yesterday, but how could I? What was I supposed to say to Malcolm? How could I face him when I'd been such a fool?

I played it over and over in my mind. There had never been any signs that he was married. Yes, there were times when I couldn't reach him, just like there were times when he couldn't reach me. It was because of our jobs. We were attorneys in a high-powered law firm. We were busy.

Besides that, I'd been to his condo, and he'd taken me away for the weekend just a few weeks ago. He was at my apartment four, sometimes five times a week. How had he pulled all that off?

And why hadn't anyone at the firm told me? Because no one knew about the two of us. Still, shouldn't there have been some mumblings about him being married? But I tried and tried and tried to remember—and there was nothing.

Malcolm displayed none of the signs of marriage—no pictures on his desk in his office, no ring on his finger . . . nothing!

Still, I felt like a fool!

All I could think about was his wife. His beautiful wife. Kayla. And I wondered, why would he want me?

I'd been fighting it, but my tears started all over again. I rolled up onto the couch—there was no way I could go to my bed. I hadn't slept in there since I'd come home from the gala. There was no way I'd be able to sleep with all those memories in that room.

Even though the outside hallway had thick carpet, I could hear the heavy steps coming toward my door. I was sure it was Skye; Devin was much more graceful than Skye or me.

She pounded on the door, and I wished she'd had a key so that I wouldn't have to move. But I pushed myself up, dragged myself across the room, and let her in. The moment she stepped inside and wrapped her arms around me, I cried as if this was the first time I was letting all this anguish out. I was still crying when Devin busted in, carrying two large grocery bags.

Without saying anything, Skye led me back to the couch, and Devin started unpacking the bags. Right on the coffee table, he piled up every kind of snack that I loved: white macadamia nut cookies, brownies, and my favorite Chunky Monkey ice cream. He also had a bottle of my favorite red wine—I guessed Skye had kept my secret.

While I stretched out on the couch, Skye and Devin moved around my apartment as if they had lived there. In just a few minutes they had plates, glasses, and silverware laid out before they sat down in front of me.

For the last three days, I'd thought of nothing but Malcolm . . . and his wife. I hadn't thought about what

I was going to say to my friends. Now, while they sat there staring at me, waiting for me to speak, the tears came to my eyes.

"Oh, no, you don't," Devin said. "You're not going to cry when I don't know what we're crying about yet."

He poured a glass of wine, handed it to me, and I burst right into tears. I couldn't help it.

"What?" Devin asked as Skye came up onto the couch to hold me again.

"She can't drink."

"Why not?" Devin frowned. And then his eyes got wide. Slowly, he put the glass down. "You're pregnant?"

I nodded because I couldn't speak. Tears were coming out of my eyes too fast.

"Get out. Is that what this Code Red is about?"

"Yes," Skye said.

I got myself together enough to say, "No. It's not."

It was Skye's turn to frown.

I said, "It's about the fact that my baby's father, Malcolm . . . is . . . is married."

"What?" my friends said at the same time.

I took a deep breath, then told my friends about all that had happened since they'd seen me off to the gala. When I got to the part about Malcolm's wife, they both leaned forward, as if they were sitting on the edge of their seats, watching some Academy Award–winning movie.

"When she introduced herself, what did you do?" Devin asked.

I shook my head. "Nothing. I just told her it was nice to meet her."

"Hmph! I would've snatched that weave right off of her head."

"It's not her fault," Skye said.

"That's right. *I'm* the other woman!" Just saying that made me start crying all over again.

This time Devin joined us on the couch, and both of my friends held me.

Devin said, "Well, I think what we need to do now is just figure out a way to kill Malcolm."

"Dang, Devin!" Skye said.

"Don't jump on him. I've been trying to figure out the same thing. But I'm not sure that I'm a good enough lawyer to get myself off."

My two friends tried to laugh, but it didn't sound as if anyone was happy.

"So, I take it you didn't tell him that you're pregnant?" Skye asked.

I shook my head.

"Are you going to tell him?"

I shrugged. I hadn't thought that far ahead.

"Have you spoken to him at all?" Skye continued her questioning, as if she was the attorney.

"No."

"What?" Devin jumped up. "He hasn't even called you?"

"No, no. I mean, yes. He's called. About one hundred times. Telling me that he wants to explain. But I haven't answered."

"I'm surprised that he didn't try to come over here."

I shrugged; I had been thinking the same thing. "I don't know what to say about Malcolm anymore. It's like I never knew him."

"Well, I know one thing," Devin piped in. "You need to get yourself together. Ain't no reason for you to let a man take you out of the game like this."

"Devin's right," Skye agreed. "You can't sit at home forever. What about work?"

This was why I'd called a Code Red. I knew my friends would be able to get me to do what I hadn't been able to talk myself into.

"Get up," Devin said, pulling my hand. "Go in there and take a shower," he demanded. "Skye, you help her," he continued, as if he was in charge. "And then I'll hook your hair up, and we'll all go out to dinner and figure this thing out."

I stood, not only because I had no choice, since Devin had grabbed my arms. But I also stood because my friend was right. I couldn't afford to miss any more time at work, and I didn't want to stay locked up in my apartment anymore. Plus, I had a baby growing inside of me and decisions had to be made. I couldn't make any decisions, locked up in here, lying down and crying all day.

So, I moped into the bedroom, with Skye right behind me. It was time for me to get my life back.

Chapter 20

Skye

It was amazing the way life changed so fast. Just a few weeks ago Chyanne, Devin, and I had gotten together to celebrate Chyanne winning her first case, and we were all on top of the world. But now Chyanne was so far at the bottom that I didn't know what was going to happen.

Chyanne still didn't know what she was going to do, but at least Devin and I had gotten her cleaned up and out of the house last night. Then she'd called me this morning—she was going to work. I hung up from her only after she promised to call me as soon as she got home from work.

But the thing was, I was exhausted. I hadn't taken a sick day since I'd started work, and right after I took that call from Chyanne, I called my boss, disguised my voice, told her that I had some kind of bug that I was sure would be over in twenty-four hours, then rolled back over in the bed.

Now, two hours later, I had finally made my way into the living room, but as I curled up on the couch, I looked straight at the sketch that Noah had done of me.

I still couldn't believe it—it looked just like me, and I couldn't figure out when he'd done it.

"I caught a little bit here, a little bit there," he'd said to me. "Every time I'm with you, I capture another facet of you, your loveliness, your peacefulness, your joy. I had to put that down on canvas."

"But . . . when? I never saw you sketching me."

"You're in my mind all the time. Your image is always in my head."

Even now I sighed as I thought back to those words. That was the moment that I knew for sure that I was falling in love with this man. He was just so wonderful, unlike Malcolm.

I shook my head. I wasn't going to sit here and waste my day off thinking about Chyanne and how horrible Malcolm was.

Yeah, Noah. That was where I needed to have my attention, especially since he already had my heart.

I glanced up at the sketch again and realized it had been two days since I'd seen him. Noah and I never got to spend much time together during the week because of my schedule.

I got the idea and jumped up at the same time. What had I been thinking? I had a day off. How many hours could I spend with Noah? I couldn't get to the shower fast enough. But it was there, under the spray of the water, that I began to think about what this day would bring.

Even though we hadn't spoken the words to each other, I was in love with Noah, and it was so clear that he was in love with me. So, what was I waiting for? Maybe it was time to commit myself fully to him. Maybe it was time for us to sleep together.

That thought was still in my mind as I got dressed. I'd never taken sex lightly and, really, still had the same values that my parents had instilled in me as I was growing up. Sex before marriage was not the best of things. But now that I was with Noah, I felt different. It was so clear to me that Noah and I were going to be together. It just felt right.

Yeah, this was the time. Today was the day. And the best part was that Noah didn't even know it.

I checked myself out in the mirror before I left my apartment. My jeans and halter top were casual enough, but sexy. And easy to get off—that was important. Outside, I stopped at the deli on the corner and purchased Noah's favorite: a pastrami sandwich. Next, I grabbed a bottle of white wine and glanced at the cheesecake that I knew that Noah loved. But then I decided that he didn't need any dessert—I would be more than enough for him.

I smiled all the way down to his loft, imagining what it was going to be like to be with Noah fully. I was nervous—I admit that. But nervous in a good way. Nervous in the excited way. I didn't have anything to be afraid of. I loved every part of Noah's body. And, I was in for some good stuff, because sometimes when we kissed and he pressed up against me, I could tell just how much he wanted me.

Talking about getting hot and bothered! Just thinking about what was to come had me ready. Stepping out of the cab, I glanced up at Noah's window—not that I expected him to be looking out. He was working. . . . I was sure of that. Well, he was just going to have to stop for a while.

Inside the building, I could already hear the music coming from his loft—John Coltrane. That was interesting. I didn't know he worked to music. But I guess there wasn't a lot that I did know about his work, since I was usually at work myself at this time.

At his door I took a deep breath and knocked. I waited, then knocked again.

The door suddenly opened, and I grinned. "Surprise!" I stepped past him before he could stop me, but then I stopped myself.

It was hard for me to wrap my mind around the scene in front of me. In the middle of the room stood a woman, an attractive woman with her arms folded, looking me up and down.

At least she was still dressed except for her shoes; she was barefoot.

It took me only a couple of seconds to take in the scene—the flowers, the candles, the plates from which they'd eaten on the floor. And still, John Coltrane played in the background.

My chest was hurting from the way my heart pounded, and I turned to Noah with so many questions. But I couldn't get anything out. Finally, I cried, "Noah!"

"Skye," he said, taking steps toward me. "I didn't know you were coming over."

It was probably the fact that that was the first thing he said to me that made me flip out. I threw the little sandwich I'd bought for him right at his head. He ducked, and it was a good thing, because the bottle of wine was right after that. The bottle crashed onto the hardwood floor, spilling all over the place.

"Skye!"

Behind me, ol' girl said, "Uh, Noah, I think I'm gonna get out of here!"

I whipped around and faced her. "You better!" I screamed.

"Skye!" Now Noah was on top of me, as if he was afraid that I might take a swing at the woman. And he was right, because I was two seconds off her butt.

She rushed out of there like the loft was on fire. Well, I guess in a way it was.

"How could you do this to me?" I asked Noah the moment we were alone. "I came over here to surprise you. To bring you lunch," I screamed, pointing to the sandwich on the floor. "To spend the day with you."

"You should've called."

"What? Is that all you have to say to me?" This time I did start swinging, but Noah caught my wrists.

"Why are you acting like this?"

"Are you kidding me? I find you up here with another woman and . . ."

"So."

So? Oh, it was on now. I tried to wrestle away from his grasp, but he held me tight.

"Listen to me," Noah said.

I calmed down only because I had to.

He held me as he explained, "I care for you, Skye, but we weren't in a committed relationship."

"What?"

"We've never established being in a relationship," he said. "We were taking it slow, seeing where things go, but we were both free to see other people."

"That's not what I thought," I said weakly. "I thought we were together."

He shrugged. "We are . . . in a way, I guess, but I'm not ready to commit to anyone."

Noah must have seen it in my eyes—my defeat. And he let go of my hands. I stood there as still as stone as he continued.

"I'm sorry, Skye, if you thought this was more than it was. But trust me, you don't want to get serious with me."

How could he say that?

"I've been there once. I tried to be committed. And my fiancée cheated on me. My heart's not ready to go there again."

I wanted to tell him that I wouldn't do that to him, that he could trust me with his heart.

But then he said, "And, really, we've only known each other a few weeks. I've been seeing Monique"—he pointed to the door—"for a lot longer than I've been seeing you."

Those were the words that crushed me. Our relationship flashed through my mind. I thought about how we met, how he'd been so kind, so sweet, so loving. I thought about the way he'd kissed me and touched me as if he cherished me.

But all of that had just been a man getting his freak on.

Then I thought about the way I'd come over here today, fully prepared to give myself to him. My humiliation was complete.

First, Chyanne and now me.

I guess we weren't ready for the big city.

I grabbed my purse from the floor, and without looking at Noah, I walked across the room, trying my best to keep my head high. At least I wanted him to think that I still had some dignity.

"I really do care about you, Skye, and I would really like for us to stay friends."

Friends? How could I be friends with him? Why did men think they could be selfish and then attach "I want to be friends" to the end of things and we'd accept that? I didn't say anything and kept walking.

"I'm sorry," Noah said right before I got to the door.

I wiped my tears away before I turned around to face him. "You sure are."

Outside, I just let the tears fall. That was probably why the first cab that rolled down the block stopped.

"Are you all right, Miss?" the man with the turban asked me over and over.

I didn't bother to answer him. I didn't feel like talking to any man.

Inside my apartment I curled up on the couch and wondered what would've happened if I had just stayed here today. But I hadn't, and now I knew the truth.

We were both free to see other people.

Those words that he'd spoken played over and over in my head. No, we weren't! If we were, I would've gone out with the first man who'd come along. I would've gone out with Trent.

Trent. Trent Hamilton.

I sat up, rummaged through my purse, and his card was exactly where I had tucked it inside the pocket.

Now all I could think about were the flowers that he'd sent me. Wasn't that just yesterday? Yeah, yesterday, when I'd told him that I couldn't go out with him because I was seeing someone else.

I laughed, though I was hurting inside. And it was because of that hurt that I decided to make the call.

Chapter 21

Devin

God had given me the wrong mother! And He was probably laughing about it. For real, I had the wrong mother, 'cause Juanita Williams was not supposed to be related to me in any way. No! Juanita Williams needed to have a daughter. Yeah, a daughter who was perfect and caused her no grief.

And a daughter who was as nosy as she was.

It wasn't that I didn't love my mother; I did. It was just that we weren't all that close. So, what was she doing sitting up here in my brownstone in Brooklyn, in my kitchen, complaining about this coffee that I had just made for her?

"Are you surprised, Devin?" she asked me for the one hundredth time.

Hell yeah, I was surprised. I had no idea who was knocking on my door at seven o'clock in the morning, and I had started not to answer it. But I had crawled out of bed, slumped down the stairs, opened the front door to "Surprise" and Juanita Williams standing on my steps.

I must've stood there for five minutes with my mouth open.

"Ma! What are you doing here?"

While I let her in and closed the door, she explained to me how her group of church members and friends, known as the Getaways, was on its way to Italy.

"Why didn't you tell me you were coming?"

"'Cause I didn't want you pretending that you weren't going to be home," my mother said like she knew me. "And I'm only going to be here a couple of hours. I booked my flight so that I have this six-hour layover, though that doesn't give us much time."

Six hours? That sounded like a lot of time to me.

"So, are you surprised, Devin?"

Oh, yeah, I was surprised. But she was lucky that she wasn't the one surprised. On any given night, Antonio could've been up in here. And what would my mother have said then? Not that she didn't know and not that she made a big deal about my being gay. But I could just tell that she wasn't happy about it. She never talked about it, never asked me a thing about my life. I was sure that every night she was on her knees, trying to pray my gay away.

"So, how are the girls?" my mother asked.

After she hadn't seen me since the holidays, and after just talking to me about five times in the last six months, this was her first question to me? See what I was talking about? Juanita didn't want to know a thing about what was going on with me.

"They're fine," I said, though everything about Chyanne ran through my mind at that moment. I guess "fine" wasn't really the right way to describe my girl right now, but what was I supposed to do? Tell my mother the truth—about the married man and her pregnancy? I don't think so!

"Either one of them married yet?"

"No, Ma!" I said, as if I thought that was a stupid question. "You know we just got here. And if they had gotten married, it would've been back home with Reverend Davenport."

"Mmm-hmm." She took a sip of her coffee. "So either one of them engaged?"

I sighed. "No, Ma!"

"Those girls better get moving. Neither one of them is getting any younger."

I didn't have anything to say. And that was too bad, because the silence between my mom and me lasted for at least five minutes. That was just how it was with us. We loved one another but didn't have anything to say to each other.

Five minutes of silence and then, "So either one of them dating anyone serious?"

Dang! My mother still didn't have a thing to say about me. I guess I should've seen that as a blessing, but I didn't. Why had she come over here, anyway? What time was she supposed to leave?

"So, are you going to show me your shop?" she asked.

I guess that was as close as she was going to get to my personal life, which made me happy and sad at the same time. "Yeah," I said. "Let me get dressed."

I tried to take as much time as I possibly could getting ready. I had to find a way to use up some of the hours. When I got back downstairs, my mother was still right where I left her.

"Ma, what time do you have to be at the airport?" I asked. It wasn't until the question was out of my mouth that I realized how it sounded.

"What? You can't wait to get rid of me?" She didn't sound mad, though. Just sounded like she accepted it all—this was just how she and I got down. "Don't worry. After I see your shop, it'll be time for me to take a cab back to JFK. I don't wanna take any chances in New York." She paused. "You still gonna let me see your shop, right?"

"Oh, yeah, Ma!" I said, now feeling bad for what I'd said. "It's too early for anyone to be there, but I think you'll like it."

Usually, I walked the nine blocks to work, but because my mother was here, I was going to catch a cab. But Juanita wasn't having it. She wanted to hang with me.

So, we walked the streets of Brooklyn as if she were a New Yorker. It took me longer than normal, but I have to admit, it was kinda good to have my mother next to me, even if we didn't say much of anything.

Finally at the shop, I unlocked the security gates and the door, clicked on the lights, and right away my mother gasped. "Oh, my," she said as she held her hand against her chest.

I hoped that was a good thing.

Slowly, she walked through the shop, examining every station, every picture on the wall, checking out the shampoo room. I stayed up front until she came back, and I was shocked at the way I shifted from one foot to the other. Why was I nervous? I mean, I had stopped trying to get my mother's approval a long time ago.

When she came back to the front, her head was down and my heart dropped. She was disappointed? Oh, no! Why? I guessed I cared more than I thought.

But then she looked up. And she smiled. "You done good, son," she said. "This place is wonderful."

I grinned like a kid on Christmas. "Thanks, Ma!"

She sat in one of the reception chairs by the window. "So, the shop is doing well?"

"Yeah!"

"You just came up here and did your thing, huh?"

I nodded. "I'm living my dream, Ma."

"Does that include having someone special in your life?"

For a moment, I froze. Never in my entire life had my mother asked me that.

"Uh . . . yeah . . . actually . . . yeah . . ."

"Why you stuttering, boy? Just get it out. You seeing someone?"

"Yes," I said before I sat down next to her. I had to sit. My legs were too weak for me to keep standing. "Yes, Ma. I'm seeing somebody."

My mother nodded a little. "You like this . . . guy?"

It was my turn to nod. "Yeah, I do."

She paused for a moment. "Well, don't keep me waiting. Tell me about him. What's his name?"

"Antonio!" I said. And then I went on to tell my mother everything about the man I fell in love with, from the art show to the dinner we had last night. I told my mother everything.

She sat there, listening, nodding, and sometimes even smiling. It was the most time I'd spent talking to my mother since she'd helped me with my fourth grade science project.

Once I finished, I had to sit back and take a deep breath. I had never used so many words at one time, and that was saying a lot since I loved to talk.

For a long time, my mother didn't say anything. And then, "Well, that's all nice, dear."

That's it? That's all she had for me?

"Okay," she said as she stood up. "How am I going to get a cab to take me back to the airport? Do I have to call one?"

"No." I shook my head, still a little stunned that that was all she had for me. "We can just go right outside, and one will pass by. It'll take a little longer than being in the city, but we'll be all right."

I helped my mother gather her things, then helped her step through the door. Once again, I had that feeling of being sad and happy at the same time. I was so happy that my mom had finally asked something about me, something meaningful. But sad because it didn't seem to affect her. She didn't have a word to say about it.

God was on my side with this, though, because we weren't outside for five minutes before I hailed a cab.

"Take her to JFK," I told the driver as I gave him a fifty-dollar bill.

"You don't have to do that," my mother said.

"I know, but I want to."

My mother and I stood there for more silent seconds as the traffic on Atlantic Avenue began to thicken with the morning rush hour. Finally, my mom reached up and hugged me.

"Thank you for coming," was all that I could think of to say.

She nodded and pulled away. She turned toward the cab, but then, a second later, came back to me. "I'm really happy for you, Devin. Really so very happy. And proud." She kissed my cheek before she slid into the car. And just as the driver pulled away from the curb, she said, "Tell Antonio I said hello and I can't wait to meet him."

She waved and I did the same. But I just stayed there, right in that spot for a minute, because I had to stay still so that I could figure out if that had all really happened or if it was just a dream.

Finally I smiled. I couldn't wait to call Antonio and tell him that my mother wanted to meet him!

Chapter 22

Chyanne

Work had turned into a sport. I was doing more ducking and dodging than handling my cases. It was working, though. A week had passed, and Malcolm hadn't been able to corner me . . . not that he hadn't tried. But my assistant had been put on high alert, to let me know whenever Malcolm was near, so that by the time he got to my office, I was already pretending to be on a very important call.

Even in the meetings he called to discuss my cases, I made sure that we were never alone. Someone was in the room with me at all times, and when Malcolm asked for me to stay afterward, I always told him that I had somewhere else to be. Then, with a glare, I dared him to pull rank. Because if he would have in any way demanded that I stay behind and talk to him, I would've blown up his spot.

I had to give it to Malcolm—he kept trying to get at me. He was still calling me at home, still trying to corner me in the office. But I was smarter than he was—at least when it came to hiding from him. When it came to lying, he was still the champion.

But while I seemed to have my interactions with Malcolm under control, the rest of my life was still in complete chaos. I didn't have any idea what I was going to do—not that I could afford to take my time making a decision. If I was going to have an abortion, I needed to do it now. But I kept using the excuse of this case I was working on: I couldn't afford to take any more time off, couldn't afford any more distractions. This case was in a month, and I had at least that much time to decide if I was really going to go through with an abortion, since I would still be in my first trimester.

Skye kept telling me that I shouldn't wait, that I had to make the decision, that I couldn't keep putting it off. But she just didn't understand that this decision was not one that could be made in a vacuum. There were so many other parts, like did I want to tell Malcolm first? And if I told him, was I prepared for his reaction? Whatever it was? What about the firm? Did I want to keep working here now that I knew Malcolm was married? How many times would I have to see him and his wife together?

There were just too many questions—that was why I wanted to push them all aside.

And that was why this trademark dispute was a good case for me right now. Because the larger team and the more complicated case kept me busy and away from my thoughts—and away from Malcolm.

The papers were piled high on my desk, even though one of my team members, Lacy, had already sorted through the cases. These were just the ones that she wanted me to be familiar with when our case began.

I was so engrossed in the paperwork that I didn't even hear my office door open, then close. But a second later I felt him, and my heart began to beat faster even before I looked up.

I knew it was Malcolm . . . and I was right.

I didn't know how he got past my assistant, but whichever way he did it, she was going to be so fired.

"She's not at her desk," Malcolm said, as if he read my mind. "I guess she went to lunch."

Well, if that was what she'd done, I was going to make sure that she never had a lunch break again!

Malcolm stayed way on the other side of my office, still by the door—as if he was scared to come any closer. Good! He was afraid. He needed to be.

"I just want to know . . ." Malcolm's voice was so soft, I had to lean forward to hear him better. Not that I really wanted to hear the lies that I was sure were going to come out of his mouth. "I just want to know," he began again, "why you haven't answered or returned any of my calls?"

Was he kidding me? Did he want me to talk to him? About what?

Well, I didn't want to talk all those times he called, and I certainly didn't want to talk now. So, I said nothing and just stared him down. Which seemed to make Malcolm uncomfortable, because he shifted from one leg to the other.

Good! He needed to be uncomfortable. He needed to be so uncomfortable that he marched his behind right out of my office. But for some reason he stayed, like he was determined to have his say.

I sighed. Maybe I needed to just let him talk so that we could once and for all get this over with.

He said, "I know I should have told you about my wife."

I leaned back in my chair and laughed because that was the funniest thing I'd heard all year. "You think?"

"And I want to thank you." I frowned when he said that. He kept on. "Thank you for not saying anything to her at the gala."

The little bit of a smile that I had went away, and all I wanted to do was to jump over my desk and wrap my hands around his neck! With everything I'd had to deal with—the humiliation of meeting his wife in a public forum, not to mention carrying his baby, which he knew nothing about—those were the first words he had for me?

I shook my head. Now I was mad, but it was my own damn fault. This was the man I'd fallen in love with.

"So, you want to thank me?" I said, finally standing up. "After the way you humiliated me, you want to thank me?"

"Chyanne," he said, coming a step closer. "You never let me explain. You've got to listen to me."

I didn't know if it was because a week had passed or if it was because he was already in my office, but I decided that it was time to hear something. So, I motioned with my hands for him to speak.

Malcolm released a breath, as if he was relieved. "When I met you," he began, "my wife and I were separated, headed for divorce. I had already moved out. That's the condo that you've been to."

"Well, something must've changed," I said in a tone that was meant to let him know that I was not impressed with what he'd said so far.

Malcolm said, "But my wife pleaded with me to come back. And she wore me down, and wore me down." He paused as if the next words were hard to say. "Finally, I went back home so that we could work it out."

"When did this happen?"

"About four months ago."

I shook my head in disbelief. "And, you never felt the need to tell me any of this?" I asked incredulously.

"I wanted to. Believe me, I did. I didn't want anything but the truth between us. But I was always afraid."

"Of what?"

"Of losing you. I never had the courage because my feelings for you were so real. I didn't have enough inside of me to tell you, but I didn't have enough inside of me to let you go."

His words, his tone, were so earnest, I began to melt. But then I caught myself and remembered the truth of what was going on here. Malcolm—the man who stood in front of me, the man whom I'd called my boyfriend for a year—was married! There were no excuses for that, not in my world. I wasn't raised this way, and I wasn't going to go out this way. I wasn't going to be anyone's mistress.

"Chyanne . . ." I held up my hand to stop him, but he kept talking. He said, "I never meant to hurt you."

Yeah, right! Well, I wanted to hurt him, and I knew the exact way to do it. If I told him about this baby, his baby, he'd be worried and hurt the same way I was.

But something held me back—I don't know what it was. Maybe it was the lawyer's instinct inside of me that said that I didn't want to throw that out there without knowing what his reaction would be.

So I kept quiet. But I crossed my arms and started tapping my feet, letting Malcolm know that I was getting bored with this conversation.

"Is there any chance, any way . . ."

What was he asking me? "No!" I said to whatever he was thinking.

He stared at me for a moment, then nodded, as if he finally believed me. "I'm so sorry, Chyanne. I never meant to hurt you, and from the bottom of my heart, I do love you."

His words were like an arrow that hit my heart. But I wasn't about to let him see that. So, I just stood there, with the same stance and the same face.

Malcolm turned toward the door, and before he opened it, he glanced over his shoulder, as if he needed to get one last look at me. As if he knew this would be the last time we'd ever be together this way.

But I didn't move.

It wasn't until he walked out that I plopped down in my chair. I could feel the tears trying to press forward. But I had promised myself that I wasn't going to shed another tear. Crying was over.

But one thing that Malcolm's visit did do was convince me that it was time to move into action. Maybe I didn't want to wait until after this case. Maybe Skye was right, and it was time to come up with a definitive plan . . . now!

Chapter 23

Skye

It had been four days of anticipation. Four days of wondering if I'd done the right thing by making that call. Four days of wondering what was going to happen with Trent and four days of wondering what had happened with Noah.

Even though I was trying to move on, I couldn't get Noah out of my mind. I couldn't figure out where I'd gone wrong or what had gone wrong. No one would have been able to convince me that Noah wasn't into me as much as I was into him. But it was clear that I had no idea what was going on. Which made me have serious doubts about Trent. With my track record, did I really want to keep doing this dating thing?

Admittedly, I'd called Trent only because I'd been so hurt by Noah. But then he had charmed me right away when he picked up the phone.

"Skye?"

I frowned. "How did you know it was me?" I asked. I'd never called his number before.

He chuckled. "I told you that you'd made an impression on me, and once I was able to track you down at work, I was able to get your cell number as well." He paused. "I have connections, but you don't have to worry. I'm not a stalker. I'm nothing but a complete gentleman."

It was only because I'd been so hurt by Noah that I even continued talking to this man. But a few minutes later I was glad that I did. He was charming and he was gentle. It had only been the day before when I told him that I was involved with someone, but even though I'd stated that fact, he didn't ask me any questions—trying to protect my feelings, I'm sure. And, I'm glad he did, because if he had asked me anything about why I was calling or what had happened to my man, I would've probably burst right into tears.

But he had kept me on the phone and, even after a few minutes, had me chuckling about how we'd met.

"You know you bumped into me," he joked. "You took one look at me from behind and bam! Just admit it."

It was only because I laughed that I agreed to keep Sunday totally free for our first date.

"I'll send a car for you," he said. "Remember, keep the whole day free."

And that was the last time I'd spoken to him—in four days. So, as you can imagine, I was ready to see what this man was all about.

I was putting the finishing touches on my makeup when my apartment intercom buzzed.

"Ms. Davenport," a man said, "I'm here for Trent Hamilton."

After telling him that I'd be right down, I grabbed my purse, took one last glance in the mirror, then hurried out the door. Just like Trent had promised, a car was waiting for me—a limousine, to be more specific. The driver tipped his hat exactly the way they did in the movies, then held the door open for me.

"Where are you taking me?" I asked the moment the car edged away from the curb.

"I'm sorry, Ms. Davenport. I've been instructed not to say anything, except to tell you that you will not be disappointed."

Okay. I couldn't imagine what Trent had planned for the day. He'd told me to dress casually, and I knew I looked good, kind of preppy, in my jeans, T-shirt, and navy blazer, which I wore just in case we were going someplace where I needed long sleeves.

I was still trying to stay positive about this date, but I couldn't say that I was feeling great about it. My heart was still with Noah, and because of that, I knew I shouldn't be going out with anyone right now. But I consoled myself by thinking that this wasn't really a date—Trent and I would just be kicking it. So there would be no harm, no foul!

When the car slowed down as we approached the South Street Seaport, I peeked through the window. And there was Trent, waiting for me. The extra moments that it took for the car to stop gave me a chance to check him out. I had to admit he looked great in his jeans, starched white shirt, and a sweater tied around his neck. I glanced down at my outfit. Without knowing it, we'd dressed almost exactly alike. Did that mean something?

But all thoughts of what we were wearing went away when Trent held my hand as he helped me out of the car, hugged me, and then thanked me for joining him. He was still holding my hand as we maneuvered through the Sunday crowd and walked onto the pier. We were a few steps away from the end when I saw it, a yacht, with THE HAMILTON written across the side.

My mouth opened wide. A yacht. I had never been this up close and personal with a yacht.

"My goodness," I said as Trent helped me to step over the edge of the pier and onto the plank. "Is this yacht yours?"

"It belongs to my family," he said, following me. "But I take it out for special occasions."

Okay. There were two questions I had about that statement. First, who was his family? And did he really think that being out with me was a special occasion?

Inside, the yacht was just like the ones I'd seen on TV, with mahogany wood throughout, leather sofas and chairs everywhere, and even crystal chandeliers hanging from the ceilings. We settled in the dining area, and that was the first time that I saw another person.

"Mr. Hamilton," a man wearing a white suit called out as he approached the table.

"Hey, Joe." Trent shook the man's hand, then patted him on his back, as if the two were longtime friends. "Haven't seen you in a while."

"It's good to see you." Then the man turned to me. "Nice to meet you, Ms. Davenport."

Dang! Trent had really planned ahead. This man knew my name.

I sat back as Trent and Joe discussed the brunch menu, and my stomach started growling just at the mention of all the dishes Joe said were waiting.

"I'm sorry we won't be able to take the boat out today," Joe said. "The city ordinance won't allow it as they start preparing for the holiday."

"Yeah, I knew that," Trent said. "We'll be fine just docked."

"Okay, then. Brunch will be right out, and I'll be back with your mimosas."

When we were alone, Trent said, "I hope you will indulge in a little alcohol—champagne and orange juice?"

I nodded. This man didn't know me at all. "I love mimosas," I said.

"So," Trent said, leaning back in his chair, "have I impressed you yet?"

It must've been all that I'd just been through with Noah and what Chyanne was going through with Malcolm that made me answer his question with one of my own. "How many women have you tried to impress this way? On your yacht?"

My question seemed to surprise him, and he stared at me for a moment before he chuckled. "Trust me, I've dated a few women, but no one has ever gotten this on a first date. I've never pulled out the stops this way before."

"So, why me?" I asked. I knew I sounded cynical, but could anyone blame me?

He leaned forward and peered into my eyes. "Because you're worth it."

I laughed, but Trent didn't.

"What's wrong? You don't think you're worth it?"

That was a good question. Of course I was worth it. Just because Noah didn't know it, and none of those other guys I'd dated seemed to know it, didn't mean I wasn't worth it. Yeah, I was worth this yacht and a whole lot more.

So, I smiled and sat back and decided to enjoy my time with Trent—no strings attached.

As we feasted over a brunch of eggs and waffles and turkey bacon and grits and home fried potatoes and all kinds of fruit, Trent and I chatted like we were old friends. I told him all about my job and my desire to become a top designer. He told me about his investments and how this was actually a great time to be in real estate.

"People think the economy is bad, but they don't know that this is the time to get as much as you can. Real estate is at bargain basement prices. There's lots of money to be made in this market."

We talked about our pasts—in terms of school. He'd gone to Harvard, which didn't surprise me. What did surprise me was that his father and grandfather had gone to Harvard as well. It was his grandfather, Richard Hamilton, who was the first real estate mogul in the Hamilton family, buying property in Harlem back in the 1950s, when that was unheard of for African Americans. His father, though, had taken a different route. He'd become a prominent surgeon, while Trent's mother, who had also attended Harvard, was the CFO of one of the country's largest banks.

Impressive was the only word that I could think of, but it wasn't impressive enough to keep my mind off of Noah. As Trent talked, I compared him to the man I was still in love with. I watched his lips move when he talked; his lips, which were thinner than Noah's juicy ones, didn't impress me. And I waited for his hair to sway like Noah's, but that would have been quite a feat, since Trent was completely bald.

The two men were nothing alike. Noah was creative and expressive. Trent was cerebral and contemplative. But he had a sense of humor, which was most important to me, and I laughed through the entire brunch.

"Are you ready to get going?" he asked after we'd been there for about two hours.

"Okay," I said, though I hated to leave. I was surprised that we were leaving so quickly. Trent had told me to clear my Sunday, and I thought I was going to spend the entire day with him. But maybe he wasn't as impressed with me as he thought he was going to be. Maybe he'd had enough.

Trent helped me off the yacht, took my hand, and led me back to the limousine. With each step we took toward the car, I became more disappointed. Even though I was thinking about Noah, I was having a good time and I didn't want the date to end. I didn't want to go back to my apartment and sit and wait for a call to come—a call from Noah, which was never going to come.

But then Trent climbed into the car with me. "Bob, you remember where we're going next?" he asked the driver.

"Yes, Mr. Hamilton." And then the car took off.

I twisted my head so that I could look into Trent's face. "Where are you taking me?"

"Can you do me a favor?" He grinned. "Can you just sit back, relax, and enjoy me?"

I laughed. "Okay. You got it."

Thirty minutes later we were in the Brooklyn Botanical Garden, which was one of the places I had on my list to visit in New York.

"How did you know I wanted to come here?" I asked, knowing for sure that I sounded like a kid, I was so excited.

He shrugged. "A good guess."

I had read all about the fifty-two-acre specialty gardens, and I couldn't wait to stroll through the landscape, ready to be inspired.

"Where do you want to go first?" Trent asked, showing me the map.

I knew exactly where I wanted to go. "The cherry trees!"

He laughed as he took my hand. We strolled through the cherry tree gardens, and even though we'd missed the cherry blossom festival by a few weeks, the trees were still gorgeous and full. During our leisurely walk, we continued the conversation about our lives, and when he took my hand, it felt like the most natural thing in the world. We wandered from the cherry tree gardens, to the Japanese Hill-and-Pond Garden, then to what became my favorite, the Shakespeare Garden, which had more than eighty plants, all of which had been mentioned in Shakespeare's writings.

For hours we wandered and talked and appreciated the beauty of God's hands all around us. But then, as the day's heat bowed to the evening's chill, my stomach began to rumble. We'd done so much walking, and now I was getting hungry.

But it had been a great day, and by the time we got back in the limousine for Trent to take me home, I was happy that I'd made that call to him four days ago.

"I've really had a good time," I said once we were in the car.

"I'm glad," he said. "But you talk as if the day is over. It's not."

I couldn't imagine what we were going to do next, and so I asked him.

"Have you heard of that new restaurant, Vibe?"

"Yes," I said, kind of excited. "They just opened. My friends and I want to go there, but I heard they have a waiting list that's over three weeks long!"

"Well, a friend of mine owns it, and we're going tonight."

"Are you kidding me? Oh, my. Well, I have to get home and . . ."

Trent glanced at his watch. "There's no time for that."

"What?" I knew this man was not going to make me go to the hottest club and restaurant in the city dressed this way.

He said, "Trust me."

"But . . ."

He took my hand. "Have you enjoyed this day so far?"

I nodded.

"Good, then trust me."

"Okay," I said right as the limousine stopped again, this time in front of Barneys. I couldn't wait to see what Trent had planned now.

The moment we walked in the door, two sales associates greeted us.

"Mr. Hamilton," the man and woman said at the same time. They both shook his hand, and I had a feeling that they knew him well.

The woman turned to me. "Ms. Davenport, please come with me."

I stood still for a moment, as if I couldn't follow instructions. Where did she want me to go?

"Go ahead," Trent said encouragingly.

So, I followed her to a room already filled with shoes and dresses.

"Mr. Hamilton thought that something here would be to your liking for your dinner tonight."

Okay, this man was going too far and not in a good way. I mean, don't get me wrong. I was appreciative of all that he'd done for this day, and even now, bringing me to Barneys. But didn't he know that I was a designer? I had a certain flare, a certain flavor that couldn't be found on just any rack. And certainly couldn't be found by a man who didn't know me.

But then I looked at the dresses. And I couldn't believe it. It was like Trent had been in my closet. Every single one of them was something that I would have bought—if I could have afforded the prices. I chose my favorite, a mini Tadashi formfitting sheath. If Trent wanted to play, I was going to show him what he was playing with.

I had just slipped into the dress and shoes when I heard "Wow!" right behind me. Turning to the door, I didn't know why I was surprised to find Trent standing in the entrance of what was supposed to be a women's dressing area. Like I said, I shouldn't have been surprised. This man didn't seem to follow any rules.

"You look amazing," he said.

I knew I did. That was what I liked about the Tadashi line—if a woman had curves, they were going to show . . . in a good way. I let my eyes wander over him, taking in the black suit that someone had just sewn onto him, 'cause that was how good he looked.

Trent took my hand. Then, with a thank-you to the sales associates, he swept me away, back to the limousine and to the fabulous Vibe on Fifty-second Street, and into one of the private rooms, where we feasted on steak and lamb and new potatoes. Then we went into the main room, where we danced and laughed, and laughed and danced, until my feet hurt.

It was well after midnight when Trent walked me to my front door, planted a soft kiss on my cheek, and told me that he couldn't wait to do this with me again.

Neither could I.

Inside my apartment I ran to the window to watch Trent and the driver pull away in the limousine, and then I turned toward my bedroom.

My last thought before I fell asleep that night was, *Noah who?*

Chapter 24

Devin

Dang! I couldn't remember the last time I'd been so bored in my life. It was my Monday off, and I had absolutely nothing to do. It was the first Monday that I was alone; since I'd met Antonio, I'd spent every single Monday with him. He'd been able to use sick days and vacation days, but not today. He had important meetings with new teams who were interested in using his company, and Antonio had put in long, long hours last week, and I had a feeling it was going to be exactly the same thing this week.

I sighed as I walked through the empty salon. All the stations were straight, all the towels had been washed, and the floors were sparkling clean. There wasn't a doggone thing for me to do here.

Plopping down in the chair at my station, I scrolled through my cell phone. See, this was what happened when your friends were just limited to a few. It wasn't like I could call Skye or Chyanne. Both were at work, and truly, while I loved my girls, they both certainly had their own problems. It was too much drama for me.

I still couldn't believe what Chyanne had decided to do, because of how we'd been raised in the church and everything. But whatever, Chyanne knew that I was down and had her back. At least Skye was happy—for the moment. She was with this new guy, Trent, though she didn't talk about him at all in the way she'd talked about Noah. I hoped that her heart still wasn't with that cheater.

I scrolled down to Leigh's name. Heck, I'd even take some of her drama right about now. But she and Michael had taken my suggestion, and they were away in the British Virgin Islands, hanging out on the island of Tortola, trying to bring back that honeymoon feeling.

I was truly by myself.

I pushed myself up from the chair. I needed to stop this pity party and enjoy this time. When was the last time I had a chance to think without someone else in my ear? Shoot, and I was with my favorite person, any-way—me!

So, I decided to walk back home. After locking up the shop, I took my time, wandering down Prospect Park West past all the trendy shops—boutiques, specialty stores, even restaurants—that made Park Slope such a desirable neighborhood. Even though I tried to slow down my steps, I was home in less than twenty minutes.

Inside my apartment, I kicked off my shoes, turned on the fan, and stretched out on the couch. I didn't know why I was trippin'; I didn't have a thing to complain about. I was living the life! I was in New York City, in one of the best neighborhoods in Brooklyn; had my own shop, which was already turning a profit; had my best friends here in the city with me, even though they all had their major share of drama. And then there was Antonio.

My Antonio.

He was the part that I had never expected. He was the only part of this dream that I hadn't prayed for. I didn't want to be involved with anyone, not while I was building my business. But the thing was, I'd been wrong about that. Antonio actually enhanced my work. I was more focused because I was satisfied at home.

I closed my eyes and imagined Antonio right here beside me.

And then I began wondering something I'd never thought of before—what would it be like to have Antonio with me twenty-four—seven? Seriously, how wonderful would my life be if this man was by my side all the time?

I sat up straight on the couch. Dang! It was clear that not only was Antonio all up in my head, but he had to be in my heart, too, for me to be thinking something ridiculous like that. Living with a man? Please! I was so glad to get out of my mama's house, I didn't know what to do. Having this place to myself was what I had dreamed about. It was stupid to think about being with Antonio all the time.

But then I wondered, what was stupid about it? What would it be like, and if it was as wonderful as I thought it would be, why wouldn't I want Antonio here all the time?

That was it—the only thing missing from my life. I was going to do it.

I was going to ask Antonio to move in with me!

Chapter 25

Chyanne

Morning sickness was no joke!

This was the third month of my pregnancy, and I just prayed that it would get better in the fourth, fifth, sixth, seventh, eighth, and ninth month.

Yes! I had decided to keep my baby. That was a huge decision, but I just couldn't think about killing this baby inside of me. Just having that thought now made me put my hand over my stomach. So, I was going to keep what God had put inside of me. There must have been some reason why he allowed me to get pregnant—even in the middle of the sin of fornication. And actually, I'd been all up in the sin of adultery, too, without even knowing it.

Oh, God! I was going to be sick again.

But then the feeling passed quickly, and I held my face down in the sink and rinsed out my mouth, then splashed water onto my face. Reaching for a paper towel, I dried off, then stared at my reflection in the mirror. No matter what I did, my eyes still had nothing but sadness in them. I guessed it was because I still loved Malcolm, and it was because I just prayed that I was doing the right thing.

I had actually decided to keep this baby. I still couldn't believe it, didn't know how I was going to do it. But I would survive. I just had to put my big girl panties on and handle it.

With my eyes still on the mirror, I pleaded to God: "Lord, I don't know how I got here, but please see me through!"

I straightened my clothes, smoothed out my jacket, then headed back down the hallway. I was ready to face the rest of my day. My thoughts were on how many times I'd have to run from Malcolm today, since my assistant had called in sick. I couldn't believe she wasn't here to protect me, but I didn't really expect things to be that bad. Ever since Malcolm had come into my office to *explain,* he'd pretty much stayed out of my way.

I stepped into my office but then stopped right at the edge. I stood frozen as I stared inside. I stood frozen as I stared at Malcolm's wife.

Her back was to me as she strolled in front of my desk, lifting picture after picture that I had displayed of my family and friends.

Why was she here? Did she know? Oh, God, I didn't want any type of confrontation. That was when I decided to just turn around, sneak out before she even knew that I was here. But I was too late. She turned around before I could.

"Chyanne," she said. "I was waiting for you."

Talking about wearing big girl panties! I took a deep breath, stepped into my office, and closed the door, though I wondered if that was such a good idea. I walked past Kayla and stood behind my desk.

I looked into her eyes for a hint of what was to come and released a breath of relief—she didn't look like a crazy woman ready to kill, though what I did see in her eyes was much worse. What I saw in her eyes was a sadness that matched the sadness that was in mine.

Slowly, I sat down in my chair. I still hadn't said one word to this woman. I didn't know what to say. But then she started talking . . . and I just listened.

"I met Malcolm when I was just eighteen years old," she said. "And that man . . . he swept me off my feet. He was so charming and so debonair."

She had said only a few words, but I totally understood. I was older than she was when I met him, but not by much.

"He told me that with me by his side, he could go far! And that every place he went, he was going to take me with him. He promised me a life that was better than what I had—which was going to be difficult since my father had provided so well for me and my mother."

She paused, and I wondered if I was supposed to speak. But I still didn't have anything to say. I mean, she still hadn't said anything about the fact that I'd been sleeping with her husband.

Kayla said, "And for a year or two, it was working." She shrugged. "I couldn't really tell you when it began to fall apart. Maybe it was when we realized that we had nothing but lust in common."

Whew! This was some deep stuff, and now I wished I had just turned around and run the other way.

Suddenly, she looked straight at me. "It's not that way with you two, is it? You have a lot more in common than just lust."

My heart was beating so fast and hard that I wasn't sure if I'd be able to answer her and sound coherent. So I just nodded—a little. And then I prayed for my life.

Kayla nodded, too. "How long have you been with Malcolm?"

I swallowed. "A little over a year. But, Mrs. Parks, I didn't know he was married." I knew that line was a sorry line. How many women had said that?

But for some reason, Kayla didn't look at me as if she thought I was lying. She looked like she believed me.

Then she asked, "How far along are you?"

What? Shocker! Oh my God. What was I supposed to say?

"You can tell me, Chyanne. It's all over you. You're pregnant, and it's Malcolm's child, I'm sure. How far along?" she asked again.

"Three months," squeaked out of me.

She nodded. "Then I'm doing the right thing. I'm going to divorce Malcolm. I'm going to give him what he wants, which is his freedom. I'm going to let him go."

I felt as if I was beginning to hyperventilate. I had to tell myself to breathe in, breathe out. I just prayed that Kayla didn't blame me for all this.

She said, "And I would like you to represent me."

"What?" I screamed, then got myself back under control. "I can't represent you, for lots of reasons. I'm not a divorce attorney, not to talk about the conflict of interest."

She shook her head at my words. "I don't care, Chyanne. I know you can handle it, and I want you."

I sat there and stared at Kayla as if she had lost her mind. But she just stared back as if she meant exactly what she said. This was incredible—the wife and the mistress on the same side.

What had my life come to?

Chapter 26

Skye

I had been through this list before: smart, sweet, kind, and fine—exactly like Noah. Though, Trent wasn't anything like Noah. Not only were they different physically, but they were completely different in every other way. Trent was all about making money, and he never stopped thinking about it, never stopped trying to make it. We'd been dating for a month now, and though we talked on the phone every day, I could still count the number of times we'd gone out together.

"There's always money to be made, baby," he often said to me.

Not that I was mad at him. 'Cause when Trent Hamilton did go out, he knew how to treat a lady. He took me to the most exclusive restaurants in Manhattan. He showered me with gifts, everything from flowers to a gold bracelet, which I told him I couldn't accept and he told me he couldn't take back. The thing that I loved about Trent was that though he came from privilege and absolutely wanted nothing but the best in his life, he didn't act like a spoiled brat. He always asked where I wanted to go, what I wanted to eat, what I wanted to do. It was always about me first.

It would've been easy to fall in love with a man like Trent, if I didn't still have Noah all up in my heart.

I cannot explain why Noah was still in my head. I don't know—maybe it was because I loved his passion. Maybe it was because he was so different from anyone I'd ever dated before. Maybe it was because we were both creative and I could talk to him for hours about my career.

I could talk to Trent, too. He was always interested in me. But there was a difference. Trent listened to me; Noah felt me.

But whatever mixed-up feelings I had in my heart, Trent was still here making each time that I spent with him more romantic than before. And tonight was no different. We were in one of his homes, this one in Greenwich, Connecticut. And once again, I was sitting, watching a man prepare a meal for me. Only this time, I wasn't in a studio loft. We were in a massive mansion. Trent said that it was eight thousand square feet and housed seven bedrooms, an office, a library, a gym, and a host of other rooms.

"Are you ready for this?"

I'd been waiting for Trent outside, on the deck that overlooked a golf course that was part of one of Connecticut's many country clubs. It was one of the most peaceful places I'd ever been—the thick green trees that surrounded the course made me feel like I wasn't anywhere near New York City.

I grinned as Trent rested the salad bowl in the middle of the wrought-iron table. "Are you sure I can't help with anything?"

"Nope." He shook his head. "This is my show because when you finally invite me to your place and offer to cook, I'm gonna sit back and let you do your thing." He went back into the kitchen and returned with the platters of rice pilaf and grilled shrimp.

After he blessed the food, which was something else that I loved about Trent, and he served me, I sat back and enjoyed the light dinner, trying my best not to compare it to the Jamaican lamb stew I'd had with Noah.

"So, I want to talk to you about something," Trent said.

Uh-oh! I never liked it when conversations began with that. "What?"

"I know you want to have your own label and your own studio. When are you thinking of getting started?"

I waved my fork in the air. "It won't be for a while. Not only do I have a lot to learn, but it takes a lot to step out there on your own."

"A lot? Like what?"

"Like connections and money." I laughed. "All the things I don't have."

"But all the things I do." He paused. "That's what I wanted to talk to you about. Why don't you start your own company now? I can help you with the money and the connections."

Talk about being stunned. This was not what I expected. "I . . . I can't let you do that."

"You're right. You can't let me but it's what I want to do. You are talented enough to step out there on your own, and it would be a great investment for me." He put his fork down. "Plus, Skye, I really do care about you . . . deeply care. You've made such an impact on my life, and I want to do the same to yours."

"Wow!"

He chuckled. "So, is that a yes?"

I shook my head. "No, really, Trent. I can't let you do that."

"Not even if I want to? Not even because I care so much for you?"

"I care for you, too, a lot. But I'm not there yet and I don't think you and I are there yet."

"But we can be." He stared at me as if he was trying to see right through me. "What's holding you back, Skye? What's stopping you from loving me the way I'm falling in love with you?"

Another wow! The *L* word. I really wasn't ready for this.

"Is there someone else?" he asked.

"No! Not at all. It's just that . . . I've dated a lot. And I want to be . . . careful. I want for both of us to be sure."

He nodded. "I can respect that." He lifted his fork and slipped a jumbo shrimp into his mouth. "So, time . . . that's all we need, right?"

"Yes."

"Okay, I'll give you some time. But I just want you to know that while we have all this time, I'm going to pull out all the stops. I'm about to sweep you off your feet."

I laughed. "Even more than you've already done? I can't imagine that."

"You right about that, baby. You can't even imagine what I'm about to do." He grinned. "Think you can handle it? Think you can handle me?"

I took his hand and curled my fingers around his. "I can handle it! Just bring it on."

When he leaned over to kiss me, our lips lingered together. And, I forgot all about Noah—at least for the moment.

Chapter 27

Devin

It was girls' night out—or should I say "girls' night in"? 'Cause my girls and I were having our first New York City slumber party. It was something that we always did back in Atlanta, but we'd all been so busy trying to be successful that we just didn't have the time to get together like we used to.

"Okay," I said, slipping a piece of pizza from the box on Skye's coffee table. We had all the goodies, everything that could do damage to a girl's waistline: pizza, fried chicken, french fries, and hamburgers. And in the kitchen, dessert waited—ice cream and all kinds of cheesecakes, and my favorite, double-chocolate, double-decker chocolate mousse cake. "So, who's gonna go first?" I asked. But then, before Skye or Chyanne could say anything, I said, "I am!"

My girls laughed, just like I wanted them to.

"I got some big news," I said. I paused for dramatic effect. "I'm gonna ask Antonio to move in with me."

Okay, my news must have been more shocking than I thought, because my girls sat there for a full two minutes, not saying a word.

"What?" I said, looking at them. "You seem surprised."

"We are," Chyanne said, putting down the fried chicken leg she held in her hand. "I mean, moving in together . . . That's a big step."

"Yeah," Skye said. "And we've only met the brother once, and that was only for a hot second."

Yeah, that was a problem. We were here in New York City, and although the three of us were close, we didn't know much about each other's significant others. Part of the reason was that time thing I was talking about before, but sometimes, I wondered if it was just so that we could keep our times together special. You know, not letting anyone step into our space when it was just the three of us.

"So, you got to really meet Antonio before he can move in?" I asked. "What's that about?"

"You know how we do," Skye kidded. "We have to approve."

"Well, if you guys have to approve of Antonio, then I have to approve of Trent," I said, pointing to Skye. "And . . ." Oops! When I turned to Chyanne, I didn't have anything to say.

Chyanne lowered her eyes and head, and I felt bad. So bad that I grabbed my fifth piece of pizza.

"I'm sorry, Chy," I said with my mouth stuffed.

She shrugged, but she didn't pick up her chicken leg. I hoped I hadn't messed up her appetite. "It's okay. I'm not with anyone right now"—she placed her hand on her belly—"since my priority has to be this baby."

It was still hard for me to believe that Chyanne was going to keep the baby. This was a big move. I mean, the way we'd been raised. She was going to be a single mother and a lawyer, living in New York City, all by herself. Whew!

"Have you thought about all of that?" I asked, pointing to her stomach.

She shook her head. "It gets overwhelming at times. I try not to think of anything more than taking care of her while she's growing inside of me."

"But she's gonna be here soon, sweetie," Skye said. "You gotta start making plans, right?"

Chyanne nodded. "But I don't have to start tonight, do I?" She paused. "And how did this subject get about me? Weren't we grilling Devin?"

"Yeah," Skye said as they both turned to me.

"Nuh-uh! I wanna talk about your man, Trent," I said, diverting the topic away from me. Not that I didn't want to talk about Antonio. I could talk about him and think about him and do all other kinds of things with him all night long. But I enjoyed playing with my girls this way. "So," I said to Skye, "what's up with your new man?"

She smiled, but it wasn't the way she glowed whenever we had mentioned Noah's name in the past. "Trent is cool. He's great, actually."

"And isn't the boy rich?" I laughed.

"First of all, he's not a boy, trust me."

"Ooohhh!" Chyanne and I laughed together.

"And second of all, yesss, he's rich!" Skye fell back onto the couch and kicked her legs in the air.

"Well, that's all I need to know, " I said. "'Cause you know my motto." And together we all said, "Date cute, marry rich!"

After we laughed for a little while, Skye said, "But you know what I've discovered? Rich isn't everything. You've got to really connect with the person."

I waved my hands, trying to wipe those dumb words away. "Please, rich can buy a whole lot of connection. Now, poor? Ain't nothing you can do with poor."

"I know. I'm just sayin' . . . I like Trent and he's rich. . . ."

"But . . . ," Chyanne and I said together.

"There are no buts," Skye said quickly, as if she didn't want to talk about this anymore. "Trent and I are fine. We're getting to know each other, and we're taking it slow." She turned to Chyanne. "So have you spoken to Malcolm any more?" she asked, changing the subject fast.

Chyanne shook her head. "No more than the stuff in the office."

"I don't know how you do it," Skye said. "I don't think that I could work all day around . . ." She stopped, but Chyanne and I knew what she was going to say. She couldn't work around Noah.

Dang! I was right. She was still feeling ole boy, even though he had done her so wrong. She needed to drop that boy from her thoughts and she needed to do it quickly.

"It's not that bad. I'm able to avoid Malcolm a lot more than you think." Chyanne paused. "But one person I haven't been able to avoid is his wife."

I dropped my pizza right onto Skye's cream-colored carpet. Not that Skye noticed, because her face was as frozen in shock as mine.

"What are you talking about?" I asked.

Chyanne leaned back on the couch, as if what she had just told us was no big deal. "His wife came to see me."

"When?" Skye and I sounded as if we were singing together.

"She came to my office." And then Chyanne went on to fill us in about how Ms. Kayla just marched into her office one day and started talking about her husband. "And then she asked me how far along I was."

"What?" Skye and I sang together again.

"Girl, I would've had the baby right there." I raised my hand in the air as if I was about to testify. "I'm telling you, I would've given birth right in that office."

Chyanne and Skye laughed at me. Okay, it was a minor technicality that I couldn't give birth. I was just sayin'.

Chyanne said, "But there's more."

"Oh, Lawd!" I said.

"How could there be more?" Skye asked.

"Well . . ." Chyanne did one of those little dramatic pauses that I always did. "She's divorcing Malcolm, and she wants me to represent her!"

That's it! I was done! I fell out on the floor as if I'd fainted. I felt like fainting. Shoot, did anyone in the world have more drama in their lives than Chyanne Monroe?

When Skye and I lifted our mouths up from the floor, Skye asked, "You told her no, right?"

"I told her I'd think about it."

"You can't do that," Skye said.

I kept my mouth shut because I had nothing to say. Nothing at all.

"Well, actually, I can because it will probably be a simple divorce."

"But what about conflict of interest?" Skye continued to drill her.

"What? You mean the fact that I used to sleep with her husband and now I'm carrying his baby? You think that disqualifies me?"

"Yes!" Skye said.

"No!" I yelled out, finally finding my voice. "I mean, yes, do it! I think it would be wonderful. And then you can end up on one of those *Snapped* episodes on Oxygen, and we'll all be famous."

"Nobody is going to snap anything," Chyanne said. "It's going to be a very cordial—if you can use that word with divorce. It's going to be a cordial divorce."

"Well, I say do it," I piped in.

"And I say don't," Skye said.

"And I say I'm not sure what I'm going to do, but whichever way I go, I know y'all will have my back, right?"

"Yeah, right," I said.

Skye nodded.

We all looked at each other for a moment, because Chyanne asked, "Does anyone have any more questions?"

I raised my hand like I was back in school. "I have a question." Doing one of those dramatic pauses, I asked, "What color is my godbaby's room going to be?"

And my girls laughed.

Which was exactly what I wanted them to do!

Chapter 28

Chyanne

I was surprised that Kayla wanted to meet me so close to the office, but I was glad that she did. I wasn't too worried about Malcolm seeing us together; he left the office only in the middle of the day for business meetings, and he certainly wouldn't be having a meeting at Trio, the little café five blocks away.

I was actually glad that Kayla had chosen someplace so close. I could walk to the restaurant, and since I knew this meeting was going to be quick, I could get in and I could get out and get back to work. I wasn't even going to order anything. Not a cup of coffee, not even a glass of water . . . nothing!

This meeting actually seemed so unnecessary to me. When Kayla called me yesterday, I tried to tell her that I'd decided not to represent her. It wasn't fair, it wasn't ethical, and I didn't need this kind of drama in my life, anyway—certainly not while pregnant. But Kayla had insisted that we meet face-to-face.

"You can tell me tomorrow what you're going to do."

I had no idea why she wanted to do this in public, but whatever. Like I said, I was going to be in and out.

I rushed into the café, and the hostess led me to the back, where she said my party was already waiting. It was interesting that she had seated us so far to the back, since it was only ten thirty and the lunch crowd had not yet arrived. Maybe Kayla was concerned about Malcolm seeing us, after all.

But as we got closer to the table, I noticed that Kayla was not alone.

"Hello, Chyanne," Kayla said, rising to greet me. The man—a tall, sandy-haired, blue-eyed white man— stood, too. "Thank you for coming."

"That's okay," I said, still eyeing the dude. Who was he? Her man?

"Hi, Chyanne." He held out his hand to me. "I'm Marvin Whitley, Kayla's attorney."

Her attorney? Okay, what was this about? I slid into the chair that he held out for me, just because now I was nosy. If she already had an attorney on the case, why had she asked me and why was I here?

"You probably are wondering what's going on," Kayla said.

I nodded, looking back and forth between the two of them.

Marvin spoke. "Well, I'll actually be handling Kayla's divorce negotiations."

"Okay," I said, releasing a long breath. I didn't realize how relieved I was. I guess I really didn't want to handle this and had only been thinking about doing it as a way to get back at Malcolm. "That's fine. It's better this way, anyway." Looking straight at Kayla, I said, "I really shouldn't be involved in this."

"But you are involved. That's why I asked you here." She motioned to Marvin as if she wanted him to pick up the conversation, and I turned to him.

He said, "To get to the point and keep this simple, there was a prenup that Kayla signed, and we want to break it."

"Oh, really? A prenup?" That surprised me. Prenups were normally reserved for people who had something to lose. I mean, Malcolm made quite a bit of money as one of the partners, but surely, most of his money had been made after he was married. So, why had a prenup been necessary?

Marvin answered my question. "Malcolm Parks is worth quite a bit of money. Several million dollars." He paused and then repeated it, as if he needed to make the point. "Several million dollars."

"Really?" Dang! I didn't know that. All that from the firm?

"He was left quite an inheritance," Kayla explained, "by his grandparents, who had bought bonds during World War II. He was eighteen when they were killed in a car accident, and he received the bonds. It was only about a million dollars."

We all kind of chuckled a little when she said *only*.

Kayla continued, "But within five years, with some savvy investments, he'd quadrupled that."

"And we're sure that over the years his fortune has grown even more," Marvin finished up.

"But Malcolm is hiding money." It was Kayla's turn to speak. "He has properties overseas, and we're sure he has offshore accounts, all kinds of things that I don't know about."

Wow! All that time I was sleeping with this man and I didn't even know who he was. "This is all very interesting, and I wish you the best with this," I said. "But what does this have to do with me if I'm not going to be representing you?"

Kayla and Marvin exchanged a glance, and I had a feeling I was not going to like the answer to my question.

She said, "I'm going to need to get a statement from you. I need you as a witness. You're proof of Malcolm's infidelity."

Damn! This was getting worse and worse. They wanted me to stand up in court and testify that I'd been with a married man? That I was the other woman? That I was a home wrecker? Hell, no, I wasn't going to do that! Not only would that be beyond embarrassing, but if this got out, got back to the firm, I could end up losing my job.

"I know this puts you in quite a position," Marvin said, as if he could imagine what I was thinking. "But, I can protect you. We're hoping to do this all through depositions, and once Malcolm knows we have you, we're hoping that he will give us what Kayla wants."

"Whew!" I shook my head.

"I know you don't want to get involved this way," Kayla said.

"I don't."

Kayla sat back and stared at me for a moment. "Is it because you're in love with Malcolm?"

I shook my head. "I haven't seen him since the night of the gala—except for at work. After his lies, I'm not interested," I said, telling her more than I'd planned to.

"So he still doesn't know about . . ." Her eyes drifted down, and at the same time I put my hand over my belly.

"No. I'm going to raise my baby by myself."

She nodded. "That's your choice to walk away." She looked me dead in the eyes when she said, "But that's not mine. I'm not walking away from anything. Not until I get what's mine."

I inhaled and said, "I'm sorry," and at the same time I prayed that she would respect my wishes.

"Why don't you think about it, Chyanne?" Marvin said. He reached into his pocket. "Here's my card."

Standing up, I took his card and said, "Thank you."

This time Marvin stood, but Kayla didn't. She said, "I hope to be hearing from you soon."

I didn't give her a yes or a no. Just turned and walked out of that café. I couldn't believe these people wanted to get me all up in their drama like that. And the thing was, there was really nothing I could do about it. Marvin was being kind, but he could have me subpoenaed. They knew about me, they knew about the baby, and I wouldn't be able to lie about it. Malcolm was in trouble, and he didn't even know it.

My first thought was that I needed to tell him. And then I was mad at myself for thinking that. After the way he lied and cheated and humiliated me, why was I thinking about protecting him? Naw, he was on his own.

I wasn't going to say a word. All I was going to do was sit back, watch, and wait this out.

Chapter 29

Skye

Meet the parents. Wasn't that the name of some movie? A comedy?

Well, what I was about to do wasn't even funny. It was meet the parents, all right, but it felt more like a thriller to me. What was I doing? Why was I doing this? Did I really want to meet Trent's parents? I mean, that was always a big step in a relationship—only one other time had I actually formally met the parents, and that was with Chuck in high school. So, why was I putting myself through this when I wasn't even sure that Trent was the one?

My nerves had been frayed ever since Trent asked me to go with him to some end of the summer party that his parents were having out at their vacation home in the Hamptons. Now, trust, at first I had been so excited. I mean, the Hamptons? Really? Where Sean "P. Diddy" Combs and all the other stars hung out? I'd always wanted to go to the Hamptons!

But not to meet anybody's parents—not to be on display. Not to have his father look me up and down and have his mother hate me. Because surely, that was going to happen. With all the money that the Hamiltons had, I was sure they didn't think that any girl was good enough for their son.

"Don't you think this is too soon?" I'd asked Trent when he'd asked me, and I'd thought about it for a while. "I mean, meeting the parents. That's serious."

"It is," Trent said, hugging me. "And right after this, we're gonna fly to Atlanta and I'm gonna meet your parents, too."

I didn't know if I was feeling all of that. I mean, Trent and I hadn't even had sex yet, though we had gotten close a couple of times. That was one place where he made me forget all about Noah. I mean, Trent could kiss! For real, because he took his time—slow and easy was what I liked to call him. His kisses took my breath away! And his touches made me lose my mind.

But a good kisser, a good fondler, did not make a relationship.

Still, here I was, sitting in the front seat of Trent's Mercedes coup and heading to the Hamptons. The air felt good, the sights were wonderful, and I still wanted to throw up.

As if he knew what I was thinking, Trent reached over and held my hand. "My parents are going to love you," he said, trying to reassure me. "They adore you already."

"How? They don't know me."

"They know you through me, and if I like you, then they'll love you. And trust, baby, I love you." He kissed the tips of my fingers.

Trent had said that before—that he loved me. And what I loved about this man was that he didn't say it, waiting for me to say it back to him. He said it because he meant it.

I wanted to mean it, too. That was why I had never told him that I loved him. I just wasn't feeling it . . . not yet.

It wasn't that Noah was still in my mind. Slowly, he was melting away from my heart and my head. But he'd left such a gaping hole in me. I guess I was kind of gun-shy. I wanted to take my time. I wanted to be sure. I didn't want any surprises.

Although the Hamptons were still part of New York, they were at the tip of Long Island. Trent's parents' home was in the village called Sag Harbor, in Southampton. It was only about ninety miles from Manhattan, but it took us more than two hours to get there. I mean, dang! I'd heard about New York traffic, but living in the city had spoiled me. I could walk or cab it anywhere.

I couldn't wait to get out of the car! That is, until Trent started slowing down the Mercedes and I could tell that we were getting close.

"Oh, God!"

"What, baby?"

Dang! Had I said that out loud? "Oh, nothing," I said.

He glanced at me sideways and chuckled. "You nervous?"

"Should I be?"

"No."

"Then why am I?" I almost felt like crying.

He laughed. "Trust me. Today is going to be a fantastic day."

Everything else he'd ever told me had been true, but there was no way he would be right about this. Parents never liked the girlfriend—especially the mother.

Trent slowed down in front of a house that had a boatload of people in front of it. There was a line of cars waiting for a valet to park for them.

"We're here," Trent said.

A valet! I knew these people were rich, but they were taking this money thing to levels I'd never seen.

Trent pulled up to the end of the line, but instead of waiting, he jumped out of the car and then took my hand. "Come on, baby!"

I had to trot to keep up with his long, quick steps, and since I was hyperventilating, it was even harder. In front of the house, he tossed his car keys to one of the attendants.

"What's up, Kenny!" he said.

"Hey, Trent, man!" They did that brother man hug thing before Trent introduced me. "This is my girl, Skye Davenport."

"What's up?" The attendant grinned, then winked at Trent. "A keeper, dog," he said before he ran off to take care of the next car.

We stepped onto the long porch, then inside the house, and I gasped out loud. I couldn't help it. I'd never seen anything like this, except for in the movies. There was a winding staircase—actually, two of them— that was the centerpiece of the foyer.

"I thought you said this was their summerhouse," I whispered.

"It is. Come on. Everyone is out back." He led me across the marble floors and down a long hallway, and then I heard a shriek.

"Tee-Tee!" A heavyset woman ambled from the kitchen and wrapped her arms around Trent. She was so short that her arms reached only to his waist.

"Hey, Miriam, honey." When Trent pulled back from the woman, he said to me, "Skye, I want you to meet the first woman I ever fell in love with."

He laughed, and Miriam playfully hit him on his arm. "Get out of here, boy, with that craziness!"

Trent said, "Skye, this is Miriam. She's been with our family since I was born, and practically raised me!"

She grinned. "Don't let your mother hear you saying that!"

I held out my hand to shake hers, but she slapped my hand away. "Girl, we don't do no handshaking around here. Especially not with someone as special as you. Come here and give me a hug."

Before I could say anything, Miriam had me wrapped up so tight in a bear hug that I could hardly breathe.

"Trent has told us some wonderful things about you," she said, finally letting me go. "Welcome to the family!"

"Uh . . . thank you?" I said as if that was a question. What was she talking about? Welcome to the family? But I didn't say anything else; I just grinned as she told us that Trent's mother and father were already in the backyard, greeting their guests.

Trent was still holding my hand as he led me through the French doors into the most fabulous backyard I'd ever seen. It felt like it was as large as Central Park and as beautiful and colorful as the botanical garden.

We pressed through the crowd of people, and though many called out Trent's name, he only smiled and waved. It was like he was on a mission to get to his parents.

"Trent!"

Instantly, I knew that this man in front of me was Trent's father. He had to be. . . . They practically looked like twins. Everything about them was the same—their build, their height, their bald head, their light brown eyes. Even the facial hair that covered their face was cut the exact same way, only Mr. Hamilton's slight beard was sprinkled with gray.

"Son," Mr. Hamilton said, grabbing his son into a bear hug. "What's good?"

"What's up, Pops?" Trent asked his father. And then his eyes softened as he looked down at the petite woman standing next to his father. She'd been so quiet, I hardly noticed her. But there was no doubt in my mind that this was his mother. It was the way they looked at each other that let me know.

Mrs. Hamilton was really a beautiful woman. She and I were about the same height, maybe even the same size. She had a golden complexion, and her hair was pulled back into a soft ponytail. She hardly looked old enough to have a son Trent's age. And she was the CFO of a major bank? Dang!

"Trent," she said quietly. "How are you, son?"

"I'm great." He hugged her, then stepped back and presented me as if I was some sort of trophy. "Mom, Dad, I want you to meet Skye."

My heart was pounding so hard, but the way they looked at me, the way they smiled, made every apprehension I had fade away.

"Finally!" Mrs. Hamilton said, taking both of my hands into hers. "We are so happy to meet you, Skye."

"Yes, indeed," Mr. Hamilton said. "I couldn't wait to meet the woman who had finally convinced my son that there was more to life than just work."

"Trent," his mother said, "would you mind if I borrowed Skye for a moment? I want to show her the grounds."

"Go ahead." Trent winked at me. "I want to talk to Dad about something, anyway."

"No business!" his mother admonished. She was still holding my hand as she led me through the backyard. "I am so glad to finally meet you."

"Me, too," I lied, though I was feeling bad about all the things I'd been thinking about this wonderful woman.

"Let me show you around." She pointed out the flowers, and then on the other side of the backyard, she showed me the Olympic-sized pool, where kids were already splashing around.

"Wow, this is amazing," I said.

"Have you ever been to the Hamptons before?"

I shook my head. "No."

"Then, you must come again and soon. The beach is only two blocks away."

After we toured the grounds, Mrs. Hamilton took me through their six-bedroom house. "I hope you and Trent will join us for one weekend before the season officially ends," she said. "We don't see enough of him, and I think you are the only one who can convince him to spend more time with his mother."

I laughed. "I'll see what I can do."

"Trent tells me that you're a designer—a fashion designer."

Uh-oh. I knew this was too good to be true. There was no way the Hamiltons would want their son with anyone who wasn't as high powered as they were.

"Yes," I said, ready for the fallout.

Mrs. Hamilton clapped her hands. "My husband and I are having a winter gala the night before Thanksgiving, and I would love for you to design something for me. I'll pay you, of course."

These people were off the chain! "I'd love to do that."

Back outside, Mrs. Hamilton introduced me to her friends and family as Trent's girlfriend. It was surprising at first when she said that, but really, I guess I was Trent's girlfriend.

At least an hour had passed by the time I found Trent, still with his father. But when he saw me, his face lit up and the way he smiled at me warmed my heart—and did a few other things to my body, too. It felt good to look into someone's eyes and know that they were glad to see you.

"Gotta go, Pops!"

The rest of the day was a whirlwind to me. All the people I met, including Trent's younger sister, who kept telling me that she had always wanted a big sister, embraced me as if I was already a part of the family.

At one point, his sister, Tracie, pulled me aside to tell me, "Trent has never brought a girl home. You must be special." And then she wrapped her arms around me, and all I could do was think that this was one hugging family!

I was exhausted when, at eleven o'clock, Trent and I climbed back into his car after promising his parents that we would see them soon. As I leaned my head back on the soft leather headrest, I closed my eyes and thought about what a wonderful day I'd had.

Trent was silent as we maneuvered through the streets of Southampton. It wasn't until we were on the highway that he asked, "So, did you have a good time?"

I opened my eyes, and when I looked at his profile, I couldn't help but smile. What had I been thinking? This man was everything that any woman could want. Maybe, just maybe, if I opened my heart, he could be the one.

"Yeah," I said. "I had a wonderful time." Then I reached for his hand, and Trent drove with one hand all the way back to New York City.

Chapter 30

Devin

This was the night. The night that I'd been planning. The night that I was going to pop the question to Antonio.

It was about time! I'd been thinking about this for almost two months now. It was just that I could never find the right time to ask him. But tonight he was coming over to my place, my territory, and we were going to have a fantastic dinner and everything else that followed.

Already the music was playing. Antonio loved salsa, especially Héctor Lavoe. I laid the spread that I'd picked up from the Caribbean House on the warming tray at the center of the table. I'd told Antonio that I'd fix dinner for him, but he knew what that meant. Lawd knows, he didn't want me cooking. I could whip up a fierce hairstyle, but in the kitchen it was all about making reservations and good takeout!

As I moved back toward the kitchen, I stopped and glanced at the velvet box that I'd left on the buffet table. I couldn't help but smile as I picked it up. When I peeked inside, my smile became even wider. There it was. The shiny silver key that I'd had made just for Antonio. I was pretty sure that Antonio was going to say yes. I mean, it made perfect sense—we spent most of our time together, anyway, and the money we could save was major. I earned way more than Antonio, and this would give him a chance to save some money. And if he could save some money, he'd be able to go after his dream. That was what I wanted for my man.

So, if this made so much sense, why did I have a bunch of butterflies fluttering around in my stomach?

And then my doorbell rang, and those butterflies really took off.

Until I opened the door and looked at my man. Mr. Dark and Lovely. Mr. Antonio. Wearing his signature all black. I swear, he needed to trademark that look. No one else in the world should ever be able to wear all black because my man wore it so well.

"Hey, baby," he said and hugged me.

Oh, yeah. This was going to be a very good night.

"This is for you," he said, handing me a bottle of wine.

"You mean, this is for us, right?"

He laughed. "Whatever."

Antonio followed me into the dining room, and his eyes got big when he saw the spread I'd prepared— well, not prepared, but it looked like I had.

"This looks fabulous, and it's a good thing, because I'm starving!" Antonio rubbed his hands together and sat down.

I placed a plate in front of him, then one at the setting right next to him. And after I served him, we feasted on the fantastic Caribbean meal. By the time I finished my first glass of wine, every single butterfly inside of me was dead. I was fine, and I knew that Antonio and I would be fine, too.

Antonio filled me in on work and a new deal he had just signed with another team, and that was when I popped the question.

"Antonio, where do you see yourself in the future?" I asked. "I mean, when you look down the line, am I there?"

"You know you are important to me. We've talked about this."

"I know you get busy, but if you could, would you like to spend more time together?"

Antonio took a long sip of wine. "Of course I would, but you know how it is. I'm working extremely hard so I can keep up with everything I got going on right now."

He'd said the magic words—exactly what I was waiting to hear. I stood from the table, grabbed the box from the buffet, and then handed it to my man.

It took a moment for Antonio to open it—he was so busy staring at me, as if he was scared to open it.

"That's for you," I said. "Something to help you with your dream."

It took him a couple of seconds to flip the box open, and then he frowned. "A key?" he asked, as if he'd thought it was going to be something else.

"Yeah!" I said and clapped my hands. "To my place. To here. I want you to move in with me."

Antonio sat so still, not saying a word, not doing anything.

Okay . . . that was not the reaction I expected. I mean, it wasn't like I really thought that he was going to get up and do the happy dance, but I was expecting something more—at least a smile.

Finally, Antonio did smile and I breathed again.

"You can move in here," I said. "That way your workload won't be so tedious, because your expenses won't be as high. And we would have more time together." I knelt down beside him. "I just want you to be happy. I want us to stay happy."

There were tears in his eyes when he looked down at me. "You would do this for me?"

"Yes. Don't you know how I feel about you?"

He nodded. "And I feel the same way." He took a deep breath and said, "But I can't do this." He closed the box. "I can't move in with you."

Stop the presses! What did this man just say to me?

"I have a lot of love for you, Devin. I really do. But it's too soon for us to be making a major move like this."

"Too soon? How many months has it been?"

"Exactly. It's only been months. I think we've got to really get to know one another. I think I'd like to be with you at least a year before I even start thinking that way."

A year? Dang! Why that long? It didn't even take a year to have a baby. Why would it take him a year to know if he wanted to be with me?

"And it's not just my year rule that I'm thinking about," Antonio went on to explain. "I'm just not settled enough—not at work, not in my life—and I wouldn't want to bring that drama and stress to you."

"What are you talking about? We talk to each other every day. We go out twice a week. I'm already completely in your life."

"But every night you get to go home and not have to deal with all of me." He took my hand. "Trust me. It is much better this way. It is much better for us."

I wasn't really feeling Antonio's answer. I mean, I thought we were close enough to do this, but I guess I was wrong. I guess I'd read this whole thing wrong.

"I want you to know, Devin, that I'm not saying no. I'm just saying not right now."

Well, that was a little better . . . but still.

A couple of seconds passed before I said, "Well, then give me back my key." I said it as a joke that was meant to make both of us laugh, make both of us feel better. It worked. He laughed, and I did, too, though I wasn't really laughing inside. I wasn't crying, either. I mean, I was a big boy. But I was disappointed.

That was okay, though. Antonio and I would still have a good time. We would see what would happen after a year. And who knows? By then, he might be begging me to come live with him.

I poured another glass of wine for both of us, and then we sat on the couch together and talked away the rest of the night.

Chapter 31

Chyanne

I'd made a lot of decisions in the last three months, but none were bigger than what I was going to do today.

I'd hired a car for the occasion—not that today was special in that kind of a way. But I didn't know what was going to happen afterward, and I didn't want to be waiting for a cab.

Inside the car I rubbed my belly. It was getting harder and harder to hide my pregnancy, but after today that wouldn't be a problem.

We were stuck in traffic, but I didn't mind. I'd given myself an extra thirty minutes to get downtown. I'd be on time. Looking out the window, I thought about all that Kayla had told me. It was almost like we were friends now—though, we really weren't. Really, I never wanted to speak to her again. Not that I was mad at her. It was just weird. But what was weird for me wasn't weird for her. She wanted to include me in all the details of her divorce, which was far from cordial.

It had begun when she served Malcolm with the papers. It seemed that Kayla had a flair for the dramatic—down to something as mundane as serving papers. She could have just told Malcolm when he came home one night. But no . . . she waited until the monthly partners meeting and then had the server make a big deal serving Malcolm the petition for divorce in front of his partners and the staff.

Kayla told me that by the time Malcolm stomped out of the office and made it to their Westchester home, his clothes had been tossed across the front lawn, the locks had been changed, and she'd left a note taped to the front door that said simply: *Dear Malcolm: I'm done!*

It was very *Waiting to Exhale*-ish!

And so, the first blow went to Kayla. At least, that was what she told me when she'd called to give me the news that the divorce proceedings had begun.

"So, you know you're in this with us, right?" she'd asked.

I knew what she meant. I could join them . . . with or without a subpoena.

"I hate to ask you to do this for me, Chyanne," she had said to me. "But really, he messed over you, too."

She was right about that. Malcolm had messed over me. And with this baby that I was carrying, I needed to remember that.

But one thing I could have told Kayla was that Malcolm wasn't about to take this sitting down. If I knew nothing else about the man I'd slept with, I knew that he was a fighter who believed only in winning.

I was right. The divorce that I had once told Skye and Devin would be cordial turned into a war. Kayla and Malcolm had been battling it out—he was trying to enforce the prenup, and she was telling him to go to hell! He wasn't budging, and neither was she.

That was where I came in—the secret weapon. Kayla had never once mentioned Malcolm's infidelity, and so he was sure that he was going to win this in front of the magistrate. But while Malcolm was sitting back, believing that he had the victory, Kayla's attorneys had me in meeting after meeting, going over the details of my affair with Malcolm. They asked me how many times we were together, how many trips we'd taken, how many gifts he'd given to me. It was all so personal, so difficult to speak about, and so very embarrassing.

But I'd gotten through those days with my head up. Though, I didn't think they were really any preparation for what I had to go through today. This was going to be much worse. It was all about to hit the fan.

In front of the courthouse, the driver gave me his card to call him when my testimony was complete.

"I'm hoping I'm not going to be more than an hour," I told him. "But I'm not sure."

I knew how legal proceedings went, though I'd never been part of something like this before. I was used to litigating in front of judges and juries. This was more of a civil matter, family court, and was handled much differently.

I moved slowly up the courthouse steps, feeling the extra weight of my baby. It might have all been in my mind. Maybe it was just a trick to delay my getting to the courtroom. But there was nothing that was going to be able to keep me away, and just five minutes after I'd been dropped off in front of the courthouse, I stood in front of Room 721.

Marvin had told me to wait on the bench right outside of the room until he came out to get me. They wanted me to make an appearance, and part of me wanted to make an appearance, too. I couldn't wait to see Malcolm's face when I walked in there, and I wondered if he would take back his thank-you—the thank-you he had given me for not telling his wife.

But while I felt a lot of satisfaction at what was about to go down, there was a part of me that felt sorry. I had shared a lot of good times with Malcolm. He'd given me a lot of joy for more than a year. But there was no way for me to find happiness in that time, because he was married. That was a point that I just could not get around.

The door to the courtroom opened suddenly, and Marvin stepped out.

"You ready?"

I popped up from the bench and nodded.

"Don't worry," he said to me. "You're well prepared."

And I'm an attorney, I said to myself. *I know what to expect.*

So, I followed Marvin into the catastrophe that had become my life.

The one thing that I hadn't allowed myself to think about was what Malcolm would do when he saw me. The moment I walked into that room, Malcolm gasped. And then he started coughing and coughing and coughing . . . as if he had suddenly caught something.

On one side, I saw Malcolm's attorney asking him if he was all right. On the other side, Marvin was leading me to the chair where I would speak to the magistrate.

From that point on, I kept my eyes away from Malcolm. Instead, I focused on the woman who swore me in, and then I kept my eyes on Marvin.

"For the record," he said to me, "would you state your full name?"

"Chyanne Brielle Monroe."

Marvin smiled, as if he thought I needed to be reassured. "Do you know Malcolm Parks?"

"Yes. He's my boss at Bailey, Booker, and Smith."

"Do you know him in any other capacity?"

I nodded, took a deep breath, and said, "I was involved . . . personally . . . with Mr. Parks."

"By personally, do you mean that you had an affair with him?"

"Yes," I said, trying to keep my voice strong. "I had an affair with him, though I didn't know I was having an affair. I didn't know that he was married."

"So you worked with him and didn't know that?"

I shook my head. "No. He didn't wear a wedding ring, and there were no pictures on his desk or anywhere in his office. I even visited his apartment, his condo, a few times, and there was nothing that led me to believe that he was married."

"What about gossip?" Marvin asked, as if he couldn't believe my answers. But I knew that he did. We'd rehearsed these over and over again, and like a good attorney, he knew exactly what I was going to say. "Didn't anyone in the office pull you aside when they found out about you and Mr. Parks?"

"Malcolm told me that I couldn't let anyone at the firm know about us, because it could cost both of us our jobs. And since working at Bailey, Booker, and Smith was my first position out of law school, I didn't want to take that chance."

"So, you met Mr. Parks at work?"

"Yes."

"And he was your boss?"

"Yes."

"Do you feel like you were taken advantage of?"

If this had been any kind of trial, Malcolm's attorney would have been on his feet, objecting. But this was a hearing. And, anyway, Malcolm's attorney would get his chance to make me look like a fool.

"Ms. Monroe," Marvin said. "Do you need me to repeat the question?"

"No." For the first time I looked at Malcolm, and my heart melted. His eyes were as sad as mine, and I could see his hurt. But didn't he know how much he had hurt me? Though, I wasn't here because of that. I was here because his wife had tracked me down. I never did ask Kayla how she'd known about me. I had a feeling it was just a wife's intuition. "In some ways, I do feel as if Mr. Parks took advantage of me. He lied to me by omitting the fact that he was married, and he lied about why we had to keep our relationship a secret."

Marvin smiled, but then I did something that we hadn't practiced.

"But even with all of that, I'm a grown woman and should have seen some of the signs." The color drained from Marvin's face when I said that, but he didn't have to worry. I was about to give him a gift. "But no matter who took advantage of whom, the fact remains that I had a yearlong relationship with Malcolm Parks. And now"—I rested my hand on my belly—"I'm going to have his baby."

This time it was Malcolm who lost the color in his face.

"Thank you," Marvin said, and he really did need to thank me. He had told me that he wanted to tell the magistrate that I was pregnant, and I had shut that down before. I didn't want my baby to be any part of this. But at just this moment I decided to tell the whole truth. I had nothing to be ashamed of. Malcolm was going to find out, anyway.

When Marvin sat down, I took a deep breath and braced myself for Malcolm's attorney. But as the man stood, Malcolm put his hand on his arm and whispered in his ear. My heart pounded; Malcolm was about to come after me—hard.

But what was he going to say? Every word I'd spoken was true.

Then the attorney said, "Your Honor, I have no questions for this witness."

On one side of the room, I thought Kayla was about to jump up and dance, knowing that this meant victory. Malcolm was not going to deny his infidelity. On the other side, Malcolm sat defeated, though his eyes never left mine.

The magistrate told me that I could leave and informed the others that there would be a short recess.

Pushing back my chair, I was hardly standing before Kayla was in front of me. "Thank you," she said, shaking my hand so hard, I thought it was going to fall off. "Thank you so much."

I just nodded, because I didn't have any words to say. I wasn't there by my own volition. I'd been forced there by her.

I stepped around the table and moved toward the door—which meant that I had to pass Malcolm's table. Good. I needed to. I needed to speak to him, if only for a moment.

"Chyanne," he whispered as I got closer. "You're pregnant?" His eyes were now on the center of me, the place where I carried his child.

I nodded.

"Why didn't you tell me?"

"I didn't know what the point was. You were *married*. But now I've seen things a bit differently." I reached into my purse and took out two envelopes. Handing them both to him, I said, "I'm sorry. But I was only telling the truth."

"What's this?"

"My resignation. And an order for child support. I'm putting your name on my baby's birth certificate."

I didn't wait to see his reaction. I just marched toward the door, keeping my head up and my hand on my belly. But once outside, I had to pause for a moment just to catch my breath, just to get my bearings.

What had happened in that courtroom was one of the most difficult things I'd ever had to do, and at the same time, I felt as if a weight had been taken from my shoulders.

It was over.

There were still many things I had to do—like find a new job . . . and an apartment, because I didn't want to spend all my savings on such a high rental place. Devin had found a few places in Brooklyn, which I was going to check out, and I prayed that something good would come through. I had a feeling that I was going to be fine, though.

I was about to start a new life, a new chapter, and surprisingly, I couldn't wait.

Chapter 32

Skye

"We ask at this time that you turn off all electronic devices. We will be arriving in Atlanta shortly." The flight attendant's voice did not soothe my nerves at all. We were actually doing this. I thought I was going to throw up on the way to the airport, but now I thought it actually might happen.

I had really fallen for Trent. He had definitely put in some overtime to woo me. He sent different types of flowers every week to my office, he wined and dined me like no other, exposed me to things like ballets and operas, and he even remembered little things about me, like how I loved chocolate, and made sure I never ran out. Even with all that, nothing could make me want to take this trip.

"Babe, I'm glad you've finally agreed to do this." Trent's voice had so much sincerity and excitement in it.

"Honestly, I'm scared out of my mind." I tried to empty out the little bottles of alcohol the flight attendant had brought me over an hour ago, but there wasn't even a drop left.

"Why would you be scared? I think your parents will love me, just like my folks love you."

Trent took the bottles, which I was still feverishly shaking up and down on my tongue, and grabbed my hand. His touch always calmed me, and he knew it. I took a deep breath to slow my heart rate down because I could feel my heart jumping out of my chest. Trent stroked my hand and waited for me to say something.

"It's not you, babe. My parents aren't the easiest people to please, especially when it comes to me."

Trent gave me the sweetest smile. It was comforting, and I knew that something profound and genuine was sure to follow. He always gave me that smile to ease my mind of whatever I was stressing about.

"Everything is going to be fine, love. Your parents just want to see you happy. You are happy, right?"

"Of course I am happy with you." I laid my head on his shoulder and rubbed his arm. He was really an amazing man, but for some reason things never felt perfect.

"Then this weekend will go better than expected." He gently kissed my forehead before he whispered, "I promise."

Landing and the baggage claim went by relatively quickly, and it felt so good to be home and breathe Georgia air when I stepped outside. Trent and I had convinced my parents last week on the phone that it would be better for us to rent a car instead of having them pick us up so that we wouldn't have to bother them for their car all weekend. I really just wanted as much time to prep Trent as I could possibly get. The whole ride from the airport to Sandy Springs, I coached Trent, mainly about my father.

"And make sure you give him straight answers. My father hates it when people dance around a subject."

"Babe, I think I got it," he said with a chuckle.

"Trent, I'm serious. My parents aren't like your parents. It takes a lot to impress them."

Before Trent could say another word, I turned into our driveway. I had no idea how this would go, but it was no turning back now. I looked into Trent's eyes, and all I could do was nod my head. I had to get out of the car. At that point I realized I wasn't afraid of what my parents would think of Trent, but what they would think of me. I was living the life I'd always dreamed about, and I wanted them to be proud of me.

Trent held my hand all the way to the door, and I took a deep breath with every step. I tried to find the key my parents hid in the flowerpot for Simone and me whenever we return home, but the door swung open and my mom came rushing out.

"My baby, my baby, my baby." She wasted no time wrapping her arms around me and almost squeezing the life out of me.

"Hey, Mom." I pushed out with as much air as I could muster.

"We are so happy you decided to come home. You look good." My mother directed her attention to Trent, looking him up and down. My mother and I had always been close, so I knew that look of approval of his appearance.

"You must be Trent. I am so glad we get to meet you. Well, ya'll don't stand out there on the porch. Come on in. Skye, I made your favorite meal, so I hope you're hungry."

"Yes, ma'am, I am. Where's Dad?"

"Right here." The strong voice that I knew so well resounded behind us. My father and I had had our differences in the past, but I was very happy to see him, and I found myself leaping into his arms. His hug reassured me that he was happy to see me, too, and that was a good feeling.

"I'm glad you came home, Skye. You've been missed."

I couldn't even form the words to give him a re-
sponse. I just smiled and hugged him a little tighter.
After we finally let go of each other, he wasted no time
turning all his attention on Trent. My father could be
intimidating, but Trent looked like he was prepared to
hold his own.

"You must be the young man we've heard about." He
shook Trent's hand and tried to size him up.

"Trent Hamilton. It's nice to finally meet you, sir.
You have a lovely home."

My mother didn't allow them to chat long before she
called all of us into the dining room. My mom went all
out for my homecoming. Fried chicken, macaroni and
cheese, sweet potatoes, greens, corn bread, and her
famous chocolate mousse cake were spread out on the
table. Trent was accustomed to catered food and fine
cuisine, but he threw down on my mother's Southern
cooking.

The conversation was surprisingly pleasant. We
chatted about Trent's background, his career, his hob-
bies and interests, and, of course, his religious affilia-
tion. Trent seemed so comfortable around my parents,
and it made me see him in a whole different light.
Could this man really win my family over?

"Well, son, I must say you seem like a fine individual." The inflection in my father's voice told me that
the big question was coming up. He was impressed
with Trent, but that meant nothing if he didn't have
an honest and genuine answer to why he wanted to be
with me.

"What exactly are your intentions with our daughter? That is a very special person you have on your
hands, and it takes a strong kind of man to love her the
way she deserves to be loved."

I had never heard those words come out of my father's mouth about me. It took me by surprise, and when I looked up from my plate, we gave each other such a genuine and loving glance. My father had really changed, and at that moment I didn't really care what Trent had to say, because the most important man in my life had given me what I needed and wanted all these years.

"Well, Reverend Davenport," Trent began, breaking my stare with my father. "I care for your daughter more than I have for anyone else before. She is the most amazing woman I have ever met, and my intentions are to be with her as long as she'll have me." Trent grabbed my hand and softly kissed the back of it.

That was it. My parents had fallen in love with him. I mean, he was incredible. Handsome, intelligent, wealthy, cherished family and loved me wholeheartedly. What was there not to love? He was the man that women prayed to God for, so why did I have a sick feeling in the pit of my stomach?

Chapter 33

Skye
One Year Later

It looked like my dream was finally going to come true. I had designed enough pieces to do a full show, to have my own line. It had been a few years coming, but nothing good came easy, right?

The sound of the key in the door made me lift my head, but only for a moment.

"Hey, babe," Trent said as he balanced three brown bags in his hands.

"Hey." I stayed in place, sitting at my coffee table, with all my sketches stretched out in front of me. I had decisions to make. Which ones should I choose?

With the bags still in his hands, Trent leaned over and kissed my nose, breaking every part of my concentration. I looked up and inhaled his cologne—Issey Miyake, my favorite. Then, when he turned around, I kept my eyes on his butt as he strolled into the kitchen.

Trent was my man—he had been for a year—and it was hard for me to believe that. Not that he wasn't wonderful; there was so much to love about Trent. Forget about the fact that he spoiled me rotten with trips and gifts, that he had charmed my parents when we flew to Atlanta to meet them, that he gave me plenty of space to work and pursue my dream. All of that was important, but the best part was that he loved me. I mean, Trent really loved me, and he had from day one.

Which was why I couldn't figure out why I didn't love him.

No, that wasn't quite true. I did love Trent. How could I not? But I wasn't *in love* with him. I didn't have the kind of love where you heard bells ringing or saw fireworks exploding. My love for Trent was calm and constant and lacked the passion that I'd had with Noah.

I sighed and closed my eyes. I got so pissed at myself every time I thought of that man. Why was he still in my head? I mean, a year had gone by and I was so much further along with Trent than I'd ever been with Noah, so why did he still jump into my mind during the most inopportune times?

"Here, babe." My eyes snapped open, and above me Trent stood, holding a plate packed high with Chinese food. "I bet you haven't eaten in hours," he said as if he knew me well.

And he did. "Not since breakfast."

I took the plate from him, and he returned to the kitchen to retrieve his own. Then he knelt beside me, blessed the food, and we ate for long minutes in silence.

It was so comfortable being with Trent—and this was the thing I had to remember. We fit together. Everyone said so.

"So, how are things going?"

I nodded. "I got a lot done today, but there is still so much to do."

"Well, I have full confidence that my baby will get it done in a spirit of excellence."

See what I mean? How could I not be in love with this man? I needed to stop trippin'!

I placed my plate on the coffee table, took Trent's plate from his hands, and put it on top of mine. Then, right there on the floor, I sat on his lap and kissed him with a passion that I pulled from deep inside of me.

"Wow!" Trent said when we finally pulled apart. "What was that for?"

"For being you."

He grinned. "I'm a much better me when I'm with you."

I reached back inside, wanting to say something as loving, as profound as what Trent had just said to me. But when I couldn't find anything to say, I leaned over and kissed him again.

This was always my answer—if I couldn't say it, I could show it. I could make love to him all night long.

We pulled away, breathless as usual, and Trent stood, pulling me up with him. We took two steps toward my bedroom, and then a knock on my door stopped us.

I frowned. No one could get inside the building without being buzzed in, so this had to be one of my neighbors. With his arms around my waist, Trent and I walked to the door. I opened it and screamed.

"Oh my God! Simone! What are you doing here?" I yelled at my younger sister as I pulled her into my arms.

"If you let me come up for air," Simone said, coughing, "I'll tell you."

I stepped back, and Simone grinned at me. And that was when I noticed that Jaylen, her husband, was with her. "You better get over here, boy!" I said before I hugged him, too. "Oh, my God!" I said again. "Come in, come in!" I closed the door. "Oh and this is Trent!" I grinned at my sister and brother-in-law. "My boyfriend."

"I know who he is," Simone said as she wrapped her arms around him. "Nice to meet you, though I feel like I know you already. You made quite an impression on my parents— especially my mother." Simone leaned in close, as if she was telling Trent a secret. "You know, she's already planning your wedding."

Simone winked, and I rolled my eyes.

Trent said, "Well, she can keep on planning because I plan on making your sister an honest woman as soon as she says yes."

This was not something that I wanted to talk about, so I introduced Trent and Jaylen so that the men would start talking.

From the corner of my eye, I could see the look on Simone's face—like she had more questions—but I wasn't about to let her ask me anything right now.

"So," I said, leading them both to the couch, "what are you doing here? What are you doing in New York?"

My sister and brother-in-law sat on the couch, while Trent and I returned to the floor.

"Well," Simone started, "I guess you don't spend too much time watching those entertainment shows. I'm performing at the Garden tomorrow."

"What?" Trent and I said together.

"I thought you weren't coming to New York on this tour?" I asked my sister.

"She wasn't supposed to," Jaylen said. "But Ciara got sick, and the promoter asked if we could fill in for her in a couple of cities."

"So"—Simone held her hands up in the air like she was doing a red-carpet pose—"I'm here."

I laughed. I was just so proud of my sister and what she'd accomplished. She was an amazing singer, and America thought so, too, since she'd had five number one hits in the two years that she'd been singing professionally. It had been a long road for her—from singing in the church choir to convincing my father that she wasn't doing the devil's work by singing R & B, to marrying Jaylen and becoming the first singer on his now rising and successful Tru Harmony record label.

As my sister chatted away, telling Trent and me about her adventures on her latest European tour, I sighed inside. But it was a happy sigh. I was so content and proud that my sister was living her dream. She was singing and was married to a man who adored her. Even now I could see how much Jaylen loved her—it was in his eyes when he looked at her.

He looked at her the same way Trent looked at me.

"So, what's happening in New York tonight?" Simone said as she glanced at the storyboards piled on the table and stacked on the floor. "Don't tell me you're not hanging out."

"Uh, li'l sis, in case you haven't noticed, tomorrow is a workday."

"Bump that!" Simone said, and I laughed at the term that we used to use when we were kids. It was the closest we could get to cursing, and we couldn't even say that around our reverend father. "I'm in town. We better go out and do something."

Trent said, "You know what? There is a new club opening tonight. Actually, it's reopening. Twenty-Twenty."

"Yeah, I heard about that," Simone said, as if she was up on everything cosmopolitan. I laughed. This was the same woman who used to be the shy, overweight girl. Well, my sister was holding it up for thick women everywhere. She'd lost a lot of weight, but she wasn't trying to get down to a size six. She was happy with her size twelve and was flaunting her curves all over the place. I couldn't count the number of magazines that had her on the cover, and she was even talking to me about doing her own line of clothes one day.

"I can get us into the club," Trent said and then stopped himself. "I mean, it's not like they're not going to let *you* in."

Simone laughed. "No, I know what you're saying, brother-in-law," she kidded. "Mom said you were connected." She crossed her arms and looked Trent up and down. "Mmm-hmm, I think my mom was right." Turning to me, she said, "What are you waiting for? You need to marry this man."

Okay, I needed to stop this right here. "First of all," I said as I stood up, "he hasn't asked me to marry him. And second of all, if you want us to go out, I gotta go get ready. I can't be letting my little sister steal my shine when I'm the designer."

"Well, you better hurry up, then," Simone said. "What about you, Trent? I know you're going with us, too, right?"

"Definitely. I got some stuff here that I can change into."

"Oh! It's like that, huh?" Simone grinned. She lifted her hands in the air and pumped them like she was raising the roof. "Hey, hey, hey!"

"Jaylen, would you control your wife, please?" I asked as I pulled Trent into my bedroom.

"I've *never* been able to control my wife." Jaylen laughed. "And that's a good thing."

Inside my bedroom I rushed to my closet, but Trent wrapped his arms around me from behind, stopping me.

He spun me around and kissed me.

It was my turn to ask, "What was that for?"

He said, "You told your sister that I never asked you to marry me."

Uh-oh. "You . . . haven't . . . ," I stuttered and then prayed inside that he wouldn't ask me right now.

He said, "It's not because I haven't wanted to. It's because when I do, I want to make sure that you're going to say yes."

Again, I reached down inside for something wonderful to say to him. But I found nothing, so I hugged him as tightly as I could and held him there for at least a minute.

When I pulled away, I said, "We'd better hurry, or else they'll think we're in here doing something else."

Trent laughed. "Okay. I just want you to know that I love you, Skye."

I nodded. This I could do. "I love you, too, Trent." And those words were the truth.

Chapter 34

Devin

I was walking to the front of my shop and then stopped. I closed my eyes slowly, then opened them again. But the vision was still there. So, I blinked over and over, like, ten times.

But that didn't help.

It was only when the receptionist started screaming that I knew what I saw before me was the truth.

Simone!

Well, she was Simone Davenport to me, but the rest of the world knew her only as Simone!

"Girl!" I yelled out as I ran to her. "What are you doing here?"

She wrapped her arms around me and hugged me while the women in the packed shop started pulling out their cell phones. They were snapping away, but it didn't seem to faze my girl. I guess she was used to it.

"Uh, Devin, you're cracking my lungs," Simone kidded.

Well, maybe she wasn't kidding. I was holding her kind of tight. It was just that I hadn't seen much of her since she'd become a big star.

"What are you doing here?" I asked her. "What are you doing in New York?" But then I held up my hands. "Wait," I said to her. To everyone else, I said, "You heffas have taken enough pictures. Put your daggone cameras away!"

The women were squealing all around us, making calls to friends. Lawd, you just couldn't buy enough class for Black folks.

I grabbed Simone's hand and dragged her to my station.

"Uh, Ms. Thang, you're gonna have to get up."

"Why?" Jennifer, my current customer, asked me. "You in the middle of doing my hair!" But though she had an attitude with me, she was grinning away at Simone. "I am such a fan of yours," she gushed. "I'm probably your biggest fan. I have all of your CDs. Will you take a picture with me?"

"Yes," Simone said.

"No," I said, pulling Jennifer out of the chair. "If she takes a picture with you, then she'll have to take a picture with everyone, and I ain't having that."

"Hater!" Jennifer growled. "And what am I supposed to do about my hair?" she said, swiveling her neck at me.

"Katrina will take care of you," I said, pointing to the only stylist who didn't have a customer at the moment. "She'll whip you up something fierce. Don't worry. She can handle you. That's why we call her Katrina, like the storm!"

Katrina sucked her teeth as she led my customer to her station. "Y'all call me Katrina 'cause that's my name."

"All of y'all need to go back to work," I said to the rest of them as Simone sat in my chair. I wished there was someplace else where we could talk, but all we had in the back was a storage area and a bathroom, neither of which was fit for my girl, Simone, the superstar.

"So, what're you doing in New York?" I asked her again.

She filled me in on how she was taking Ciara's spot at Madison Square Garden tonight. "That's why I'm here. I want you to come to the Garden early to do my hair."

"Are you kidding me?"

"No, I'm not kidding," she said as she slapped my arm. "You know that I would have you on the road with me if I could afford you."

"And you know if you could afford me, I'd be right there."

We laughed together.

I said, "It would be an honor to hook you up tonight, Ms. Simone. So, how long are you here?"

"I got here last night, and we're leaving first thing in the morning. Jaylen and I hung out with Skye and Trent last night."

"And y'all didn't call me?"

"I'm sorry, boo. I just wanted to spend some time with Skye since I hadn't seen her in over a year. And I wanted to meet her man." Simone leaned back in the chair. "So, tell me about Trent. What do you think?"

"He seems really cool," I said. "We haven't spent that much time together. But I like him. And, I can tell that he loves your sister."

"That's what I'm sayin'. You should see the way he looks at her. He is so far gone, which is why I can't figure out why they're not married already."

I shrugged, though I had an opinion about this. I was sure that Ms. Skye was still hung up on Mr. Locks and Lips. Yup, that was what I was thinking. I wanted to shake her out of it, tell her that she was living the epitome of my motto. . . . She had dated cute—Noah. Now it was time to marry rich—Trent. But I wasn't gonna say a word to Simone. I valued my life, and Skye would kill me if I told her sister about the man that was surely still in her heart.

"So, what's up with you?" Simone asked. "What's going on in your love life?"

It must've been the way my lips spread into an instant grin that made Simone gasp.

"Oh my God!" She put her hand over her mouth. "I was just kidding. Don't tell me that you're dating, too?"

"Ssshhh!" I said, looking around the shop. I whispered to her, "I don't want these people in here all up in my business."

"Okay," she said, standing up. "We'll talk later."

"What? You're leaving already?"

She nodded. "I have to. We have to do sound checks at the Garden. But here . . ." She pulled a ticket from her purse. "This will give you full access to get to me tonight. I wanna have my hair done around five, 'cause I've gotta look fresh. Will that work for you?"

"I'll be there at four!" I said. "Shoot! I'll go with you now."

She laughed. "No, five will be fine." She hugged me. "I can't wait for us to hang out a little bit tonight. Skye has Chyanne's ticket." She leaned in closer and whispered, "Do you need an extra one for your man?"

"Nah! Antonio won't be able to go," I said, knowing that I could never get him to do anything with me at the last minute.

"Okay," she said as she hugged me again.

The women all squealed, "Bye, Simone," as she trotted out of the shop and into the waiting limousine.

Dang! My girl was all the way famous now. For real!

And that made me feel good! I just wished that I could celebrate tonight at the Garden with Antonio. But he hated it when I sprang anything on him at the last minute, so I would just tell him about it tomorrow.

Anyway, I had enough to do. I began packing my bag with all my tools and supplies so that I could hook my little sister up tonight. When I finished with Simone Davenport, aka Simone, she was gonna look something fierce!

Chapter 35

Chyanne

"Oh, my goodness," I said. "Yes, definitely. I'll be there," I told Skye before I hung up the phone.

So Simone was in town. How cool was this? Our little Simone, now the superstar.

I shook my head, so happy that I was going to see her tonight. And in concert, too. But then the love of my life interrupted my thoughts, and I rushed into my bedroom.

Justice, my eight-month-old daughter, was awake, and she wanted me to know it.

"Sssshhh," I whispered as I cuddled her into my arms. "What's wrong with Mommy's princess?"

Can I tell you how much I loved this little girl? And, the best thing of all was that everyone loved her, too. Not that my mother had been thrilled when I told her the news about my pregnancy.

"What are you gonna do up in New York all by yourself?" she had asked me. "You need to come back to Atlanta."

"I'm not by myself. I have Skye and Devin. They're gonna help me. Plus, I'm going to go back to work. I want to be a lawyer right here in the city."

The hardest part for me had been breaking this news to the Davenports. But surprisingly, they'd done nothing but tell me that they loved me, and then they sent me a check every month.

Just a little something, the check always said. And, no matter if it was a fifty-dollar check or a one-hundred-dollar check, it always made me cry.

But like I'd told my mom I would, I'd been handling it. Yes, I was in a one-bedroom walk-up in Brooklyn, but it was still Park Slope. And I was saving almost a thousand dollars a month in rent.

Before I left the firm, I made a few calls to other companies who had been interested in me at the start of my career. With my growing reputation at Bailey, Booker, and Smith, it was pretty easy to find a position at Parker Graham as a freelance attorney. The money wasn't as good and court wasn't as often as I was used to, but it allowed me to be an attorney and a full-time mom. Really, I thought that my child support would've been settled by now, but I'd just gotten the summons for family court last week. I was pretty sure that if I'd contacted Malcolm, he would've given me something to help with his daughter. He wasn't a monster. . . . He was just a cheater. But I wanted everything to go through the court so there would never be any misunderstandings.

Malcolm hadn't tried yet to see his daughter, which wasn't really his fault. He didn't know where I was. But once we had things settled, I wasn't going to keep Justice from him. If he wanted a relationship with her, I was going to make sure that happened. I wasn't going to be one of those bitter women, standing in the way of my daughter having a relationship with her father. Especially since I'd lost my father when I was so young.

As I rocked Justice back and forth, I began to wonder what I could do about tonight. I really wanted to go to Madison Square Garden to see Simone, but life wasn't as easy as it used to be. Not that I cared—all I had to do was look down at the face of this little girl and I was done. I never knew this kind of love was inside of me. My love for Justice came from deep inside of me. So even if I had to miss Simone tonight, even if I had to miss a million concerts, even if I had to miss days hanging out with my friends, I would give it all up for Justice.

The knock on my door interrupted all my thoughts.

"Hey, Mari," I said to my seventeen-year-old neighbor. "What's up?"

"My mom told me to give you this," she said, handing me an envelope. "It got mixed up with our mail."

I balanced Justice in one arm and took the envelope from her with the other hand. "Thanks," I said.

"Can I play with Justice for a minute?" she asked.

"Sure, come on in. I wanna ask you something, anyway."

With the door closed behind her, I asked if she was doing anything tonight.

"Nah!" She was standing right in front of me, cooing at Justice. "I was supposed to go out with my boyfriend, but I found out that he's been kicking it with one of my girls, so I'm just pissed and . . ."

I held up my hand. I had to stop Mari right there, or else she was going to go into one of those long teenage soliloquies. "So, then . . . can you babysit tonight?"

She grinned. "Oh, yeah," she said, taking Justice from my arms.

My baby cooed when she looked into Mari's face, and that pleased me. I often asked Mari to babysit for me when Mrs. Wallace—the woman who watched Justice during the day—was unavailable at night.

"That's great. Now, it may be a late night."

"That's okay," Mari said. "I'll just sleep on the couch, if that's all right with you."

I told her what time to be back here, then took Justice from her arms and closed the door behind her. Now that that was settled, I had to find something fabulous to wear, which wasn't going to be easy since I was still ten pounds over my pre-pregnancy weight. But I had a lot of faith in that new Pilates video I'd bought.

Inside my bedroom I tucked Justice inside of a fort that I made with six pillows so that she could sit up and watch me. She gurgled and smiled and made my heart melt.

Oh, yeah. I was in love.

I turned toward my closet, but then I remembered the envelope, which I'd dumped onto the dresser. Grabbing it, I looked at the return address. It was from Kayla.

I sighed. I hadn't heard from Malcolm's wife since I'd testified at that hearing, and I had been glad about it. I didn't want anything to do with Kayla or Malcolm, and my life had been good that way.

But somehow, this woman had found me.

I ripped open the envelope, pulled out the letter, and groaned. *What now?* I wondered as I read through Kayla's words. She thanked me for all my help, told me that she'd won and that she had some news she wanted to share with me.

I wasn't interested in a thing with Kayla, but she promised that after next Tuesday I would never hear from her again. She wanted to meet me at the café where we'd met before.

One last time, was the last line in the letter.

Already I was thinking about not going, but the thing was, I had a feeling that Kayla wouldn't leave me alone until she had the last word.

Okay, I would meet her. But after next Tuesday I wanted Malcolm's wife to be out of my life.

Chapter 36

Skye

In my head I could still hear my sister singing. And, I could still hear the crowd roaring. From our first row seats we'd seen everything up close and personal, and my sister had done her thing on that stage, a force to be reckoned with.

I couldn't have been more proud of Simone.

But now it was time to get up. Even if it was Saturday, I didn't want to sleep the day away. I let my eyes kinda just flutter open, then reached across the bed. But the space where Trent was supposed to be was empty.

I sat up and let my eyes wander around my bedroom. His slacks and shirt were still tossed across the chair, right where he'd left them last night. So, I plopped back down.

As soon as my head hit the pillow, Trent came strolling in, carrying two cups of coffee. I was surprised he was already dressed.

"Good morning," he said and kissed my lips.

But I kept my mouth closed—morning breath!

He sat on the edge of the bed as we sipped, but Trent was quiet. Usually by now he'd ask me what I wanted to do for the day, or he'd tell me if he already made plans. Or he'd apologize if he had to go out and work. But this morning he just stared straight ahead, gazing out the window, as if there was something deep on his mind.

"Did you enjoy the show last night?" I asked as I rested my cup on the nightstand.

"What?" he asked, as if I'd interrupted his thoughts. "The show? Oh, yeah. Your sister was great." He looked at me. "Greatness just runs in your family, I guess."

I chuckled. "I'm not doing anything great. Not like Simone."

"No, you're living your own dream. And now you're part of mine." He kissed my forehead. "Okay, get dressed."

I frowned. Obviously, he had something planned for the day, but usually he told me what we'd be doing. But that was it? Just get dressed?

"Where are we going?"

He smiled. "It's a surprise."

I studied him for a little while, trying to figure out what he was up to. I never did like surprises, but that was before I met Trent. This man was all about surprising me, all the time. No matter how many times I told him that I would rather be involved in whatever he was planning, he just kept shutting me out and surprising me.

So, I had given up a long time ago. I'd learned to go with Trent's flow.

"What am I supposed to wear?"

He wrapped his arms around me. "Well, I prefer you naked, but that won't work for today."

Now, that got me. I laughed. "Okay, I'll choose something besides being naked."

It never took me long to get ready. My closet was so organized, it was easy for me to see what I had and what I could pair together. Plus, I cut my hair a lot shorter, so it never took me long to style it, which drove Devin crazy!

In just under an hour I stood in the living room, wearing a sweetheart sundress that I knew for sure showed off all my curves. And, I had hit all the right notes with this outfit, because the moment I sauntered into the living room and Trent saw me, he jumped up from the couch and grinned.

"Damn!"

I laughed as I grabbed my purse and a shawl. "I aim to please."

"If that was your aim, you hit your target," he said, putting his hand over his heart.

Right then I decided. I was just going to have to find a way, find a way to love this man, who loved me without even thinking about it. I was just going to love him, and maybe one day it would come as easy for me as it did for him.

Outside, after we got his car out of the garage, I asked him again where we were going.

"What part of 'It's a surprise' didn't you understand?"

So, I did what I always did—I just sat back in Trent's car and enjoyed the ride. As he drove, all kinds of thoughts swirled through my head. I thought about Simone and Jaylen and how both of them were living their dreams. I thought about Chyanne and how she had turned her challenges into a joy. I thought about Devin and his love for Antonio, whom we still hadn't met, and how he'd found his tempo in New York, too.

And then I thought about my life. I was happy, no doubt about it. My career was coming together, I loved the city . . . and then there was this man sitting next to me, this wonderful man who deserved to have my heart. I was going to find a way to give it to him.

When we pulled up in front of Vibe, I remembered the time we'd come to this restaurant together, and I was thrilled to be back. It felt like we were coming full circle, being here today.

The hostess smiled at us as we came in.

Trent told her, "You have reservations for Trent Hamilton."

"Oh, yes." Her smile seemed to widen as she looked at me. "Right this way."

I followed the hostess and was surprised as we kept walking farther back, past a bunch of empty tables. I frowned. Trent had probably gotten another private room. But why? We were just having brunch.

At the very back of the restaurant, the hostess swung open the double doors, and a rush of "Surprise!" screams came at me.

I stood there, stunned for a moment, because surely I had to be dreaming. How could this be?

Before me stood my parents and Trent's parents and Simone and Jaylen—who were supposed to be gone— and Trent's sister, Tracie, and Chyanne, with Justice in her arms, and Devin.

"What . . ." I said to the crowd, and then I turned to Trent. "What is this? Why is everyone here?"

It wasn't my birthday; it wasn't Trent's birthday; it wasn't any kind of holiday. I couldn't imagine what this celebration was about.

Until Trent took my hand and said, "Sweetheart, I asked all of our family here today because I'm praying that this is going to be a day that you'll never forget. And, I want all the people who are important to us to be here with us."

Okay, but I still didn't get what was going on.

He said, "Skye, I have loved you for a long time. I never believed in love at first sight, until I met you. And over the year that we've dated, my love has just grown stronger. When we're together, I feel complete. When we're apart, I can't wait to get back together with you. Not a moment goes by when I don't think of you. Even when I'm asleep, I dream about you."

"Awww!"

I wasn't sure who said that, but if I had to guess, it was Devin!

But I couldn't turn my head away; I couldn't look at anyone except Trent. I was mesmerized by his words, by this moment.

When he slowly dropped to one knee, I was sure that I was going to faint. My breath caught in my throat as he slipped a velvet box from his jacket and opened it for me to see. I was almost blinded by the diamond that shone back.

"Skye Davenport, would you do me the honor and give me the blessing of becoming Skye Hamilton, of being my wife for the rest of our lives?"

A hush hovered over the room, and I just stared at Trent. I couldn't believe this. Hadn't I just been thinking this morning about loving him completely?

My eyes went from Trent's to the ring, then back to the man who loved me without question. In an instant the last year played in my mind. There hadn't been a day or a time when Trent hadn't shown me that he would love me forever.

"Skye?" Trent called my name.

The only thing that was in my future was happiness with this man. So, the word just flew out of my mouth. "Yes!" I said. "Yes! Yes! Yes!" I exclaimed, pulling him from his bended knee.

Our friends and family cheered as Trent slipped the ring onto my finger. And then I kissed him with a passion that I usually reserved for our bedroom.

There were whistles and heartfelt jeers behind us, and when we separated, I looked into his eyes. Trent Hamilton was going to be my husband.

And I knew in my heart that that was a very good thing.

Chapter 37

Devin

"So, Skye is getting married," Leigh said. "Do you like the guy?"

"Yes, and yes," I said. "But, no!"

Leigh frowned. "No what?"

"No, we're not gonna talk about Skye and her four-carat diamond ring. . . ."

Leigh's eyes got wide. "He gave her four carats?"

I waved my hand in the air. "Of course he did. He's Trent Hamilton, real estate mogul, or whatever. But like I said, boo, we're not gonna talk about this, 'cause that is not why you asked me to come to lunch." I picked over my salad, wishing that I'd ordered what I really wanted, a hamburger. But I was trying to keep my girlish figure for Antonio. Not that my man had any complaints—I just wanted to make sure it stayed that way between us.

I said, "So are you going to tell me what this is about?"

When Leigh sighed, I knew. Really, I knew even before she did that. The only thing that Leigh ever talked about these days was her husband and her marriage. And the way she just exhaled, I guessed things with her and Michael weren't pretty at all.

Leigh still hadn't said a word, so I said, "Please don't make me have to pull it out of you. I don't have that

kind of time. I've gotta be back at the shop in an hour."
I was losing my patience. It wasn't that I didn't want to
help my friend, but the thing was, it was getting hard
with Leigh. Skye and Chyanne didn't take this much
trouble—even with all the drama in their lives.

And my girls had lots of drama, for real. First, there
was Skye, who could not forget about that loser, Noah,
but at least she was putting Mr. Locks and Lips behind
her and had finally agreed to spend the rest of her life
with Trent. And Chyanne had a beautiful daughter
and a baby daddy that she was about to take to court.
But even with their lives, my girls smiled a little and
laughed a lot.

Leigh hardly ever did either, and it was beginning to
wear hard on me.

"I'm sorry to always call on you, Devin," she said.
"It's just that I don't have anyone else to talk to."

"Oh, it's no problem, girl," I lied. "You know I got
you." Even though I was tired of hearing it, I couldn't
leave my girl out there like that with no backup. And,
really, it was only because I was involved with Antonio
that this was a problem for me. If it wasn't for him, I
probably could have hung out with Leigh every day and
every night, listening to all her problems. But it was
hard hearing her go on about her horrible marriage
when my life with Antonio just seemed to be getting
better and better. He still hadn't agreed to move in with
me, but I had a feeling, because of all the time we'd
been spending together, that he was coming close to
finally making that decision.

Leigh's voice cut through my thoughts. "I thought
Michael and I were getting closer for a while, but he's
back to being distant." She looked down into her salad
and swirled a piece of the lettuce around in the dressing. "In fact, he's more distant than he was before."

"Have you asked him about it?"

"Yeah, when I can catch him at home. But even when he's there, he hardly talks, and when he does open up, he just says that I'm imagining everything."

"Well, maybe you are."

When Leigh looked up, there were already tears in her eyes, and that was when I knew this was serious, even more serious than before. "I'm not," she said. "I'm not imagining a thing."

"Okay, sweetie," I said, wanting to make her feel better. I reached for her hand. "What do you think is going on?"

It took her a moment to say it. "I think he's having an affair."

I laughed out loud. Please! As gorgeous as Leigh was, Michael would be a fool. I knew relationships weren't just based on looks, but Leigh had it all; she was the complete package, with to-die-for looks, an amazing career, a charming personality, and all kinds of connections. If I had to bet, I'd say that she'd probably helped Michael even get his job as a sports agent.

No, no, no! I had never met her husband, but I knew he wasn't seeing another woman. No man on earth was that crazy.

"I just don't believe it," I said, still shaking my head. "Michael wouldn't do that to you."

"Why do you say that? Men have affairs all the time."

"Not your husband. You're too beautiful."

"What does that have to do with anything? Remember Halle Berry?"

Well, Leigh had a point there. But still, I had to encourage her. "This ain't Hollywood, and out there it's hard to make any kind of marriage work. We're back here with the normal people. Michael loves you."

She pressed her lips together and squinted as if she was contemplating what I'd said. "You think that I might be wrong?"

"I'd bet on it."

Leigh sighed.

"Look," I said. "Didn't you tell me that Michael had been really busy at work?"

"Yeah."

"Well, that's it. It's the stress of trying to keep a job in today's times. And I get that. Unless you're an entre-preneur, you're at the mercy of someone else. I'm going through the same thing with my guy."

"What's going on with Antonio?"

"Nothing. It's just that he's stressed out a lot, and it's hard to be all lovey when pressures are beating you down."

She nodded her head as if she believed my words. "Maybe . . ."

"I'm right," I said, trying to reassure my friend.

I could tell that she really wanted to believe me. But she said, "I just think there's something inside of a wife, some kind of radar that lets your heart know what's really going on. That's why that saying that the wife is the last to know is false. . . . Wives always know."

Wow! That was deep. I didn't know what to say, so I didn't say anything.

Leigh said, "But either way, Devin, I have to find out the truth."

It was my turn to nod. "Well, let me know what I can do to help, okay?" I certainly understood what she was saying. I just prayed that she was wrong and I was right.

Chapter 38

Chyanne

I frowned at the FedEx envelope that had just been delivered. What now?

And then I saw the return address—it was the address of my law firm. My hands were shaking as I pulled out the single sheet of paper and read the note:

My Dearest Chyanne:

First, I don't want you to think that I'm stalking you. I found you through the court records from the child support claim that you filed. That brought tears to my eyes, and for many days I wondered if you and I would somehow be able to work it out since I am now officially divorced. But in my heart, I know the truth. Your integrity would never allow you to become involved with me again; you would never be able to trust me, and I understand that. We have a court date next week, but I just want you to know that you don't have to go through this. I know that your daughter is mine. Yes, I know we have a daughter. I overheard Nicole whispering it to your assistant. But I do want you to know that you will not have a problem with me paying child support—whatever the court decides will be fine with me.

*I am asking you for a favor, however. I love
my daughter already—sight unseen. I found out
her name is Justice from the court papers. How
appropriate for our daughter. Chyanne, with all
my heart, I want to be a part of her life. But I will
leave that up to you and will respect your wishes.
I just want you to know that I have never stopped
thinking about you. You truly were a great love
that I lost, and I apologize again for what I put
you through. Thank you for the joy that you did
bring into my life, and I'll see you in court.*

I could almost see Malcolm smiling as he wrote that
last line. Those were the words that we usually said to
our opponents, though I could tell that Malcolm wasn't
saying it in a negative way.

Wow, was all I could think as I stared at the letter.
This was not the way I expected this to go down. I had
dreamed about facing off against Malcolm in court. I
had imagined that he would be pissed that I'd testified
for his wife, so that he would get back at me by denying,
denying, denying that Justice was his and then fighting
giving me any money.

But then the second part of my dream—the best
part—would kick in, and that was where a year's worth
of my hurt and anger would explode onto Malcolm.
Through my screams, I was going to make sure that he
understood all the pain that he'd inflicted upon me. I
was going to make sure that he felt the physical horror
of having his heart ripped apart.

"I loved you on purpose!" I imagined myself shout-
ing at him.

And then, in part three of the dream, my words
would cut through to Malcolm's heart, and I'd watch
him crumple to his knees as he begged for my forgive-

ness. But I wouldn't give him the satisfaction of accepting his apology. I would just step right over him and march away, never looking back and leaving him sprawled in the middle of the floor like a fool!

I sighed; I guessed all of that was going to remain a dream. None of it was ever going to happen now.

As I tucked the letter back into the FedEx envelope, I had to admit that I did feel relieved. Up until this moment, I'd been dreading seeing Malcolm again, but there was no need to fear him. Yes, he was a dog, but I was grateful that he hadn't turned into a pit bull.

I still had decisions to make, like, was I still going to do this through the courts? And as for a relationship between him and Justice, how exactly was that going to work?

But I had time to decide how all of that was going to go down. Right now I had to deal with the other person in the Parks household, Kayla Parks.

It was interesting that Malcolm had sent this letter so that it arrived on the same day that I was to meet his wife. But I knew that God didn't deal in coincidences, so this had to mean something.

Not that I felt any better about seeing Kayla. I just prayed that after this meeting today, Malcolm's wife would be out of my life.

Kayla was sitting at the exact same table where I'd met her over a year ago, but this time she was alone. When I slipped into the chair across from her, she smiled, and I couldn't help it. . . . I smiled back.

Being an ex-wife had done Kayla good. She'd always been beautiful to me, but she'd also always been angry, which I could understand. Before, she'd worn her pain all over—it had been in her eyes, on her face, even in the way she stomped when she walked.

But now she looked relaxed, almost ten years younger, and that made me wonder, what kind of marriage had those two had? Not that it was my business, not that I cared.

"How are you, Chyanne?"

"I'm fine." I paused. "You look great."

She tossed her hair—which was only shoulder length now—over her shoulder and grinned. "I do look good, don't I?" Her words were arrogant, but her tone wasn't, and I chuckled with her.

She said, "This is what happens when you lose over two hundred pounds."

I frowned.

"That's how much Malcolm weighed," she told me.

This time I laughed. "That's a good one. I'm going to have to remember that."

"I hope not," Kayla said, suddenly serious. "I hope you don't ever have to go through what I just went through."

To this point, I'd heard only Kayla's anger. Today I heard her sadness.

But just as quickly, she recovered and was perky again. "I don't want to keep you very long." She paused and looked away when she asked, "How's your . . ."

"Daughter," I said. "I had a daughter."

She looked back at me and nodded. She tried to smile, but there was no joy on her face. "Are you happy?"

"I am," I said. I knew what she was asking me. "I am so happy that I kept Justice. . . ."

This time when she smiled, it seemed real. "What a beautiful and appropriate name."

I nodded. "I had to keep her. I would've never been able to abort. . . ." I couldn't even say the rest of that.

"I understand."

She looked straight in my eyes when she said, "Malcolm and I wanted to have children. But I wasn't able. . . ."

Oh, God! It was too hard to be here. To face the woman whose husband I had in ways that should have been reserved for her. I couldn't do this. What did she want from me, anyway?

"Kayla, I don't want to be rude, but I have to get back to Justice."

"Yes, of course," she said, as if she was snapping out of a trance. She reached into her purse and pulled out an envelope. "I want to give you this."

I glanced at it for a moment. What? Another letter?

But then I opened it, and my mouth got as wide as my eyes.

"What is this?"

"A thank-you . . . for helping me."

"But . . ." I looked down again, then shook my head. "There is no way I can take this. All I did was tell the truth." I slipped the check and the envelope back across the table to her.

She slid them right back to me. "No, please, this would mean a lot to me. Because of you, I found out that Malcolm was worth far more than I even thought. I was thinking he had hidden five, maybe six million dollars. Well, it was much more, and I walked away from my marriage a very wealthy woman."

"But . . ."

"If you can't take it for me, please, take it for Justice. I feel . . . in a way like I'm connected to her."

I looked down at the check again. Justice. This check would mean a lot for my daughter.

"You have to take it," Kayla pressed. "Haven't you ever heard the saying 'Don't block anyone else's blessings'?"

A blessing. That was what this would be. For me. For Justice.

There were tears in my eyes when I looked at Kayla Parks. This was a woman who could have hated me. Instead, she'd chosen to not only befriend me but also to bless me.

"Thank you," I said, my voice coming out in a whisper. "Thank you so, so much."

She stood; I did the same. We hugged.

"Take care, Chyanne," she said, as if she knew this would be the last time we would see each other. "And please take care of Justice."

I nodded, then walked slowly away from her, feeling like I was in a trance.

Outside, I stood for a moment, not sure what to do. I decided to walk the few blocks to my bank. I needed to open a new account, for Justice, and make her first deposit.

A deposit of two million dollars.

Chapter 39

Skye

I couldn't remember a time when I was so early for a date with Chyanne and Devin. But these days, whenever I had a chance to hook up with my crew and see my little goddaughter, I made sure that I was on time.

Justice—she had her little fingers wrapped around everyone's heart, and I couldn't wait to see her today.

Glancing at my watch, I saw I still had thirty minutes before Chyanne and Devin would arrive, so I strolled down Prospect Park West to check out some of the stores. I didn't come to Brooklyn all that much, but since Chyanne had moved here and since she was the one with the baby, I made the sacrifice to come over the bridge.

Two doors down from the restaurant where we were meeting was a variety store—one of those small shops that sold a little bit of everything. I strolled inside. I was always on the lookout for something I could buy for Justice.

I stopped to skim through the card display. I loved writing little notes to Justice. It was important to me that once she grew up, she knew just how much she was loved—even if her father wasn't living with her.

Not that I was mad at Malcolm—he had certainly stepped up. The court had awarded Chyanne twelve hundred dollars a month in child support, but Malcolm sent her two thousand dollars every time. That man might have been a dog, but he'd turned out to be a paying dog.

I was thrilled for my girl because between not having to worry so much about Justice because Malcolm was accepting responsibility and the money she'd received from Malcolm's wife, she was set. She had stopped doing freelance work with that new law firm and had opened her own little storefront legal practice right here in Brooklyn. Another entrepreneur added to the mix. Chyanne was living her dream, and I was so happy for her.

I picked up a card, but I didn't read it. I just stood there thinking about how wonderful life had turned out for all of us. Even though we'd had our trials, we had all become stronger.

"You might like this card better."

I didn't even turn around. I couldn't, not at first. But when I started breathing again, I did. I turned and faced him. I looked into the eyes of Noah.

"It *is* you," he said. He took a step closer. "I wasn't sure."

In my mind I told my heart to keep beating, and I told my eyes to stay away from his locks . . . and his lips. So, I kept my eyes on his eyes. But it was hard not to see all of him. Dressed in jeans and a white shirt. O! M! G!

"Hi," I said, as if more than a year had not passed since I'd last seen him.

He shook his head a little and his locks swayed and they had gotten a lot longer. Oh, God!

"You look . . . beautiful, magnificent." His eyes traveled up my body and then down again.

I shuddered and hoped that he couldn't see the effect he was having on me just by standing there. "Thank you." I needed to get his eyes off of me and my mind away from him. So I said, "What are you doing here, in Brooklyn?"

"Some of my art is on display at a gallery down the street," he said. "And, I love coming to Brooklyn. This is where we met, remember?"

Of course I remembered. All I'd been able to do for the past year was remember all the wonderful times I'd had with him. "Yeah, I remember. I'm just surprised that you did."

He held his hand to his chest, as if my words had wounded him. "I'm sorry," he said.

I frowned. "For what?"

"For letting you go."

Oh, my! I didn't have a thing to say to that.

But Noah kept going. "I thought about calling you a thousand times, but I could never pick up the phone. I knew I had hurt you, and I didn't want to hurt you anymore."

"Well then, I'm glad you didn't call, because I try my best not to be hurt."

"I should have called you, though, because letting you go was the biggest mistake I've ever made in my life."

I needed to get out of here; I needed to get far away from this man and everything he was doing to me. We'd been standing there for two minutes, and already he was in my head. I couldn't let him get down to my heart.

"Look," he said. "Can we get out of here and go somewhere to talk?"

"No, I have other plans." I tucked the card that I was still holding back into the display, then tried to step around Noah, but he blocked my path.

"Well, if not today, what about tomorrow or the next day or the next one? Now that I've seen you again, I know I have to make things right between us."

He was hitting all the right keys, hitting all the right notes. And the feelings that I'd worked so hard to press down were surging up—he was getting close, so close to my heart.

"I want you, Skye. I want you back in my life."

"You wanted me before, but I wasn't enough," I said, surprised at the hurt that was in my tone. I didn't know that it was still there inside of me.

He said, "I was a fool, but I won't be one again. I'm not going to let you go."

I chuckled, though I didn't find what he was saying funny. "You already let me go, Noah." I folded my arms. "And when you let me go, what did you think I was going to do? Did you think I was going to just sit there and wait for you to come to your senses?"

I paused, giving him a chance to say something, but he didn't.

I said, "Well, I didn't just sit there. I wasn't waiting for you, and now . . ." I held up my hand, wiggled my fingers, and let my ring sparkle in his face. "I'm engaged. So, we don't have any reason to get together. You got what you wanted, you got me out of your life, and it's been over for a long time."

Even though Noah was as brown as I was, I could almost see the color draining from his face. "You're engaged? To be married?"

" That's what *engaged* means."

"But when we were together, I could feel it. I was a part of you, and you were a part of me."

"And apparently, so was Monica, or whatever her name was."

"I didn't think you would be engaged. Do you love him?" He paused and I said nothing. "Do you love him like you loved me?"

Those words took my breath away, and it was definitely time to go now.

This time I pushed my way around him and headed toward the door. Over my shoulder, I said, "Good-bye," then rushed down the street to the safety of the Tree House, where I was meeting Chyanne and Devin.

I rushed through the restaurant doors, and never in my life had I been so glad to see Devin.

"Hey, girl," he said as he hugged me. "Who's chasing you?"

He had no idea how true his words were. I hadn't looked back and had no idea if Noah had seen where I'd gone, but I felt like I was being chased. I felt like Noah was after me and trying to steal my heart.

Before I had the chance to answer him, Chyanne came through the door, pushing Justice in a stroller, and right away all our attention turned to the baby.

Thank God for Justice! When I lifted her into my arms, I felt all the fear ease out of me. I didn't have anything to be scared of, anyway. Noah couldn't do a thing to me—Trent would make sure of that.

I had calmed down, but once we were seated and had placed our orders, I told my friends that I'd just run into Noah.

"I was looking for something for Justice and instead found my past."

"Oohh!" Devin clapped his hands. "Did you get to rub your engagement in his face?"

But while Devin cheered, Chyanne stared at me, as if she knew there was much more to this story. It was hard to hide anything from her.

Chyanne said, "Don't tell me . . ."

When she didn't say anything else, Devin said, "Don't tell you what?"

I sighed. "Yeah, I do," I said, almost crying. "Standing there in front of Noah, I did start feeling something for him."

"Oh, girl," Devin said, waving his hand in my face, "that ain't nothin' but indigestion."

"Or heartburn," I said, "because all of those feelings I once had for him seemed to come right back. I felt it, right here." I pressed my hand over my heart. My friends stared at me as if I'd lost my mind. "I know," I continued. "How could I be engaged to this wonderful man, and as soon as I see Noah, I start thinking about him?"

"Well, first of all, you need to be honest," Chyanne said. "Because this is not the first time you've thought about Noah."

My mouth opened wide. I hadn't told either one of them all the feelings and thoughts I'd had about Noah over the year. But Chyanne knew, anyway. It had to be that sister thing that we had between us.

Devin said, "Yeah, I could see it, even when you were with Trent. He would look at you all lovey-dovey, and you'd look back at him like he was just a friend."

Dang! Devin too? I guess he had that sister thing with me as well.

"I don't know what's wrong with me."

Chyanne reached for my hand. "Do you love Trent?"

I waited a moment so that I could tell her the truth. "I do. I love him with all of my heart."

"Well then, that's it," Devin said. "You're in love with Trent. Period. Look, having old flames burning in your heart is normal," he said , as if he was some kind of relationship counselor. "All you have to do is remember that you have an amazing man who adores you."

Chyanne nodded. "That's true."

"Who has lots of money," Devin added and laughed. "So even if you're not head over heels in love with Trent, just remember his money. That'll make up for a lot."

Devin was still laughing, but Chyanne and I were not.

I said, "I'm not marrying Trent for his money. What he has in the bank means nothing to me."

"Mmm-hmm," Devin hummed, like he didn't believe me.

"No, it's true. I make my own money. What I'm looking for is that passionate love. The love I thought I had with Noah, but the love I hope to have one day for real with Trent."

"Chile, please!" Devin laughed. "Forget all that passion stuff. Look, I would leave Antonio, my Mandingo, for Oprah at any time."

"Boy, you stupid!" I laughed, and Chyanne cracked up, too.

"Shoot! Y'all think I'm playing. Let Oprah call me, and I'll jump back to the other side so fast, y'all won't even recognize me."

When Justice tried to clap her hands, that made the three of us laugh even louder, and for a moment all thoughts of Noah were gone.

By the time we finished lunch, I felt better than even before I'd awakened that morning. I was going to marry Trent. After seeing Noah, I had no doubt whatsoever that I was going to live one of those "happily ever after" lives with the man who truly, truly loved me.

Chapter 40

Chyanne

Central Park tends to be so peaceful on a weekday. There aren't many people out, and the scenery is immaculate on a beautiful day like this. I parked myself on a bench and maneuvered Justice's stroller in front of me as we took in the sights and sounds all around us. Well, I more so than she. Justice was concerned about the stuffed animal she had been fighting with all afternoon.

"Sorry I'm late." Malcolm's voice took me out of my trance. "It was hell trying to get out of the office."

There he was, in all his glory. He was just as fine as the day I met him, standing there in his custom-made Armani suit. He made me feel underdressed. I was rocking mom jeans and a blouse. I had lost almost all my baby weight, but my stomach wasn't as flat as it was when he and I were together, and I was hoping he didn't notice. It was amazing that this man took me through so much and yet my heart still had a sweet spot for him. Maybe it was the fact that he wanted a relationship with Justice.

"Oh, that's fine. We haven't been here long. Plus, it's really nice out here today." I moved over a little so he could sit, but he was frozen in his spot.

His eyes locked on Justice, and it was like he fell in love for the very first time. I knew that feeling, oh, so well. It was the same feeling I got when I first heard her heartbeat, when I felt her kick for the first time, and when I gave birth to her. She was the light of my life, and the look in his face showed that she had just become his.

"So this is Miss Justice." Malcolm finally sat on the bench, and I took Justice out of her stroller and handed her to him. "She's gorgeous, Chyanne."

"Thank you. She's half yours, so I can't take all the credit."

"I know, but she looks like you."

Malcolm never took his eyes off Justice. She stood on his legs as he bounced her up and down. She giggled and grabbed his face, and at that point I swore I saw a tear form in his eye.

"Thank you again for allowing me to see her," he said, finally looking at me.

"My intentions weren't to keep you from her." I looked into his eyes, and I could see sincerity in them. "I just wanted to do what was right for me and her."

He didn't respond, but I could tell he understood where I was coming from. For the next hour it was all about Justice. We laughed and played with her. I caught Malcolm up on all her likes and dislikes and told him how smart a baby she was. He seemed so tickled when I told him she had some of his same characteristics, like how she rubbed her chin when she was sleepy just like him. It was a truly pleasant meeting, and we decided to put Justice back in her stroller and walk around the park.

"So I heard Kayla gave you a large sum of money." His tone revealed that his divorce was still a sensitive topic.

"Yeah, she did," I said hesitantly. "I opened up my own legal office in Brooklyn with it."

We walked in silence for a few minutes. I couldn't tell if he was upset with the fact that I not only helped his ex-wife in their divorce battle but took his money to start my own business. It had been one roller-coaster ride of a year for all parties involved, and I couldn't blame him if he was a little salty about the situation. I opened my mouth to lighten the mood back up, but he beat me to it.

"I'm really happy for you both." His words took me by surprise.

"Really?"

"Of course." He paused and chuckled a little. "I mean, I must admit, at first I was a little upset about the whole thing, but then I realized that I put myself in that predicament. I tried to play a dangerous game to have it all and then some, and I lost."

I didn't know what to say. I never expected for him to even think anything like that, let alone say it. I tried to form words, but nothing was coming out.

"Honestly, it was harder giving you up than it was getting a divorce."

Okay, now I was really shocked.

"You mean to tell me that losing me was harder than divorcing your wife, who you've known since you were eighteen?" I gave him a little chuckle of my own.

"I'm serious. Kayla and I lost whatever we thought we had a long time ago. We were merely keeping up appearances. I was and still am truly in love with you." He looked down at the stroller and smiled at a now sleeping Justice. "Plus, you gave me her."

I was taking his words all in. For the longest time I had struggled to see how I could have let myself be fooled by him. I had felt so used by him. I had blamed myself for even falling in love with him, and here he was, confessing his love for me. Malcolm used to tell me that a good attorney always had a rebuttal, and I was speechless.

"Listen, I was wondering if we could do this again. Maybe like dinner or something." He stuck his hands in his pockets, which was a nervous twitch of his.

"Are you asking me out on a date?" The thought of us going out on a date actually made me smile.

"Sort of. I mean, I would like you to bring Justice, so it would be like a family date." He searched my face for some sort of an answer. That was one thing I was good at that he never had to school me on, my poker face.

Was I really ready to revisit this chapter of my life? I was thankful that he wanted to be in his daughter's life, because she definitely deserved a father, but was I ready to do the family thing with him? I did not even know if he would be here after a month or so.

"We can take it slow. I know you might not be ready to do the family thing with me right now, but I would like a chance to prove that I'm in this for both of you." He said it like he was reading my mind.

The last three years quickly replayed in my mind. From the moment we met and he flashed that gorgeous smile at me, through our debacle a year ago, till this moment right now. We had had some really high highs and some pretty low lows. The logical part of me wanted to say no and kept this arrangement strictly about Justice to ensure I never got hurt by him again, but my heart took over at that point.

"Sure. We would love to." He smiled harder than a kid who got everything he wanted for Christmas. He wrapped his arm around my shoulder and kissed me softly on the forehead.

Lord, I prayed this was the right decision.

Chapter 41

Skye

I hate wedding planning. You would think this would be the best time of my life and the whole process would be an unforgettable one, but between my mom, Trent's mom, and Devin, I was another place card away from telling Trent we should just elope. They argued about the flowers. They argued about centerpieces. They argued about the cake. The only input I really had was about my dress, because I was designing it, and I talked the wedding planner into an open bar at the reception. I loved my family, but I was gonna need a stiff drink on my wedding day to forget all about this process.

Today Devin, my wedding planner, Sheila, and I were doing a tasting of the food for the cocktail hour and reception. This was the one part of the planning where I really wanted Trent to be here, but he was away on business.

"Whoo, girl, these crab cakes are the business," Devin hollered with his mouth full. "You gotta serve these."

"I told you I won't make a decision until we taste everything." I took another forkful of crab cake and let it melt in my mouth. "You know what, D? You're right. These crab cakes are the bomb. Put these down as a favorite, Sheila."

This was the most relaxing part about this whole thing. I wanted to make sure my food was on point because that was really the only thing people went to weddings for, anyway. That and the dress. The caterer brought us another entrée, and before I could stick my fork into the succulent filet mignon, my phone rang.

"Hey, future hubby," I said so that Trent could feel the love through the phone.

"Well, hello, future Mrs. Hamilton. How's everything going?"

"Everything is good today. Although I'm still recovering from the lilies versus orchids debate yesterday." I cut my eyes toward Devin, who had initiated the flower war between my future mother-in-law and the florist.

"Don't give me the side eye, Ms. Thang," Devin said, putting another piece of beef in his mouth. "That Russian heifer started it."

I could hear Trent laughing over the phone, which softened my look on Devin and made me chuckle a little bit.

"Well, don't get too stressed out. I was just calling to check in on you before I headed to this meeting. I love you, and I'll be home in a few days." This man was truly amazing.

"Love you, too, babe. See you soon." I hung up with a big smile on my face.

My wedding was getting closer and closer, and I was ready more than ever to say "I do" to Trent. I was trying to turn my mind back to food tasting and finally eat what looked to be a delicious contender when my phone rang again.

"Hello?" I was slightly annoyed and confused since I didn't recognize the number.

"I want to see you tonight." I dropped my fork on my plate when I heard Noah's voice through the receiver.

They all stared at me like I was crazy. "You all right, girl?" Devin was the only one who spoke up.

"Yeah. Excuse me while I take this outside." I put on a fake smile and rushed from the table like my hair was on fire.

"What do you think you're doing?" I gave him much attitude.

"I haven't been able to get you out of my head since we ran into each other, and I need to see you tonight."

"Noah, do you understand that I am in the middle of planning my wedding?" If he didn't want to hurt me again, he was definitely doing a bad job so far.

"Skye, I don't care about that wedding, which may not even happen. I care about you, and I know you care about me, too." He took a deep breath into the phone, like that sentence took a lot out of him.

He was right. I did care about him, a lot. He still had this hold on my heart, but going to see him was wrong. I was engaged to a wonderful man. Why would I throw that away for a man who could potentially break my heart a second time? The more I thought about it, though, the harder it was to resist him.

"Skye, I really need to see you. If you ever loved me at all, could you at least give me thirty minutes?"

I contemplated this a little while longer. Maybe if I went tonight, this would be the last I would see of him. This man confused my thoughts, and I needed him out of my system.

"Skye?" he said to see if I was still on the phone.

"Fine. Thirty minutes and that's it."

Lord, please let that be it, I prayed.

"Cool." He had both excitement and relief in his voice. "Come by my house around eight o'clock. I love you, Skye." He hung up before I could even object to coming to his house.

I couldn't move. How did I get to this place? Stuck between a man who I was supposed to marry and a man who I still had a lot of love for. I was starting to miss the days when I couldn't get a decent date, because those days were looking a hell of a lot simpler than what I was going through at the moment.

"Skye, girl, you all right?" Devin came out, breaking my daze. "Is everything okay?"

"Yeah, everything is good. That was just work." I couldn't believe I had just lied to one of my best friends, but I couldn't tell him that was Noah and I had agreed to go see him tonight. I would never hear the end of it.

"Well, come on back, then. You still got four more options to try. You were taking so long, I was going to decide for you." Devin sucked his teeth like he had food stuck in them.

"It wouldn't be the first time," I joked. "You've basically picked everything else."

"That's because our wedding has to be the event of the year. Nothing less for these divas." We both laughed and walked back arm in arm to finish eating.

The rest of my day went by like a blur. I couldn't remember anything after we left the catering place. All I knew was that I was standing in front of Noah's apartment building, wondering why I had trekked my tail all the way here. I should turn around, get in a cab, and go back home. That would be what a responsible woman who was getting married would do. Instead, I pushed the button to his loft.

"You made it. Come on up." I was surprised he answered like he knew it was me.

I took deep breaths the whole walk to his door, and before I could even knock, he swung it open. He had on a wife beater and some basketball shorts, with his hair in a loose ponytail. It was the first time I had ever seen it pulled back. This man was too fine.

"Sorry about my attire, but I just got out of the shower. Please come in." He opened the door wider and stepped aside.

I walked in reluctantly. "Thirty minutes, Noah."

"That's fine." I heard him close the door behind me. Then he came and wrapped his arms around my waist. "I've missed you so much, baby."

At first his strong arms felt so good, but then I pulled away. "You're already starting on the wrong foot."

"Skye, I don't want to play this game anymore."

"What game?" I put my hands on my hips.

"This cat-and-mouse game. I messed up, I know that, but I'm here now and I want to make everything up to you."

I didn't say a word. I just stood there with my hands still on my hips.

"A year ago I thought I wasn't ready to be fully committed, but I realized that you were everything I wanted and needed, and the thought of you being with someone else is killing me."

His words were beginning to melt me. This was what I had wanted all along from this man. This confession of love and willingness to commit. Why did he have to wait so long to give them to me?

"Why does everything have to be on your time?" I said. He looked at me in confusion. "When you weren't ready, I had to move on. Now that you want the things I wanted all along, I'm supposed to stop my whole life for you."

"It's not like that, Skye."

"This was a bad idea." I started moving toward the door. He grabbed my arm.

"Don't go." I tried not to stare into his eyes, but it was hard. I had to get out of here before this man clouded all my judgment. I wrestled my arm from his grasp and headed toward the door again.

"I can't do this, Noah. I'm happy, and I just need for you to stay out of my life forever."

I ran out of there without giving him an opportunity to say anything else. I should have never agreed to come. What was I thinking? I vowed to myself that this was the last time this was ever going to happen. I hailed a cab, and all I wanted to do was go home and talk to Trent.

Chapter 42

Devin

I finally had Leigh settled down. It had been a month since we'd gone out to lunch together and she'd talked about how bad her marriage was. But it seemed as if things had not gotten better at home with Michael and had now escalated to the point where Leigh was certain her marriage was headed toward the ultimate breakup.

"I just don't know what to do," Leigh wailed through the telephone, but at least it sounded like her tears had stopped. "He said that he needed a couple of days away, but I'm afraid that he won't come back."

Pulling the phone away from my ear just a bit, I rolled my eyes. I didn't want to tell Leigh that she needed to let it go, but it was beginning to sound like she needed to do just that. I mean, I was all for "for better or worse," but it just seemed like there was nothing but *worse* in her life. She deserved something better.

"Look, a couple of days may be good for you. It'll help you get your head together, and he'll get his together, too," I said, hoping I would get her to find some kind of bright side in this situation.

"I just never thought I'd be in this position. When we got married, I thought it was truly going to be till death."

Doesn't everyone think that? I thought.

"Honey, you need to just get a good night's sleep, and I'm sure you'll see things so much better in the morning."

It wasn't like I was trying to rush her off the phone, but I was sure glad when she sniffed and finally said good-bye.

Whew! I'm telling you. That was truly beginning to wear on me. But Leigh was going to be able to count on me, especially now, since it did look like she and Michael were going to get a divorce. I'd never turn her away; I was going to make sure that I was there to help her through.

I turned the music back up to the low level I had had my iPod on right before Leigh called, and then I settled back onto the couch.

Antonio was away on a business trip, but he was returning in the morning. Tomorrow night was gonna be all about us. But tonight—this was all about me.

I took a sip of my wine, opened up the book I was reading, snuggled into the pillows on the couch, and then the doorbell rang.

Dang bang it!

Who had the audacity to interrupt my peace? I wish there was a way people could put a DO NOT DISTURB sign on their front doors.

As I trudged to the front of my brownstone, I laughed at that. Can you imagine? All up and down the street, there would be those signs. No one would ever get the chance to visit anyone. I was still cracking up, but I stopped laughing the moment I opened the door.

There, right before my eyes, stood Antonio! Mr. Dark and Lovely. In his all-black outfit.

Hmph. Hmph. Hmph.

Before I could ask him what he was doing back so early, he said, "I'm ready, Devin. I'm finally ready to do this."

That was when I noticed it—the suitcase that was in his hand.

Oh my God!

"I'm ready," he said again as he stepped inside and rolled the suitcase in with him. "I'm ready for us to really be a couple."

It still took me a couple of moments to get unstuck, but when I did, I wrapped my arms around my man! I was finally stepping into the world of real commitment.

I helped him with the suitcase, and we settled into the living room. And as Antonio held me in his arms, my solo night was turning into the best duo night of my life.

I didn't even have the right word to describe last night: *fantastic, fantabulous, wonderful, amazing.* Nah, none of those words did justice to the first night that Antonio and I spent together as true partners.

And now this morning had gotten even better! The aroma of what he was whipping up in the kitchen for our breakfast wafted into the bedroom, and already I could tell that I was gonna wanna slap somebody's mama!

How wonderful was this?

The ringing phone interrupted my thoughts of joy, and when I glanced at the caller ID, I sighed. But I had promised myself to be there for my friend, so I tucked the towel that I had just wrapped around me tighter on my waist and picked up the phone.

"Hey, Leigh," I said, praying that she had something good to say about her and Michael. "What's up? You feel better?"

"Actually, I don't," she said. "It was horrible for me last night. Honestly, Devin, I don't think Michael is coming back. Listen, do you have a few minutes to talk before you go into the shop this morning?"

Dang! I did have some time, but with Antonio here, I hadn't planned on spending any of this time talking.

"I'll only be a few minutes. I'm thinking about getting out ahead of this, and you told me about Chyanne and her law office, and I want to—"

"Sure," I said, without letting her finish. Good. At least she was going to be proactive about her life.

I started to tell her that Antonio was here, but it didn't matter, really. My friends were going to have to get used to the fact that now I was in as committed a relationship as the ones they were in. I wasn't going to be able to jump every time they said, "Jump." "Come on over," I said. "But give me about ten minutes to get dressed."

"Okay. I'm only about two blocks away, but I'll wait."

I hung up the phone quickly, jumped into a tracksuit, and tried not to think about how my friend was really messing up my morning. But what was I to do? And, anyway, this might be a good thing. Antonio and Leigh could finally meet, and maybe Antonio would also have some words of wisdom for Leigh.

I wished that I had prepared Antonio a bit about what was going on, but I didn't bring my girls and their drama into my relationship with Antonio. When we were together, it was all about the two of us, but, honey, that was gonna change. It was going to be good to have someone to talk to about Skye, Chyanne, and Leigh. Sometimes, their drama was too much to handle.

Like besides Leigh, I was counseling Skye. That dang-blasted Noah wouldn't leave her alone, calling all the time, trying to get her to call off the wedding. I shook my head. I just prayed that Skye was going to do what she needed to do—and that was marry rich. Then love would follow.

I was thinking about Skye when the doorbell rang. Stepping quickly, I stopped to give Antonio a quick peck on the lips.

"Breakfast is almost ready," he said as I turned away. "Who's at the door?"

"Just one of my girls." I rushed out of the kitchen and down the hallway. "She won't be here long," I said as I opened the front door.

The moment I saw Leigh, I felt bad for all the thoughts I had had about how her situation was getting on my nerves. My friend was really hurting. Her eyes were swollen and bloodshot, and her lips were turned so far down, I wondered if she would ever smile again. And what did she have on? My girl was wearing some kind of flowered shift dress like my grandmother used to wear.

Oh, yeah, my girl had it bad.

"Leigh," I whispered as I pulled her into my arms.

She started crying as soon as I held her.

"Sssshhhh. Come on in here," I said, taking her hand.

"I've been trying to be strong," she whimpered. "But I guess it's hard to let someone you love go."

"Oh, sweetie, I know." I had been through this with Chyanne and Skye, but Leigh's was the most serious, because there was going to be a divorce involved. I guess this was the role I was destined to have with my friends. "Let's go into the kitchen," I said. "We were just getting ready to have breakfast and . . ."

"We?"

"Antonio! Honey chile, he moved in with me last night."

"Oh, then I don't want to intrude."

"Don't be crazy," I said. Antonio's back was to us, and I called out to him, "Baby, I want you to meet one of my friends."

He turned around, and the plate that he was holding crashed to the floor.

"Leigh!"

"Michael!" she screamed.

"Michael?" But I didn't have a chance to ask any other questions, because the petite, five foot three, 110-pound girl who had been my friend turned into Mike Tyson. She went after Antonio with everything she had—arms, legs, her teeth.

I grabbed her from behind, but not before she'd done major damage. She'd kicked Antonio in the groin, and he crumpled to the floor.

"Leigh!" he screamed, his tone filled with pain.

"What the hell are you doing here?" she cried. "I knew you were cheating on me, but I never thought this!"

It had all happened so fast that I didn't have time to think. But then it hit me. Antonio was Michael! Michael was Antonio!

I looked at Leigh standing there, sobbing so hard, it sounded like she was hyperventilating. I glanced at Antonio-Michael on the floor, his hands still clutched between his legs.

Leigh was doubled over, and Michael finally, slowly pulled himself up. He was holding on to the kitchen counter, his eyes still filled with his pain.

Antonio, my man.

I took slow steps over to him. And then I did exactly what Leigh had done. I kicked him right in his balls.

He screamed again, and while he was falling to the floor, I grabbed Leigh's hand. She sobbed, but I pulled her out of the kitchen, down the hallway, and out of my house.

I had no idea where I was going to take her, but she had to get away from there. I had to do the same, because if I didn't, I would be kicking Antonio all day long.

We walked down the block to Leigh's car, climbed inside, and for long minutes just listened to each other breathing heavily. Then Leigh turned to me, and I looked at her. I prayed that she didn't hate me, because I just didn't know. I had no idea that Antonio was really Michael. I had no idea that he'd been living on the down low.

But I didn't know if Leigh would believe me. Then she leaned over, pulled me into her arms, and hugged me.

And right there in her car, the two of us cried together.

Chapter 43

Chyanne

I hung up the telephone, and I was in a state of shock.

Devin could come up with some stories, but this one he hadn't made up. Oh, my God!

I didn't know his friend Leigh all that well. She was one of the first people he'd met when we'd got to New York; he'd met her in Brooklyn when she'd first come into the shop. Skye and I had hung out with her a couple of times, we'd gone to a couple of her openings and other events, but none of us had ever met her husband. But even though I didn't know her well, I felt every bit of her pain now. Who would have even imagined that Michael was using his middle name and a made-up last name to hide his identity?

Wow! Leigh, Skye, and I had all met up with our share of men who had done us wrong. But this, to me, was the worst, because Devin was also involved.

I picked up the phone to call Skye. I had to do it now, before Leigh got here. After that, I wouldn't be able to say a word, because of attorney-client privilege. But since Leigh hadn't said a word to me and this was all from Devin, I could tell Skye.

"Hey, girl. What's up?" she said when she answered the phone.

I didn't even say hello. I just went into the story that Devin had just told me. Finishing up, I said, "So, all of

this time, Devin was sleeping with one of his friends'
husband."

"Dang! When did this all go down?"

"He said a week ago."

"That's why he hasn't returned any of my calls. I
thought it was because he was getting sick of hearing
me talk about Noah."

"You still getting calls from him?"

"Yeah, all the time. So much that I was thinking
about changing my cell number."

"Do you really think Noah believes you'll call off the
wedding?"

"I don't know what that fool believes, but he needs to
leave me alone."

I heard my friend's words, but I can't say that I really
believed her. I was pretty sure that she was going to
marry Trent—after all, the wedding was only a month
away, and the plans were still moving forward, full
steam ahead. But I knew Skye's heart. She didn't give
it away often, and she'd given it to Noah. It was hard to
get it back.

Trust me. I knew the feeling.

"So, are you going to represent Leigh?" Skye asked,
changing the subject back.

"We're gonna talk about it. Devin was with Leigh
when he called, and he said they were on their way over
here from the hospital."

"The hospital? What is that about?" Before I could
answer Skye, she came up with her own story. "OMG!
Do you think she's pregnant?"

"I don't know."

"Well, when you find out, you have to call me."

"I won't be able to, because then I'll be a lawyer."

"You're a lawyer now!" She laughed.

"I'm your friend until Leigh hires me." The bell over the front door of my office tinkled, and I told Skye that I had to go.

I rushed into the reception area since the young girl I'd hired had called in sick this morning.

"Hey!" I said, greeting Devin and then Leigh. Taking her hand, I said, "I'm so sorry."

As I led them back to my office, Devin said, "You're gonna be sorrier in a minute."

The two of them settled onto the leather sofa, and I sat across from them in one of the two matching chairs that I had set up to make half of my office feel homier. I found that clients always talked more, always told you more when they felt most comfortable.

"So . . ." That was all I said, because often that was enough to get a client started.

"I want to hire you," Leigh said softly. She sounded like she'd been broken, and my heart went out to her. "I know Devin's told you . . . I want a divorce."

Before I could respond, Devin jumped up from the sofa. "And do you know what, Chyanne? That low-life scum gave her AIDS! Leigh is HIV-positive."

I gasped, exactly what I wasn't supposed to do as an attorney. I wasn't supposed to show shock. But what else could I do? This story just got worse and worse.

I reached for Leigh's hand. Forget about all that attorney decorum. I wanted her to know just how I felt.

"I'm so sorry," I said, wishing that what Skye had said just a little while ago was true. Wishing to God that they had been at the hospital because Leigh was pregnant.

"So, what are you gonna do?" Devin demanded to know. "How are we gonna get him?"

Slowly, my eyes turned to Devin, and my heart started beating fast. If Leigh was positive, did that mean . . .

As if he knew what I was thinking, he said, "No, I'm not. At least not yet." Devin fell back onto the sofa. "But I have to keep getting tested for the next couple of years. I do that, anyway, but now . . ."

Devin sighed, Leigh lowered her eyes, and I shook my head. Well, Devin and Leigh had come to the right place. I was going to take Michael, Antonio, or whatever his name was, for all that he had and all that he didn't have.

When I finished with him, he was going to be calling Leigh and me all kinds of dirty names.

Chapter 44

Skye

I balanced the package I held in one arm and glanced down at my cell phone. It was another call—from him. That was it. I was going to spend the money to have his number blocked, though I didn't really think that was going to stop Noah. He knew where I worked; he knew where I lived.

I sighed. From that day that I'd seen him three months ago, Noah had been relentless. The first few times he'd called, I'd actually talked to him and listened to what he had to say.

But his words were the same all the time—he kept apologizing and saying that he didn't want to let me go. Soon after, I started letting his calls go to voice mail.

Not that that dissuaded him. He sent cards and flowers to my home and job, telling me—again—how he missed me and wanted me back.

The only thing he hadn't done was show up at my door, which was a very good thing because Trent would've killed him.

And then . . . just as I had that thought, I looked up and Noah was there. A few steps away from me, right in front of my apartment building.

Oh, God! It was a good thing that Trent was in New Jersey, working on closing a deal on a property. I didn't expect him back in the city for hours.

"Hi, Skye," he called to me above all the noise of New York that was surrounding us.

"Noah, what are you doing here? I don't want to talk to you," I said as I put the key in the door leading into my building.

"I just want a few moments to say what I have to say. I didn't get to say everything last time. Just a few moments," he repeated.

"You've said it all, and I'm still getting married."

"Well if you are, what do you have to lose? Let me in, and we'll talk for just a moment. And then I'll be gone . . . forever."

This was not what I wanted to do, but it was the "gone forever" part that made me agree. Inside the elevator I tried to keep my eyes on the door, but through my peripheral vision, I could see him staring at me, his eyes intense, and his lips and his locks . . . oh, God!

I rushed into my apartment, so anxious to get this over with. I placed the bag of groceries on the kitchen table and tossed my keys there as well, then turned back to Noah, who was standing in the center of the living room.

I folded my arms, kept my eyes on his eyes and away from his lips and his locks and his jeans, which he was wearing, oh, so well. "Okay, speak," I said as if I didn't care.

He looked around, as if he was getting used to the familiar surroundings, and then his eyes stopped moving when he got to the entryway wall. "What happened to the picture?"

"What? The sketch you gave me?"

He nodded.

"I threw it away!" My words were meant to hurt him. Maybe he would now leave me alone—even though I hadn't thrown it away at all. The sketch was sitting in the back of my closet, though I wasn't sure what I was going to do with it now that I was getting married.

"I really hurt you, didn't I?" he said, and for the first time, I heard real sadness in his voice.

"Yes, you did. And you're hurting me now by not leaving me alone."

"I can't, because if there is one thing I know, it's that we belong together."

Noah had said this to me at least one hundred times since we'd met up again. And each time, I wanted to strangle him. Why hadn't he said that before? Why hadn't he known that? Didn't he know that he was the first man I ever really loved? He could have had me into eternity. But I wasn't enough for him then; I wasn't dumb enough to believe that I was enough for him now—even though the flames I had for him were still burning inside of me. But like Devin said, that was normal. After all, Noah was really my first love. Could you ever get over that?

"Is it because of money?"

I frowned. "What money?"

"The money that Trent Hamilton and his family have. I saw the announcement of your wedding in the *New York Times*. Is that why you want to marry him? Because he can give you more than I can?"

I crossed my arms even tighter across my chest. "The mere fact that you can ask me that lets me know that you don't know me at all."

"I had to ask."

"Because you can't think of any other reason why I'm saying no to you?"

"Exactly. Because I know we're supposed to be together. I can see it all over you, even now." He stepped closer, and the smart thing for me to do would've been to move back. But I didn't. He said, "It's in your eyes."

Another step. "It's on your lips." Another step. "It's in your heart." There was nowhere else for him to move. "Like I said, it's all over you." His lips were right there in front of me, juicy, wet, thick. And his locks swayed as he talked.

I couldn't figure out how I was still standing, because my heart had stopped beating. And then he lowered his face, closer, closer, closer to me . . . until his lips were on top of mine. So gentle, at first.

But then I closed my eyes and he took me into his arms and we went at it. We ravaged each other with our passion, which I could feel all the way down to my center.

This was exactly what I remembered, the fire that passed between us every time we touched. I didn't know how long we stayed connected. Two minutes? Two hours? I wasn't sure. But finally, I broke away, stepped back, and covered my lips with my hands.

Noah's eyes were filled with lust when he looked at me. And he smiled. "Finally," he said. "I knew it." He sighed. "Thank God you know it now and we can just start again where we left off."

I had to force my legs to move, and I took the twelve steps to the door. My back was to him the entire time, until I opened it.

Turning to him, I said, "You need to leave, Noah."

There was nothing but confusion all over his face. "What?"

"You need to leave. It's over between us."

His locks swayed. "After that kiss?"

"It was just a kiss," I said as I stared at his lips. "I'm still marrying Trent."

He shook his head as if he couldn't believe it. "You're actually going through with this?"

I nodded.

"What about me?" he asked. He had not taken a single step toward the door, but I still held it open.

"I loved you," I told him. "And my heart has been broken for a year. But I'm in love with another man, who loves me completely," I said. "And I cannot wait to marry him."

Those must've been the first words that I'd spoken that Noah actually heard, because finally he moved toward me. He stood at the edge of the door, just inches away from me, and asked, "Are you sure?"

I looked straight at him when I nodded. "Yes."

"You're making a big mistake," he said before he stepped into the hallway.

I didn't give him a chance to say another word—not even *good-bye*. There was no need for us to say anything else. After what had just gone down here, in the middle of my living room, I think Noah Calhoun and I were finally on the same page.

We both knew that it was over once and for all.

Chapter 45

Skye

The dressing room was tight and small in the back of this church, but it didn't matter to me. I didn't need many people back here with me, anyway. Those who loved me most were here to make sure that I didn't explode with happiness before the wedding.

It was amazing. . . . The day was finally here. I was about to marry Trent Hamilton. After a year of dating and months of doubts, today I would do the right thing.

"You look absolutely amazing," my sister, Simone, said. "But I've got to get going." She hugged me, and I closed my eyes as I held her back. "I'll see you out there," she said.

I still couldn't believe that Simone wasn't standing up for me, but she had said that she really wanted to be in charge of the music.

"I'm gonna rock that church," she had kidded at my bridal shower. "Y'all done forgot that my singing roots began in the church, and when I finish singing those songs, Abyssinian Baptist Church will be talking about Skye's wedding for a long time."

Everyone laughed, but I had no doubt about it. 'Cause there was not a singer on the market today who could rival my sister's talent.

Through the reflection in the mirror, I could see Chyanne and Leigh standing behind me. Leigh and I had never been that close, but we'd all become closer since her divorce proceedings began and her diagnosis with AIDS. It was still hard to believe what had happened to her, but you couldn't tell it in her face. Devin said that it was our friendship that gave her strength, and she was moving on, praying for a Magic Johnson kind of cure.

"Okay, I think I'm done, Mz. Thang," Devin said as he tucked one last curl behind my ear.

"Oh, my goodness," Chyanne said. "You do look absolutely beautiful." She started waving her hand in front of her face, as if that would keep her tears away.

I wished my mother had done that, because she was already crying and the makeup consultant that Trent hired had to redo my mom's makeup twice already.

"Okay," my mother said, standing up from the vanity next to me. "I promise, I'm not going to cry again."

Then she looked at me, and the tears started coming.

"Mama, you've got to stop," I said, laughing.

"I know, but I can't help it."

"Okay, that's it. It's time for you to go, anyway. Time for the mother of the bride to be escorted down the aisle."

My mother nodded, then hugged me, though she kept her face away from mine so that neither one of us would have to have our makeup done again.

"I am so proud of you," she whispered.

"For what? For getting married?"

"No, for being you, for always standing your ground and going after what you wanted, for growing up into the magnificent woman that you are." She sobbed, and I pointed toward the door.

"Devin, take her. And it's time for you to go, too."

When I stood and looked into my best friend's eyes, he was about to cry as well.

"Stop it! Stop!" I said to all of them. Now *I* had to wave my hands in front of my face. There was no way I could cry. Not now. Not yet.

"Okay, we're going, Mz. Thang!"

He hugged me one last time, and my mother blew me a kiss.

Leigh said, "I'm going to let them know that we're ready." She followed Devin and my mother out the door, and I was alone with Chyanne.

"Well, this is it, kiddo," Chyanne said.

"Yeah." I held her hands. "I always thought you were going to be first."

"Well, you got the husband first, but I got the baby first," she kidded. "Seriously, though, do you know how much I love you?"

I nodded because I was afraid to speak. Chyanne was my sister, just as much as Simone. We had been through so much together: from her father's death to going to college together, choosing our careers, and finding our first loves. We'd both lost the men who'd had our hearts first. But I had no doubt that Chyanne would find what I'd found with Trent. He wasn't the first, but he was the best.

"I am so happy for you," she said as she handed me my bouquet. "Now, let's go get married."

I stepped into the hallway of Abyssinian Baptist Church. It was quite a coup and quite special to be married here, in the oldest African American church in New York. It was only because we were being married here that my father agreed to a wedding outside of Atlanta. Plus, my father understood that the Hamiltons had so many connections in the city and really wanted the wedding here. But the kicker for my father was that our wedding would be held in this church with so much history. And when Reverend Butts, the pastor of the church, agreed that my father could preside over my nuptials, it was a done deal for Daddy, the Reverend Arthur Davenport.

The only thing, though, was that my father took his responsibilities seriously, and that meant that he wanted to stand at the altar during the entire ceremony. So, I was going to walk down the aisle myself.

I had thought of other options: walking with Simone, but she was singing, or my mother, who wouldn't have been able to handle it. So, I'd decided that I could do it alone. It was perfect, anyway, so apropos of my life.

As Simone sang "With You I'm Born Again," Leigh and then Chyanne sauntered down the aisle, looking stunning in the emerald green dresses I'd chosen. I stayed away from the doors so that no one could see me. And then, right after Simone killed that last note to the song that Billy Preston had made famous, the wedding march began.

I could hear the rustle of the crowd standing, and I took a deep breath as I turned the corner.

The gasps were immediate, and the oohs and aahs continued from the three hundred or so people who had packed the church. I knew I looked great in the custom gown that I had designed, but I didn't really care what anyone thought—except for Trent. Not looking to the left or to the right, I kept my eyes on the center, first seeing my father, with a smile so wide on his face that his cheeks had spread up to his eyes.

Then Trent came into view, and a shiver ran through me. It was a good one, one filled with all the love that I had for this man. I loved him because he loved me so much.

And Trent showed his love. For the first time ever, I saw his eyes glassy with tears. That made me smile; that made me melt; that made me love him even more.

Trent didn't wait at the altar, the way we had rehearsed. When I was just a few steps away, he came into the aisle to get me, and that made the congregation laugh.

When Trent took my hand, I was sure this was the moment I was going to burst with happiness.

The music stopped, and my father began.

"Dearly beloved, we are gathered here on this special day to witness the nuptials of two very important people to me. My daughter Skye and the man who in just minutes will be my son, Trent Hamilton."

As my father talked, I had to blink back tears. My father and I had had such a rocky relationship over the years. But finally, we'd found our groove. And as we stood here today, I no longer had any doubts that he loved me, his firstborn.

My father's words made their way back to my ears. "We rejoice and celebrate in the ways life has led Skye and Trent to each other. Therefore, if any man can show just cause why they may not be lawfully joined together, let him speak now or forever hold his peace."

"I can show just cause!"

"What?" I whipped around and watched my nightmare come to life. Noah, dressed in a tuxedo, walked down the aisle toward me.

"I can show just cause," he said again as the murmurs that rolled through the congregation became louder.

"What?" Trent said. "Who are you?"

"I'm the man who Skye should be with," Noah said.

And, I wanted to die right there. Why was this happening to me? On my wedding day!

Trent turned to me. "Skye?" he asked, his eyes filled with such confusion. "What is going on?"

I shook my head. "I don't know."

"Tell him, Skye," Noah demanded, though he was stopped in his tracks by two of the ushers. "Tell him that you love me!"

It was hard for me to get the words out of my mouth.

"Skye?" Trent called my name again.

"Skye!" my father called to me at the same time.

I felt every eye in the church on me. And my heart was beating so hard, I couldn't speak.

"You can tell him, Skye," Noah said as he tried to wrestle his arms from the grasp of the ushers. "And then we can get married. Today. Right now. Here, in front of all of these people."

It was hard for me to breathe. I glanced at Trent, and there was no longer confusion in his eyes. Now all that was there was hurt. And his pain was because of me.

I pushed my bouquet into Chyanne's arms, even though she was standing frozen. Gathering the satin skirt of my gown, I walked up the center aisle toward Noah and the men who held him.

"Skye!" Trent called, and now his voice trembled with his fear and his pain. But I was so sorry. I had to do this.

As I came closer, Noah stopped wrestling with the ushers and he smiled. There was nothing but triumph all over his face. I took a deep breath, and then, with as loud a voice as I could muster, I said, "I don't love you! I don't want you! I don't want to be married to you." I pointed to Trent. "This is the man I love, because he loves me. He always has, and he always will. Just get out of my life."

My words stunned Noah, but I didn't care. A second later I turned around and ran into Trent's waiting arms.

"Oh, God," he breathed into my ear.

"I love you," I said over and over and over and over.

It was as if it was just the two of us, but my father's voice brought us back to reality. "Get him out of here," he said.

I didn't dare turn to look, but from the applause, I imagined that Noah was being dragged away. I knew I had some explaining to do to Trent once this ceremony was over, but when I looked into his eyes, Trent told me without words that it was okay. Whatever it was, we were going to walk this road together.

Then my father said, "Does anyone want to see a wedding today?"

Again, the crowd cheered, and my father went through with our vows. Just minutes after Noah tried to destroy my life, I became Mrs. Trent Hamilton. And my heart sang!

After we kissed, we turned to the crowd, who were standing on their feet, applauding our first introduction as man and wife.

To the left, I heard Devin say, "Nothing but drama!"

I laughed. He had some nerve, but he was right. My life had been nothing but drama right up to a few minutes ago. But now there was going to be a new song in my life.

I looked up at my husband as we hurried down the aisle, and I knew that I'd never have a love greater than his. Except for the Lord, no one would love me more.

And, really, isn't that all any girl ever wanted?